CHAMPIONS ONLY

DIANA HICKS SHERER

outskirts
press

Outskirts Press, Inc.
http://www.outskirtspress.com

Paperback ISBN: 978-1-9772-1210-8
Hardback ISBN: 978-1-9772-1546-8

PRINTED IN THE UNITED STATES OF AMERICA

ACKNOWLEDGMENTS

Any book project can be influenced by many individuals. Words they have spoken can spark an idea or remind you of a forgotten memory. This is definitely true of my late husband Alex Sherer, Jr. who was a wealth of knowledge when it came to boxing. I am so grateful to have shared so many wonderful experiences with him.

I want to thank Bill "Pops" Miller and my second mom Beverly Miller for sharing my love of boxing. Their support early on in the book's development was a blessing. I have tremendous appreciation and devotion for my loving mother, Alberta Hicks for always being a stable force of influence.

Thanks to my son Anaeus Sherer who is the best decision I ever made. He's also chosen to be a writer. Much gratitude to my sister Theresa Luke for being my best friend. Thanks to my brother Ronald Brooks for having the patience to listen to this story over a hundred times. Thanks to my cousin Deanna Veasley for letting me vent and giving me a shoulder to lean on. Thanks to my sisters Sharon Hicks, Sandy Sims, Yolanda Johnson, and Debra Sherer. Thanks to my late husband's parents Willie Brown and Calvin Brown for all their love, support, and dedication. Thanks to my Forum Boxing family. They will always be special to me. I am so grateful to the late John Jackson, who taught me a great deal about the business of boxing.

IMPORTANT PEOPLE

I would like to acknowledge all the many athletes that I worked with during my career in sports. Special thanks to Ivery Black and Michael Troupe for introducing me to the business of sports. My close friends; Elan Carter-Price, Goldie Williams, Diane Blankumsee, Wuyvette Richardson, Dani Parsi, Maria Scott, Karen Toni, Lenora Scott, Crystal McCarey, Juliette Hagerman, Maurice Carter, Richard Young, Michael Peterson, Sr., Joseph Peterson, III, Wendy Williams, Daria LeSassier, Eddie Murray, James Bundy, Allanda Smith, Kevin and Ava Mack, Felecia Speaks, Edward Scott, Nicole Largent, and Chris Steele.

Chapter 1

LETHAL WEAPONS

The sport of boxing is both a strange yet unique business. It is comprised of many colorful people from all walks of life. These fascinating casts of characters have one thing in common, their love for boxing. If you take a moment to listen, they all have incredible stories to tell.

Over the years as a sportswriter, I've been fortunate to interview athletes from several sports; baseball, track, and field, football, basketball, and boxing. Though there are similarities among the athletes who participate in these sports, boxers have notable differences.

In most sports, the majority of athletes are filtered through an educational system. Whether they learn something or not is up to the individual. In boxing, this is often not the case; yet it somehow adds to the allure.

In some sports, a contract is negotiated for a length of time, such as one or more seasons, and the deal is done. In boxing, the negotiations never stop. This, in itself, allows the deadly sin of greed to flourish.

Despite the flaws that many of us debate about, if you hang around boxing long enough, you'll learn that the imperfections are what make this sport a multi-million-dollar business. In retrospect, they become memorable moments in time.

For example, I was at an awards dinner before a big fight in Las Vegas. When giving out an award for integrity, the master of ceremonies put it this way.

"I don't think I know an honest person in boxing. I guess that's why this award hasn't been given out for ten years."

No one in the audience appeared to take offense. Instead, everyone laughed at the idea that there was some truth in that statement. I'm not saying there aren't honest people in boxing. It's just that the acceptance of this fact is partly what makes boxing such an exciting sport. It is the reason so many people stick around long after the curtain has gone down. I believe boxing coined the phrase "hanger-on."

To help you better understand, I will start at the beginning. I want you to hear first-hand how greed can deceive not only a fool but the smartest of people. Let me take you back to a time in Chicago. It was on the south side, at the Savoy Boxing Gym, where hundreds of young boxers started their rise to the top. Some say they sold their soul for a bit of fame and glory. I would like to think a piece of boxing history lived within those walls. Many great champions walked through those very doors and built their careers right there in that gym. To be a world champion was their dream.

The Savoy Boxing Gym sat near the corner of Seventy-First

and Cottage Grove. At first glance, you couldn't help thinking it should be boarded up.

Inside wasn't much better. The city had provided little. A couple of ping pong tables, two bumper pool tables, and even these were well used.

There was an indoor basketball court, which was sorely in need of attention. The lighting was poor, and the rims were bent, but the kids with their dreams of becoming "Magic," "The Mailman," "The Big'O" or whomever they were enamored with for the moment, played a soulful, rhythmic, and painfully-neglected game.

There was little in the way of direction for these would be NBA hopefuls. The real attraction, and surely the most functional part of this recreational center, was in the basement. Down a short flight of stairs and through a set of olive drab double doors was the boxing gym. The first thing one noticed when they stepped inside was the intense heat. Almost furnace-like, with tropical humidity. Here scores of hungry young men (some as young as ten) came daily.

The gym was quite small, barely the size of half a basketball court. There was a boxing ring, two heavy bags, and one empty bracket for the speed bag. The activity here was always alive, like that of an anthill or beehive.

There were two dressing rooms. The largest one was old and run down. The showers didn't produce hot water, and most of the lockers were hard to open. Roaches roamed the facility freely until someone tried to stomp them, which was frequently. The boxers didn't seem offended by their presence but looked upon them as residents.

The other dressing room was smaller, with only ten lockers. This room was much cleaner, the showers offered hot and cold running water. There also was a rubbing table and a water cooler. This room was reserved for **World Champions Only**.

Every day at 2:00 p.m. Mr. Wright would open the gym. He was a large, jovial man who had once boxed professionally. All of the boxers called him Mr. Wright. The other trainers simply called him Wright. He was retired from a Chicago industrial plant and now worked for the city recreation department.

Mr. Wright started all the little kids out. He showed them how to position their feet, how to shoot a jab, and how to follow through with a straight right-hand. Then he would guide them to other trainers in the gym, all of whom were searching for the next, "Sugar" Ray Robinson, "Hammering" Henry Armstrong, Joe Louis, or the "Greatest" himself, Muhammad Ali.

For all intents and purposes, this type of boxer came along as often as Einstein, Caruso, Louis Armstrong or Stevie Wonder. Their dreams of boxing wonderment were always in precise, yet somewhat diluted, form, for this gym had several current world professional champions in residence.

Tony Speaks was a lightning-fast world lightweight champion. He wasn't particularly strong, nor a very heavy puncher. Speaks had a ton of heart and could box with speed and flair, though without the ability to dominate upper-echelon world-class fighters. He was brilliantly guided to the crown and was known in boxing circles to be just a cheese champion.

Richmond Marcellus also was a lightweight. He was recognized as a world champion by another of the governing bodies of the sport. Marcellus was known in the trade as a technician because he could perform all needed boxing skills well. He was a much better boxer than Speaks, except Marcellus made far less money because he was not that exciting to watch and was by no means box office. Unlike most former champions, Marcellus was extremely tight with a dollar. Even though Marcellus had made eight successful title defenses, he still lived at home with his mother.

His favorite quote was, "I'm not going from rags to riches to rags."

This he would tell anyone within listening distance. There was no reason to doubt him.

Charles Morgan was the welterweight champion of the world. He also was recognized by one of the alphabet sanctioning bodies. He was a competent and schooled long-distance boxer who was quick, with an educated left-hand and good endurance. Despite his more than twenty-five knockouts, Morgan was neither strong nor a devastating puncher. His record had been padded, thus making him look more impressive than he actually was. Nevertheless, Morgan stood to make several huge paydays. Every welterweight contender knew he was not a great fighter and could be taken.

Wonderful Magnificent was by far the superstar of all the champions at the Savoy gym. He was tall, just short of six-foot-three. Magnificent had been a welterweight champion, junior middleweight champion, and currently held half of the world's middleweight title.

Magnificent was blessed with a strong upper body and speed of hand and foot. He packed awesome power in his right hand. Scoring a knockout every time he entered the ring was his mission.

At will, Magnificent was a cunning and brilliant boxer with the ability to counter-punch like a master. He possessed an all-day left-jab that in seconds could close the eyes of an unfortunate opponent. The weakest punch in his deadly arsenal was his marginal left-hook, but with his right hand, who needed a left-hook. This was undoubtedly his and his manager's thinking.

Magnificent had the aura of a killer in the ring, but early on in his career, he was not very articulate out of the ring. Still, he was the shining Holy Grail to the other boxers in the sport because at one time he too was hungry, deprived, neglected and unknown.

Now Magnificent was a star. He had a fleet of a dozen cars, including exotic sports cars, luxury sedans, a custom-built limo, and a replica antique. He owned a hundred pairs of shoes, two hundred custom-tailored suits, fifty sport coats, and five custom-made tuxedos. To top it off, Magnificent had a mansion that was furnished and paid for, and investments which paid him close to a million a year.

Though hardly handsome, Magnificent had his choice of the most beautiful women in the world. As a teenager, he had been hard-pressed to get a date. Now Magnificent was the most ardent and insatiable participant in fantasy, fulfilling sexual encounters.

Magnificent appeared to have it all and recently was named "Fighter of the Year." He was finally acknowledged as a superstar in his sport; however, Magnificent was not at peace. At times he was down-right annoyed. One did not have to look far to find the object of his annoyance.

Hiwatha "Absolute" Jordan was at this time all that Wonderful Magnificent was not. He was the decade's media darling. In all eyes, Hiwatha was a great fighter. America black, white, and brown had fallen in love with him. He was fast on his feet, efficient in the ring, had a colorful personality, and was just brilliant in all aspects of the sport.

Hiwatha had been an Olympic Gold Medal-winner. He was drop-dead handsome. Young girls swooned, and more mature women stare invitingly at him with sexual hopes they desired to fulfill.

The spoken word for Hiwatha was as natural as breathing for most humans. Like an actor in a starring role, he knew where to stand, where to sit, what to say, and when to say it. He was not just a superstar; Hiwatha was the king of boxing. It was inevitable that one-day Hiwatha and Magnificent would have to meet in the ring. Not just boxing fans, but all sports fans felt that this would indeed be the "Fight of the Century."

Hiwatha held two championship belts. He was totally independent of any single promoter. He was self-managed; therefore, set a new standard in boxing. This champion was so beyond the brutal sport of boxing that it was unbelievable he could actually be such a precision fighting machine.

Hiwatha was doing American Express commercials, print ads, and television appearances. Everything he touched turned to gold. Hiwatha was rich beyond rich. He would arrive at his private gym in a midnight blue Rolls Royce convertible, but in the back of his mind lingered the reality that he must defeat Magnificent. This would be no easy task.

When questioned by the press about Magnificent, Hiwatha would gladly tell them, "I'll give him his chance. I'll destroy him physically, crush him mentally, and drain him along with his so-called Windy City and his egotistical manager."

Hiwatha knew that Chicago held Magnificent in untouchable hero status, so his comments definitely didn't sit well with Magnificent manager, Charleston Orlando who was watching Jordan's comments on WNN Sports. He became so upset he pushed his meal away, threw his napkin on the table, and retreated to his office.

Charleston was a man of small stature. He was nowhere near his listed five-foot-ten height. In public, he wore boots to boost his height. His complexion as an African American was paper-bag brown. He was the quintessential modern-day hustler, except his hustle was boxing.

Charleston was a man deeply in love with himself. He had come to Chicago as a child. His number one passion was to become wealthy and successful. He had little interest, other than sex, women, money, and himself. So, it was a blessing that he had a sharp eye for talent.

By the time Charleston was twenty, he had moved into his first home. At twenty-three, he was a foreman with the local municipal power company.

On the side, Charleston coached young amateur boxers. Arnold Thompson (now known as Wonderful Magnificent) was sent to Charleston by a friend who had seen him in a schoolyard brawl. His friend liked the skinny kid and wanted Magnificent to learn how to box. Charleston would later tell reporters that on first meeting, he thought Magnificent was a hopeless case until gradually, his athleticism began to flourish.

At sixteen, Magnificent was the National Runner-up at the Golden Gloves, and later the Amateur Boxing Federation (ABF). The following year, he won both tournaments and was named "Amateur Boxer of the Year."

The only problem was that during this same period, few would notice because a youngster from Brooklyn, New York, named Hiwatha "Absolute" Jordan won the Olympic Gold Medal and turned professional. Jordan's first pro bout was nationally televised, and he was paid the astronomical sum at the time of six-hundred thousand dollars. His star was launched.

Meanwhile, Charleston knew he couldn't keep Magnificent fighting merely for trophies forever. So, he sat Magnificent down and negotiated his first managerial contract.

"Look, man, we've got to look ahead when it comes to your career," said Charleston. "I feel you can be a world champion. I believe I'm the one that can take you to the title. All I've got to give you is me. How about we go, fifty-fifty?"

Charleston searched Magnificent eyes for a response. He knew at times, Magnificent trust in him was a bit blind. With no other prospects, Magnificent readily accepted, and this began their whirlwind professional partnership.

Charleston did everything in his scope of influence to land a promotional contract for Magnificent. None of the big-time promoters or major networks was interested. After much deliberation, Charleston mortgaged his house and solely promoted his first fight card with Magnificent as the main attraction.

Chicago was hungry for a sports hero. The pro baseball and football teams at the time were not first-place finishers.

On November fifteenth, in a converted downtown ballroom, the city of Chicago came and fell in love with Magnificent. His opponent was a living cadaver by the name of Frank Lightfoot. Magnificent impressively knocked him senseless in fewer than two rounds. Although his opponent had been no match, it was clear to the sold-out crowd that this kid had promise and destructive explosiveness in his right-hand. The gross from the live gate was just over eight thousand dollars. Charleston was off and running.

Magnificent knocked out his next twenty opponents

before one went the distance. It didn't make a difference. He went on to kayo fifteen more opponents and win two world titles before the boxing world took notice.

Charleston began to see his and Magnificent economic standing dramatically improve. Still, he was not satisfied. To his credit, Charleston was a smooth talker. He loved to talk to the press, especially if it was about himself. Since Magnificent was not a talker (though he would improve over the years), Charleston eagerly filled the void.

As Charleston fortune grew, he, too, would buy a luxurious home and later get more involved in real estate. Unfortunately, Charleston had one issue; he always worried about his looks. He finally decided to have them altered by the scalpel of a famous Southern California plastic surgeon.

Before his surgery, Charleston had been a decent-looking man. Nevertheless, he was happy to go through the pain, swelling, money, and time to give himself what in his eyesight was the ultimate gift. A "white" look. For a nice five-figure sum, he did just that. Although Charleston was no "Uncle Tom," he was a closet "Oreo" that actually distrusted his own people.

Charleston could barely control his excitement when he and Magnificent were guests at the White House. He took delight in his photograph with a president who had skillfully stacked the Supreme Court against any and all minority advancement. Charleston gladly placed the photo on his mantle and had several dozen copies made, dated and personally autographed to him.

Now in the hospital, Charleston was beginning to forget the pain of his operation. The awful swelling and discomfort were finally gone. The doctor had performed a Hollywood nose job and face-lift. He still had scars behind his ears. Charleston had hoped they would have gone by now.

As he studied his new face, Charleston was in heaven. He had loved himself unabashedly before. Now his narcissism knew no limits. It had taken almost two months for his new look to really take hold. His nose was "European" perfect, and he had a more classic jawline.

All his life, Charleston had worshiped white people. Now he was living his private fantasies by indulging himself in woman chasing. He now thought of himself as a "player."

"I don't need one of anything," Charleston was fond of saying. "One woman is not enough for me."

As the success and monetary gains from Magnificent's performances grew, Charleston slowly began to distance himself from the gym. This is why he actually never made money on his other champions. Charleston was content to build all their careers except Speaks on the undercards of Magnificent's bouts.

Charleston loved to be admired and praised by others. To keep his boxers and trainers in line, he would buy them customized jackets in silver, black or blue. For the young up-coming amateurs who had won titles or kept his favor, he would hand out fifty, and one-hundred-dollar bills.

As Charleston became more successful, he began to neglect his amateur operation. Unlike other big-time fight managers, with others actually doing the training, Charleston groomed his amateur stars from scratch. Along with the emergence of Wonderful Magnificent, this was indeed the secret to his success.

Charleston was not a man to leave himself or his interests unprotected. He knew any boxer could be beaten. His other champions were in no way Magnificent. For this reason, he was known in the boxing business to be overly "protective."

Charleston was currently having problems getting an acceptable deal for a Magnificent-and-Jordan bout. In the sporting world, such a fight was known to be a potential blockbuster. Several big-name promoters had begun to make offers. Greg Jackson, the high-profile black promoter, wasted no time.

"Hey, brother, let's make this fight happen. I can get you and Magnificent a king's ransom," he boasted.

"I don't know," replied Charleston. "Can you deliver Jordan?"

Charleston figured Jackson would say yes. Outside of hating Jackson intensely, Charleston knew Jordan dealt with no promoter exclusively. For this reason, Charleston disliked Jackson and didn't trust him. In truth, Charleston didn't like dealing with black people in any business setting.

The big promoter Shapiro Einstein, also wanted desperately to do the bout. Though Charleston would not admit it, he knew Shapiro hated doing business with blacks. After all, he promoted championship bouts in South Africa when it was taboo. His weakness was his love of money.

Shapiro had previously worked in the California District Attorney office until he helped down-on-his-luck ex-champion Willie Forello with a case. With that, Shapiro got the contagious boxing bug and jumped headfirst into promotion.

"I can get you and Magnificent ten-million," Shapiro said, hoping for a positive response.

"So, what," replied Charleston? "That may be cheap compared to what this fight can do."

"I know you've been talking to Jackson," Shapiro practically spat. "That no-good bastard couldn't be fair to Jesus Christ."

Charleston knew that this was the pot calling the kettle black, but he would do business with Shapiro again. Just not on this fight.

It was known in boxing circles that early on in his career Magnificent had made relatively low purses while fighting on some of Shapiro's cards. This would eventually become one of several sore spots between Charleston and Magnificent.

Charleston knew it was inevitable that Jordan and Magnificent would meet. Now was the time to make his move. Sure, Jordan and Magnificent were the talk of boxing. Everywhere you went, this proposed "showdown" was the main topic of conversation. There was one problem, and Charleston knew he needed to take care of it himself.

Numwar Nasser was born in Antiqua. He was one of twelve children. As a small boy, he used to swim in the ocean and fish with a spear. He had been born into grinding poverty. Until Numwar came stateside, he had never seen an indoor restroom.

As a young child, Numwar had been ashamed to go to school because his clothes were mere rags. Sometimes he would climb the walls of the elegant estates and poach the fruit from the trees. In the afternoon he would sing and dance on street corners to collect money from tourist to bring home to his mother.

While returning home one day from a poaching mission, Numwar saw a group of men in the corner store. They were shouting and cheering at the television as they watched a championship bout.

"Then and there, I wanted to become a world champion," Numwar would later tell the press.

At the age of thirteen, Numwar wandered into the Commonwealth Youth Gym in Antiqua to begin formal training. Oliver Xavier, who managed the gym, didn't know what to make of the skinny boy and didn't expect much. He usually ran the kids off, but Numwar was different.

"Whatdya want now, boy," Oliver asked in his lilting accent? "I have no time for play stuff. Got my own business to tend to."

"I want to be champion of the world," came back the calm reply from Numwar. I want to be like Muhammad Ali."

Xavier was a skilled teacher who was known in boxing as having the goods. He could communicate with a boxer, which made training fun. Xavier himself years ago had represented Antigua in the Olympic Games, winning a bronze medal.

Oliver's setback came early in his professional career when he was severely thumbed by an opponent. He suffered a detached retina in his left eye. What sorrow Xavier felt watching his dream of becoming a champion slip away.

After months of pondering, Xavier decided to help other children like himself. He finally found employment working for the Youth Authority, developing kids like Numwar Nasser.

Numwar immersed himself and his whole life into boxing. He was a sponge to all the knowledge Xavier could impart. He began to execute all the teachings of his boxing professor.

Numwar flowed in the ring and was able to master any style. He was not as explosive as Magnificent, or as lighting fast as Jordan, but in time Numwar would become more complete.

His rise through the amateurs was not that ballyhooed, but Numwar advanced nonetheless by winning the Commonwealth amateur title twice. He also defeated all the national champions in his weight class from Jamaica, Virgin Islands, Barbados, Puerto Rico, and Trinidad. He was excited to make the Olympic team until an attack of appendicitis forced him to step down. He was disappointed, but not worried. His star was still on the rise.

Xavier knew his protégé was ready to go stateside. "You ready now to go'n up ta ladder I think now," said the wise coach. "Got to send you, stateside if you go'n be champion."

Having no connections or money, Xavier sent Numwar to a small nickel and dime manager in New York. The relationship did not bear fruit and ended abruptly leaving Numwar with few options. From that point forward, Numwar changed managers as quickly as he fired combinations. He became one without trust; therefore, questioning anybody's intentions concerning him openly and often. Only in the ring was he at peace.

Numwar was a gifted artist, with an unshakable sense of timing. He was unhurried in his movements. Like a computer with memory, Numwar was accurate. He was not the puncher Magnificent was, and to a lesser degree, Jordan either; but he was better defensively than Magnificent, and equal to Jordan in this all too forgotten ring skill.

His counter-punching was untouchable. He was blessed with patience, like the great Hank Aaron in the batter's box, behind in the count. He would force the pitcher to give him his pitch and then blast it out of the ballpark.

Numwar's idol remained Muhammed Ali, but he was closer to the great Ezzard Charles in style. Like Charles before him, Numwar was a wickedly proficient body-puncher with either hand. He used body punches as knockout blows. Brilliant as any tactician, Numwar would counter with body shots as his opponents came to him. This approach was his way of maximizing the draining effect on his opponents by using their weight against them. He would systematically place his big shots at the liver, spleen, heart, kidneys, and rib cage on both sides.

Numwar was now a dangerous boxer and a threat in the middleweight division. Unlike most fighters, he could place his shots, while not being hit in return. His counter-punching was excellent, but his technical brilliance did not make him commercial like his rivals Jordan and Magnificent.

Without recognition, Numwar suffered economically at the box office. Still, he kept winning. All of the world governing bodies had him ranked as the number one contender with a record of forty wins, no losses, and thirty-eight knockouts. To his deep chagrin, only two people were keeping him from his goal, and even they could not look upon this smooth ring craftsman without silence.

Magnificent and Jordan would meet in a unification of the title. Economics demanded it, but after gaining a king's ransom, the prospect of meeting Numwar would be a fight of no gain, and possibly no win.

This depressed Numwar. He desperately wanted to be champion of the world. Bitterness was creeping into him daily. Unlike other world-class boxers who would take long layoffs between bouts, Numwar lived in the gym.

"I must be ready when my chance comes," he would tell anyone who would listen.

Numwar would rest only a week between bouts. Even then, he would go right back to the gym and work on all phases of his craft. Some days he would work on the heavy bag. On other days it would be just the rope, speed bag and shadow-boxing.

As part of his daily routine, Numwar put himself through

calisthenics, strengthening his shoulders, back, chest, abdomen, neck, and legs. In addition to running, he did sets of rigorous sprinting. Sometimes ten two-hundred yards, five one-hundred-yard, and six forty-yard sprints. He was an athlete who loved to work hard, not leaving anything to chance. Yes, Numwar would be a hard man to deny.

Chapter 2

SWEET POISON

Once again, Charleston was on the move. He was headed to New York City. "I'm going to see this Nasser kid fight," he told his wife, Danielle. "I always got to think about our future baby. You know I'm the man, right?"

Danielle didn't know this was only one of three reasons her husband was flying to New York. The others were to meet privately with Mitch Danton, and a beautiful woman named Theresa Tarver.

Mitch Danton was an attorney and the adviser for Hiwatha "Absolute" Jordan. He was the "King's" mouthpiece, and therefore was holding the goods.

Mitch lived near Hiwatha, in Virginia Beach, with his wife, Charlotte. This is how he came to represent Hiwatha after meeting him at a neighborhood party thrown by friends. The two struck up a conversation about a multitude of things, and Hiwatha was in awe of Mitch's intelligence and wisdom.

Hiwatha's only concern for Mitch was the sexual escapes of his beautiful wife, Charlotte. Hiwatha knew his friend and confidant adored Charlotte and had no idea about the smooth-talking men that graced her bed in his absence. After the loss of their two children in a plane crash two years earlier, Charlotte's heart and soul had grown cold.

Hiwatha himself, before knowing Mitch, had thrilled Charlotte with his manhood. The two had met at a party thrown for him after he'd become champion. Though Charlotte was ten years his senior, Hiwatha was captivated by her beauty and gorgeous figure. Amid his shaking of hands, he caught Charlotte studying him from her table. The black dress she wore was low-cut and revealed her well-shaped breasts, but it was her smile that charmed the hell out of him.

When the grueling task of introductions was over, Hiwatha went over to Charlotte's table and asked her to dance. They stayed on the dance floor for a long time enjoying each other's company and grooving to the beat of the music. Hiwatha knew if they stopped dancing, people would distract him by asking for his autograph or trying to be in his company. Right now, the only attention he wanted was from Charlotte.

When the D.J. paused to make an announcement, Hiwatha grabbed Charlotte's hand and headed straight for the exit.

"We must go somewhere quiet so we can talk," he whispered in her ear. "Just follow me, and don't stop."

"I have to get my purse from the table," Charlotte replied.

"Listen beautiful, take my key, and meet me in room 2213. I would like to know more about you, but with all these people, we won't be able to talk privately. If I don't get out of here right now, I will never get out."

With that, Hiwatha rushed to the front desk to get another key. On his way to the elevator, he stopped to sign a few autographs. Though he loved being a celebrity, this was one of the downsides.

Once inside his spacious suite, Hiwatha slipped into something more comfortable and waited for the beautiful woman whose name he didn't know. With a body like that, you can just call her "Diamond," he thought.

Hiwatha laid across the lounge chair in front of the fireplace as he thought of Charlotte. What a pleasure it would be to have her tonight. As these thoughts lingered in his mind, he heard a soft knock at the door. With his ego, he never doubted she was coming.

Like a gazelle, Charlotte strode into the room with confidence. Her long, beautiful, blonde hair flowed, and her scent instantly drove him wild. Hiwatha sensed his erection at the sight of her and eased up behind Charlotte and began kissing her neck. Charlotte removed his hands and let them slide gently down her sides. Hiwatha felt every curve of her body.

"I thought you said we were going to talk," Charlotte said in a seductive voice. "At least offer me a drink and pretend for a moment that I am a lady, and you still have some class."

"Oh, forgive me," Hiwatha replied as he walked over to the bar. "I must have forgotten my manners. What would you like to drink? I have soda, beer, and wine. If none of that suits your taste, I can call room service."

"Do you have red wine?" Charlotte asked. "It usually puts me at ease."

"Then red it is," Hiwatha responded. "By the way, what is your name? You never told me, and I was so taken by you, I forgot to ask."

"My name is Charlotte Danton," she said warmly. "I live here in Virginia Beach."

"Well, that's perfect, Miss Danton, because I'm here to look at some property. I saw an estate off Hungarian Road yesterday that blew my mind. I got right on the phone and told my accountant I had to have it. Now looking at you, I see why it felt so much like home."

"Hungarian Road?" Charlotte asked with surprise. "Why that's close to where I live. Do you know the address?"

"I can't recall," responded Hiwatha. My real estate agent is handling it. I've been traveling a lot, and it's time for me to settle down. When I saw Virginia Beach, I knew I could live here."

They made idle conversation as they sipped their drinks. Hiwatha studied Charlotte intently before making his move. When the time was right, he finally knelt down in front of her and removed her shoes. Hiwatha began massaging her feet and slowly moved his hand up Charlotte's leg until he reached the base of her buttock. Just like he thought, it was firm and round.

Charlotte's head fell back on the chair, and she began moving to the rhythm of his touch. Before long, they were making passionate love on the rug in front of the fireplace.

Hiwatha thought of himself as a skilled lover, except Charlotte was so passionate at her lovemaking it caught him off guard, and definitely blew his mind. There was no doubt she was the teacher and he the student.

Hiwatha wanted more of this mystery woman. After their evening together, he called Charlotte every chance he got. He also became more resolute in closing the deal on his new house.

At first, Charlotte appeared open to his repeated calls, then suddenly there was a problem reaching her, and it was driving Hiwatha crazy. Charlotte didn't respond to his voice message about sending a plane ticket to his fight or his invitation to take her to the islands.

Hiwatha was perplexed as to what the problem was. Any other woman would have forsaken God Almighty for him. He became angry but refused to show it or tell anyone what was wrong. Everyone around him just accepted that he was not in a good mood. After all, he was the man in charge.

When Hiwatha moved into his new house, he decided to give Charlotte a call. The number was disconnected. He tried to find her in the phone book, but the only Danton he saw was Mitch Danton.

One night, Hiwatha was invited to a neighbor's party, and there sat Charlotte, with a gorgeous red sundress cut down to the small of her back. Though there were other people at the bar, Hiwatha saw only Charlotte. He felt happy and upset to finally see her. Regardless of his feelings, he wanted to say something to her but didn't want to appear desperate; nor did he want her to know how much he'd longed to see her again. When Charlotte walked out on the balcony alone, Hiwatha finally decided to approach her.

"What is going on with you, mystery, woman? I've been trying to reach you. Why haven't you returned my calls? I can understand most things, but I clearly think you owe me an explanation."

"Why do I owe you an explanation?" Charlotte asked without the slightest bit of concern in her voice. "I'm a grown woman, and you, my dear, are definitely a grown man. It is not my job or duty to hold your hand. Just because we had sex one night, you think that entitles you to some type of get-out-of-jail-free card?"

Hiwatha was stunned by her response, and his ego was shattered. He couldn't believe that Charlotte, who had made love to him so passionately, was being so cold. What had he done to her, or was this lady truly a real bitch? As Hiwatha tried to gather his composure, a well-dressed man walked up behind Charlotte and grabbed her hand. Hiwatha could not make out what he whispered in her ear.

Hiwatha was clearly annoyed when Charlotte turned around and placed a kiss on the man's lips. They both looked at Hiwatha as they walked off, laughing and holding hands. Charlotte's date turned back to apologize and extended his hand. Hiwatha did not accept. He was disgusted.

"I'm sorry man," her date commented. "I was just missing my beautiful lady. Congratulations on your win over Azume. He had that ass-kicking coming."

Hiwatha was humiliated. He tried for the rest of the evening to make Charlotte uncomfortable by staring. This didn't faze Charlotte.

As time went on, there were more parties and many men that he'd see in Charlotte's company. Hiwatha decided Charlotte was sweet poison.

———— ◆ ————

As Charleston sat on the plane, he was in deep thought about his upcoming meeting with Mitch Danton. This would really get the ball rolling for the lucrative and long-awaited showdown. Regardless of the outcome, Charleston felt he would become rich beyond his wildest dreams.

His thoughts slowly gravitated to his third and most appealing reason for the trip, Theresa Tarver. Charleston had met Theresa at a press luncheon in Chicago where he and Wonderful were being honored as "Sportsmen of the Year." Charleston upon seeing Theresa was so dumb-struck by her beauty, he almost passed out.

Theresa was one to make even a preacher lust after her. She was mocha in color, with a flawless, unblemished, smooth complexion, a set of round full lips and perfectly-tapered long legs. Her shoulder-length hair complemented her dark green eyes. She was class personified, Ivy League-educated and blessed with a warm, personable charm.

Theresa worked as an attorney in the State's Attorney General's office. When she was first introduced to Charleston, Theresa did not recognize or acknowledge his statue in boxing. His ego was crushed. Despite his own vanity, Charleston knew a "superstar" when he saw one.

As his plane raced toward the Kennedy Airport in New York, Charleston could hardly wait for landing. He had pursued Theresa for weeks before realizing she was no groupie.

Theresa was in New York for the weekend visiting relatives and friends. Although she didn't think of Charleston as attractive, Theresa agreed to meet him for dinner at a restaurant called Twenty-One in Manhattan.

Charleston had repeatedly called her office to inquire about dinner, and reluctantly, Theresa finally said yes. He cared little that the date was in New York. His goal was to be in her company.

Charleston couldn't wait to get his business with Mitch Danton behind him. Numwar Nasser was merely an afterthought. Charleston was focused on the new challenge Theresa Tarver presented in his life. It had been a long time since a woman could make his manhood rise at the mere thought of her name.

Charleston rushed from the Kennedy Airport to Numwar's fight. Upon entering the arena, he took his usual ringside seat. To his surprise, Numwar was already on the money. His jab was working to perfection. With remarkable rapidity, his left-hooks thudded off the body and head of Rene Sanguillan.

Sanguillan tried to counter with a vicious right-hand, but Numwar countered by turning his left shoulder inward and allowing the punch to slide harmlessly over his neck. With split-second timing, Numwar again countered with a wicked right-uppercut to the spleen of Sanguillan, followed by a double left hook to his liver and a whistling left-hook to the chin. As Sanguillan hit the canvas, the crowd was strangely silent before erupting in a tremendous roar.

The referee didn't bother to count as he removed the mouthpiece from the unconscious boxer's mouth. It had taken fewer than four rounds to dispose of the world's number sixth-ranked contender. Sanguillan was definitely not a bum, but unfortunately, against Numwar, he had no chance. After taking such a beating, it would be foolish for Sanguillan to ever fight again.

At ringside, the precision and controlled savagery of Nasser's performance was not lost on Charleston or Mitch.

"He's a bad dude," said Charleston, confirming the obvious.

"I don't want any traffic with that son-of-a-bitch," said the astute Danton.

The two shook their heads and quickly brought up the business of the upcoming "Fight of the Century." Mitch agreed with Charleston that they should go with an independent promoter. Charleston wanted a fifty-fifty split between Jordan and Magnificent in everything. Mitch politely responded, knowing he had the upper hand.

"No way will Hiwatha go for that," stated Mitch. "We know that Magnificent is a super attraction. He's got half the title and is exciting to watch. I know Magnificent can fight, but Hiwatha is the biggest draw in boxing and the hottest ticket in the world of sports." Mitch smiled knowingly at Charleston before proceeding.

"I know why Hiwatha gets under your skin. The media loves him. All the major corporations want him for commercials and endorsements. Also, my friend, the women, love him. So read my lips. For these reasons, Hiwatha goes fifty-fifty with nobody. So, let's get down to the brass tacks," Mitch continued earnestly.

"We can do a sixty-forty split on the fighter's portion of the pay-per-view. Just let me make the deal?"

Mitch leaned back to get a feel for Charleston, who was thinking over the proposal. He let the silence linger before continuing.

"I think we can get Magnificent a purse of at least twenty-million, maybe more. You won't get that much anywhere else. Believe me."

Charleston hated the idea of not being on an equal basis with Jordan, but they were not in the driver's seat. Jordan was the draw, and Charleston knew it. He also knew Magnificent would scream to holy heaven at a deal less than fifty percent, but twenty-million was nothing to sneeze at.

Besides, this was just a low estimate. If everything turned out right, who knew how much they actually could earn.

"Okay, but no Shapiro and definitely no Jackson," replied Charleston. "Get an independent promoter. Work out the pay-per-view deal and the up-front money. You know the rest training expenses, travel, and fight site. You can do it anywhere but Reno. I'm concerned about the altitude. If these things are right, we can get it on."

Charleston had just made the biggest deal of his life. Now that business was done, he bought up the subject of Numwar Nasser. After the Jordan / Magnificent fight, someone would have to fight him.

"Not us," replied Mitch.

"I'm gonna sign him," laughed Charleston. "This way, I can keep him away from both of us."

"It could work," said Mitch. "Just remember, this guy could cause you problems. That's a high price to pay just to cover your ass," reasoned Mitch.

"Forget it," responded Charleston. "I'm not signing him."

Charleston was embarrassed that Mitch had seen through his smokescreen. Still, it was essential to cover his managerial future in boxing. With that, the meeting wrapped up, and Mitch stood to shake Charleston's hand.

"Look, Charleston, I'll keep you informed as things progress."

Charleston agreed and left the meeting in a hurry. He raced from the arena to his limo parked outback. He quickly gave instructions to the driver.

"I need you to step on the gas," said Charleston. "I'm in a hurry. Get me to a restaurant called Twenty-One in Manhattan. I've got a date with the queen."

Charleston laughed, but there was something different about Theresa. As he stepped from the limo, Charleston was careful not to wrinkle his suit.

"Give me your best table," he told the hostess, slipping her a twenty-dollar bill.

Theresa intentionally arrived late. She lived to make big impressions and grand entrances. Tonight, was no different. Her dress fit every curve of her body and gave a bold view of her long, shapely legs. As Theresa came closer, Charleston was slowly undressing her with his eyes. Theresa had Charleston dangling on her string. When she reached the table, Charleston stood to greet her.

"You look absolutely stunning tonight," Charleston stated as he pulled her seat back from the table.

"Why thank you," replied Theresa. "How was your flight?" she asked.

Theresa had inquired about Charleston through a few friends who gave her useful background information that changed her mind about Charleston. Theresa was now attracted to what she perceived to be his power and notoriety.

At almost thirty years of age, Theresa was still "shopping," as the girls would say, and just maybe Charleston could be her future husband. For Theresa, the challenge had begun.

Though Charleston knew they were worlds apart, he

was smitten with her. His only areas of expertise were boxing and being a great manipulator.

Theresa was educated and skilled in both law and economics. She was well-read and personified the word class without being a snob.

She had spent time with relatives earlier that day and shopped with her girlfriends that afternoon. Now Theresa was studying the man sitting across the table. She sensed his desire and decided he was indeed worthy of a "tryout."

Theresa seductively sat back in her chair and slowly crossed her legs to reveal just enough of her thighs to make every man sitting nearby turn to steal a peek. This move was not lost on Charleston, who was looking right into her eyes and down the front of her dress. He purposely dropped his napkin to the floor to get a better view of her, shapely thighs.

"I really don't believe I'm here," Theresa said while allowing her dress to rise another inch. "I've been out all day shopping with friends. It's been an exhausting experience."

"Well, I'm here to be with you," Charleston answered honestly. "I'd like to get to know you. Why else would I come all the way to New York for a date?"

"Oh, really," Theresa teased. "I bet there are many women in your life. I'm sure you have a few right now in New York probably waiting for your call. My instincts tell me that women come easily for you. What's your angle? The conquest or merely sexual satisfaction."

At that moment, Charleston knew this woman was

capable of causing him to seriously evaluate himself. He began to realize this piece of ass would not come cheap.

Charleston sat across the table and studied Theresa for a moment. She definitely had an agenda. Until he found out what it was, Charleston decided not to tell her about his wife, Danielle. That would be kept secret for now.

Charleston finally concluded, like most women, Theresa had to like money and pretty things. Fortunately, he was just the guy to give it to her.

"Tell me, Theresa, have you ever been to a championship fight in Las Vegas?"

"No, I'm afraid I haven't had the opportunity," she replied.

"Well, I have a fight coming up in Las Vegas next month. Do you think you could get away from work for a few days and come with me? I would love to show you Las Vegas. Maybe even take an afternoon to go shopping. You look like a woman who might enjoy that. In return, I get to enjoy being in your company. I already have a suite at The Desert Palace Hotel. What do you say?"

"I would have to think about that," replied Theresa. "I don't really know you. Besides, I have a lot of work to do in the office."

Theresa knew she was not ready to go to bed with Charleston. The days of taking trips with men and not sleeping with them were over. She was beyond playing those games. Theresa was a woman that liked sex on her terms.

Charleston was not reading her signals; therefore,

remained persistent in his pursuit. The same way he did with most women.

"I want you, Theresa," Charleston said, searching her eyes for confirmation. "There is something you do to me that I can't explain. It's just the way you make me feel. What is wrong with a man wanting more of that? What is wrong with me, wanting you?"

"There's nothing wrong with that," replied Theresa. "It's just that things in life take time. I am not in a hurry, and I would appreciate you more if you weren't either."

"Well, at least join me for a drink after dinner," Charleston said with passion in his eyes. "I am staying at the Hotel Ambassador, and it's not far from here."

Theresa was not expecting Charleston to invite her to his room on their first date. What could he be thinking to do that? Yes, she wanted his attention, but Theresa had no intentions of being just a bed partner. His approach to the evening insulted her. She politely refused his invitation and rose from the table.

"Mr. Orlando, some things in life may be free, but not this girl. And definitely not tonight. I think you have a couple of phone calls to make if you just want someone in your bed tonight."

Theresa started to walk away, then paused and looked back at Charleston still seated at the table with a surprised look on his face. Charleston wasn't quite sure what just happened.

"Please don't bother to get up," Theresa said, looking

over her shoulder. "I know my way out. Oh, and thanks for dinner."

As Charleston lay on his hotel bed, his heart was pumping a mile a minute. He hated traveling alone and would typically arrange for one of his women to meet him. He usually put them up in a hotel opposite his and saw them once his business dealings were done. He had become an expert at trickery.

This had become a sore spot in his relationship with Danielle. She was by no means a dumb woman. As Charleston's fortune grew, the more resolute she was about keeping him.

Danielle knew Charleston was not faithful to her but refused to let another woman benefit from her hard work and sacrifice. She had stood by Charleston through the tough times and raised their children. She had married Charleston at eighteen and supported him through his many failed endeavors.

No doubt, boxing was Charleston's ticket, but as his success grew, their marriage suffered. Though Danielle was in the prime of her life, she was alone, and Charleston was not meeting her needs sexually. For now, she would let him have his fun, but when it came to the money, it was hers as well.

Danielle had no intentions of leaving the mansion she called home. Being the envy of her friends and family was too rewarding. She would help them out here or there, but to be on the same level as them again was unthinkable.

As her husband became more public, the further apart they grew. His sexual conquests were no secret. Charleston was seen around town with a lineup of young bed partners. Though he had lodged in his photographic memory a mental road map of every available hotel and willing woman, in Danielle's eyes Charleston managed to keep his image of a dutiful husband intact. He always came home and never allowed himself to be photographed in public with other women. This was difficult because Charleston loved getting his picture taken, especially after his plastic surgery.

Over the past weeks, Charleston had a particular look in his eyes. Danielle knew the look but hadn't seen it in years. She sensed that he was not alone in New York, however, tonight, to Charleston's displeasure, he was by himself. He wanted desperately to be with the beautiful Theresa Tarver. No one else would do. Not even Danielle.

Unable to sleep, Charleston tossed and turned in his bed thinking of Theresa. She had left him at the restaurant. She wouldn't even allow him to escort her back to her relative's home on the east side. Charleston was upset with her rejection but tried not to show it. Instead, he decided to focus on his plan to sign the number one contender.

———◎———

Numwar was visibly upset as he sat looking at his friends. His frustration was understandable. Hadn't he been named "Fighter of the Year" by the Boxing Writers Association? He was the boxer no one wanted to fight.

Numwar could only hope to get a shot at "America's Hero" Hiwatha "Absolute" Jordan. It was also evident that the other superstar of the weight class, Wonderful Magnificent, was headed toward a multi-million-dollar collision. Numwar was definitely the odd man out.

"What do I have to do to get a title shot?" He asked himself while looking around his sparse living room. I've beaten everyone out there, and still can't get a chance to fight for the title. I know I can beat both of them."

Numwar thought back to when he had only six pro bouts. He was summoned to Brooklyn, New York to work as a sparring partner for Hiwatha. At the time, Hiwatha was barely a year away from becoming champion. He was world-rated and getting the "big pub," as Numwar was fond of saying. The first two days, Numwar didn't have the opportunity to spar with the future king, but on the third day, he did.

Hiwatha had a habit earlier in his career of humiliating his sparring partners. He would break ribs and noses as easily as taking a drink of water. He would let everyone know that these boxers were there for his personal target practice.

Hiwatha came out firing hard at Numwar, basically shaking him up. Numwar instantly tasted his own blood, caused by a laser beam right-cross-counter over his lazy left lead. Hiwatha then felt he could do as he pleased, however, Numwar found him with a few sharp jabs and began to counter with sharp-hooks of his own.

Numwar was not the master of the champion-to-be, but neither was he the buffoon. Numwar gained Hiwatha's respect. He was let go the next day after a total of four rounds. He had boxed only twice with the king but now felt he too could be king one day.

In reality, Numwar struggled with the fact he was not yet a household name. Sure, he was a national idol in the Caribbean and his native Antigua, but Numwar needed more national television exposure in the United States. How could he get better connections and still avoid the entanglements and deceit that big-time promoters were known for?

Numwar didn't want to be locked into a long-term option agreement with a particular promoter. This would keep his price down when and if he became champion.

He once thought about signing with the colorful Greg Jackson, except rumor had it that Jackson indeed only promoted heavyweights and was notorious for short-changing his fighters on their already-agreed-upon purses. Numwar and other boxers tried to avoid doing business with Jackson.

On the other side of the ring was Shapiro Einstein, a promoter who was as colorless and dull as Jackson was bombastic. To his credit, Einstein was one of the few promoters with a weekly televised fight show. He also promoted dozens of world title bouts and was known to be a shrewd negotiator. No matter how much of a gate attraction a boxer was, Shapiro never gave them their full-dollar value. He also required a four-bout promotional option, with purses already set. This is why Shapiro could never promote a Jordan title bout.

Shapiro was very successful in dealing with Charleston.

He even told his staff behind closed doors that he could get Magnificent manager to go along with anything. It was this confidence that led him to believe that he would have a hand in the promotion of the Fight of the Century, but Charleston, with the help of Mitch Danton, wanted to throw the boxing establishment for a loop.

Chapter 3

THE NUMBER ONE CONTENDER

Their lovemaking was nakedly passionate and full of sensual passion. Charleston was at the end of the earth. He could not caress Theresa' body enough. She was perfection to him. Her breasts were small melons, with nipples the color of burnished copper. They stood at arresting attention as he eagerly kissed them.

Her full legs and omnipotent buttocks seemed to flow beneath him. So hungrily did he kiss her mouth, it was as if Charleston had come out of the Sahara Desert near death and stumbled upon an oasis.

Theresa held nothing back as she raced her hands from the back of his head to the base of his clenched buttocks. Charleston had never felt such passion. Not with Danielle or any of his groupies. He could hear his heartbeat in his ears. As he met Theresa, she seemed to mesh with him. He thrust slowly at first, but could not hold himself. Lustily and without hesitation, they moved in motion.

A sexual tapestry fueled by unabated hunger seemed

to be reaching into the fantasies of his dreams, but this was no dream. Theresa kisses, touch, and scent all inspired him into a timeless sexual Shangri-La. He felt an internal sensation that left him still kissing her passionately. Charleston decided then and there never to be without her.

⸻ ((●)) ⸻

As Numwar stepped from the airport terminal, he was taken back by Charleston's limousine. Numwar had ridden in many limousines, but never a golden one.

"I do everything first class," boasted Charleston.

As the two men were ushered into the back of the custom-made chariot, Charleston continued.

"See, that's what's wrong with your career. You're not getting that first-class treatment. You need to be promoted right. You're missing someone who can pick the right opponents and get you the big fights. Pay-per-view is where it's at today, baby!"

Numwar was a very observant man. While Charleston went on about his boxing operation, Numwar was busy studying his surroundings. He was impressed with the velvet interior of the limo, which was complete with a television, sunroof, and bar. The initials C.O. lined the inner doors.

Charleston opened the sunroof as he went into his smooth recruiting pitch. His mind was set on securing another future champion, and this one was ready-made. Charleston had a way of making his visions sound inevitable.

"Look, man, Wonderful is going to kick Hiwatha's ass,

and that's a fact. With him out of the way, you can take over the middleweight division. Dominate it and clean it up."

Numwar listened intently and watched Charleston's every move. If there was a trick, he wasn't going to miss it. As he studied Charleston, Numwar had to agree, the man did know how to dress up the picture.

Charleston was wearing a custom-made beige suit, beige boots, and a cream-color silk shirt accented with a matching handkerchief in his breast pocket. His shirt was open at the collar to reveal an expensive gold chain. His wrist bore a flashy gold Rolex.

"See, Numwar, Wonderful is gonna make a ton of money with Hiwatha. After that, it's your turn to be a superstar baby. I'll get you on the major cable and television networks. You can make your first title defense in your own country."

Charleston knew Numwar had a great love for his people, so without pause, he went for the kill. Charleston was singing like a schoolboy.

"Look, you are a great fighter, maybe as good as Wonderful or Hiwatha, but who cares. You need to be seen, man. You fight in New York, and they still don't know your name."

Charleston was trying to read Numwar, so he sat back and let his last bit of rhetoric sink in. He began listening to the imperceptible whine of the smooth limo ride.

Numwar sat silent for a while, thinking. Charleston waited patiently for his answer. When Numwar finally spoke in a precise and measured tone, Charleston sat up to face him.

"I hear what you're saying, but I just want to be champion," Numwar stated in a serious tone. "I want to have enough money to care for my mother and family. Be a symbol of my countrymen and go down as one of the greatest."

"Uh-hum," replied Charleston. "I've had many world champions since I've been in the business. I think you can be a champion. You've got the talent, and I've got the connections."

"We can do business, but don't fuck with me," said Numwar. "I just want my shot. Work up a contract, and I'll read it."

Numwar grabbed Charleston's arm to make sure he clearly understood him, "Oh, and I can read, so don't come up with any bullshit."

Numwar was not like the other boxers Charleston was used to dealing with. He had been educated in the USA's "Head Start program." Numwar graduated high school with honors in English and science. In between his training and workouts, he'd attended a few years of community college in New York. Numwar knew his family was poor. When he discovered his gift was boxing, he took the sport seriously.

For a moment, Numwar thought back to a time when he almost gave up boxing. He had just arrived in New York and hadn't been in the United States very long. He'd just finished his morning classes and made the long ride back to the gym in Brooklyn. He was scheduled to spar with the then middleweight champion, Max "Sharp-Shooter" Bailey.

When Numwar walked through the gym doors, the

smell of sweat was thick in the air. Max's trainer, Davey Justice, was standing next to the ring motioning for Max to come over so he could check his gloves. His opponent, Wiley Lightfoot, stood waiting in a neutral corner to finish off the final rounds of their sparring session.

Numwar held his hand up and nodded his head to acknowledge Wiley. They were close friends and had been roommates since Numwar arrived in New York. Numwar and Wiley were both broke and struggling to make a name or leave a perceived mark in the boxing game.

Their manager at the time was a short, stout Italian man named, Shelly Dean. He owned a small house in Brooklyn where several of his future boxing prospects lived. He had hired Numwar and Wiley as sparring partners to help Max prepare for his title defense against Mark "Pretty Boy" Willis.

"Let's kick some ass today," shouted Numwar in his Jamaican accent. "We got to get my main man; Max ready to take it to the bridge. Show'em how the boys from Brooklyn handle things."

Max turned to look at Numwar as Davey finished lacing-up his gloves. Max was known to be arrogant, and Numwar was purposely playing to his ego. He had every intention of giving Max a rough time when it came to his turn to spar. In truth, he didn't really like the guy, but Numwar needed the money.

Max swiftly moved through the ropes being held open by the foot of Davey.

"Let's take it easy this last round," were the final

instructions from Davey as he hit the ring apron signaling the boxers to continue.

"Easy…I don't know what that means," responded Max. "I'm getting ready for a fight. You take it easy."

Davey shook his head. He had been in boxing a long time and was no stranger to the antics of boxers. So, Davey ignored Max comment as he watched him land several unanswered left-hands before delivering a chilling body shot to the side of Wiley, instantly bending him over. Davey called "time," but Max delivered another right-hook to the head of Wiley sending him to the canvas.

"What in the hell do you think you're doing Max?" asked Davey. "When I say "time" step back and relax, not take another shot."

It was too late. Wiley was already on the canvas, unconscious. His body jerked several times before going limp. Numwar looked on in disbelief as Davey began working to revive Wiley. Max held his gloves to his head. For the first time, Numwar saw him show some compassion.

"Man, I wasn't trying to hurt you," shouted Max. "I'm sorry, Davey. I got a little carried away. Wiley's going to be okay, right."

Davey shouted to Numwar to call the paramedics. His request was lost on the ears of Numwar who had already run to the gym office and began dialing 911. When the paramedics arrived, they tried to save Wiley. All the inhabitants of the gym were silent as they lifted Wiley on the gurney and carried his body through the gym doors.

Numwar before stumbling outside of the gym to get a final look at his friend turned to Max and landed a blow to his chin so devastating, he knocked him over the water cooler. Numwar was crying uncontrollably as he picked up the large water bottle and threw it on top of Max's head.

Once in front of the gym, Numwar watched as the paramedics drove off with his friend. There were no blaring sirens just the heavy beat of his unsettled heart. Numwar put his head in his hands to say a prayer for Wiley and his family. He knew his dream of becoming champion was being tested. It was two months before Numwar returned to the gym with a different purpose and a renewal of faith.

"Where have you been?" asked Davey. "We were all worried about you."

"I know," answered Numwar. "I had to get pass my fear of dying. I can't become a world champion unless I'm willing to put my life on the line. I'm not saying I am willing to die for a world-class title, but I am willing to die to help my family rise above poverty."

As Numwar rode in Charleston's golden limo, he thought of Wiley. He realized how much he'd sacrificed. Numwar was hoping he wouldn't have much further to go. Although he had no idea what Charleston's true intentions were, Numwar prayed they were honorable.

Unfortunately, Charleston was a man that never wanted to be left hanging. Though he felt Magnificent was the baddest boxer in the world, Charleston knew anything could happen in the ring with two super athletes. Even with his enormous ego, Charleston had to admit that as an all-around ring performer, Hiwatha might be superior.

Magnificent had a never-ending reach, probably the best left-jab in boxing and the unstoppable feared "bazooka" right-hand. He was definitely a gifted athlete that had captured his half of the middleweight title by nearly decapitating Jean Carne of France.

It all seemed perfect, but Charleston knew Magnificent still had flaws. All of them had not been worked out in the gym or under the hot lights of competition. After running up his knockout totals, Magnificent seemed to forget about defense. His stamina was suspect even as an amateur. Often, Magnificent would be gassed by the second round, but fortunately, in this area, he had improved.

Magnificent record was filled with tankers, bums and occasionally a cadaver, but there were several world-class fighters on his list of victims. Jackie Masters had given a tired Magnificent a scuffle. He finally managed to stop Masters with a left-jab closing his right eye.

There also was tough, grizzled veteran Fred Taylor, who lasted until the last thirty seconds of the tenth round. Then the bazooka right-hand found Taylor and knocked him to the canvass.

Magnificent had come a long way, but no one was unbeatable. Charleston had done an excellent job cloaking his fighter in the veil of invincibility. Magnificent had successfully defended the title ten times and proven he could dominate and crush world-class opposition. It would take an almost superhuman effort to unseat this former hungry street urchin. Just maybe Hiwatha "Absolute" Jordan was superhuman.

———————⋘⦿⋙———————

Hiwatha would strip naked after every workout. He would stand before a full-length mirror and examine himself. He checked with the eye of a surgeon looking for the slightest sign of imperfection. To his pleasure, there were none. Hiwatha was a perfect specimen. No Greek statue was any better. His face was as magnificent as his physique. Though, masculine, his features were plain, almost pretty.

The women who raced to his bed were startled to learn that he was indeed a skilled smooth and satisfying lover. Hiwatha would thrill, tease, and please them, as he would his boxing audience...fully.

Like a great artist, Hiwatha went about his training with a purposeful air. When he entered the ring, people felt as if they were being treated to a performance, like that of Andre Watts, the classical pianist, or the great trumpeter Wynton Marsalis.

Though Hiwatha did not possess the bazooka right-hand of Magnificent, his left was equal to that of "Sugar" Ray Robinson, Bob Foster, Ezzard Charles, Alexis Arguello and a few others in boxing history.

At will, Hiwatha's defense was impenetrable. His stamina was like that of an Olympic track star. He processed information faster than most mere mortals. Like all great performers, Hiwatha was versatile. He could make adjustments, analyze, and defeat any style. Although Charleston didn't want to admit it, Hiwatha had fought tougher opposition.

In his heart, Charleston envied Hiwatha, and that made him uneasy. His master appeal galled Charleston, and to a lesser degree Magnificent. When Hiwatha entered a room, there was a noticeable shift in focus. It didn't help that he was a cunning boxer who could take advantage of the least mistake of an opponent. This concerned Charleston.

His saving grace would be the big payday. Charleston knew their match-up would rate up there with Ali / Frazier and the Holmes / Norton war. Despite his feelings, Charleston decided to be patient, something he couldn't do when it came to Theresa Tarver.

Her answering machine had gone off for the third time in an hour. Theresa would not answer.

"Hello, this is Charleston," he growled. "It's eleven o'clock. I've been calling you steadily since eight o'clock this evening. Where are you?" Charleston demanded. "When you get in, call me." With that, he hung up.

Theresa was already in the bedroom Charleston desperately wanted to sleep in. Their affair had been going on for almost a year. They would make love passionately all over the country, then without notice, fight like heart-broken sailors. Charleston would curse her unmercifully. His jealousy was sickening. He couldn't stand the thought of another man touching her.

Charleston brought Theresa a brand-new red Mercedes and a cell phone, so he could contact her twenty-four hours a day. He spent thousands of dollars on diamond rings, ten thousand on a gold-encrusted tennis bracelet laced with diamonds, and forked over the money to buy her a home in a money enclave just a short ride away from him.

Charleston was obsessed with Theresa, and after finding out he was married, Theresa was obsessed with becoming Mrs. Orlando. Once on a trip to Los Angeles, the lovers had quarreled so vehemently Theresa hid from Charleston for over an hour. This sent him into a panic until he later found her in the closet. Charleston was furious.

Due to her work with the State Attorney General's office, Theresa was well known and highly respected throughout the state. She was seen as a rising star in political circles, and Theresa no longer wanted to play the back-up role. She had fallen in love with Charleston.

"Where have you been?" Charleston demanded.

"Out," Theresa responded.

"Why didn't you call me when I phoned?" He said, almost with a whine. "You know how much I need you,"

"Well, where are you when I need you?" she asked. "Where are you when I want to make love? Yes, you're at home with your wife, or off with one of your groupies."

Charleston was livid and began to curse profusely. He had promised to get a divorce, knowing full well he would never leave Danielle. That could generate negative publicity and definitely not be suitable for his image. There also was the financial aspect. No, things were okay just the way they were.

The same way Charleston used everyone else, he was going to use Theresa. Unfortunately, he hadn't realized Theresa was a worthy adversary. One Charleston could not emotionally live without.

"Goddammit, I want to see you right now," he shouted into the phone.

"Come on over," she teased.

Theresa knew Charleston could not leave home at this late hour without another lie.

"Better still," she cooed. "I'll come over there right now."

With that statement, Theresa hung up. Charleston was still frantically whispering into the phone.

"Wait a minute, Theresa. Theresa!"

Chapter 4

LET'S MAKE A DEAL

Mitch Danton had never seen a home so awe-inspiring. It seemed to be a never-ending mural painting come to life. It was an estate of the first magnitude. Marble statues graced the entrance with lawns manicured to perfection. There was a private nine-hole golf course, a private helicopter port, Olympic-sized swimming pool, lighted tennis courts, a horse stable, and a fully stocked wine cellar.

Mitch was surprised to see a well-manicured polo field. As a child, he loved to ride horses. The home was a cross between Disneyland and Buckingham Palace. This was "Oakridge," and it was said to be worth fifty million dollars. A high price by even Hollywood mogul standards, and yet it was the private home of the most prominent and most influential mogul in Hollywood, Antonio Rosanni.

Antonio was the head of the Unlimited Entertainment Studios. He was the unquestioned king of entertainment. His studio and other investments grossed more than thirty billion dollars a year.

Antonio loved sports. His father had left the family a major league baseball franchise, and his deceased uncle had left them holdings in a highly successful European soccer team. They also owned the stadium and the arena where they each played. Antonio himself had vast holdings in prime Southern California real estate. It was conceded that he belonged to one of the wealthiest families in the world.

Antonio was a distinguished-looking man, with a stern face, almost cold in appearance. He was in his early fifties, but you would never know it. He kept himself in great shape. It was said that his grandfather made the family fortune in the underworld before becoming legitimate and buying a small Hollywood movie studio in the early 1930s. Now their family name was associated with other American royalty.

Until now, Mitch couldn't conceive of such wealth. He was a modest man and a diligent worker. Every step of his life had been well planned. Even as a boy, he had decided to become a lawyer working his way through both college and law school. After graduation, he became an outstanding public defender.

Mitch finally decided to open his own practice. He soon met Charlotte, who came to him seeking legal advice regarding a contract she was trying to get out of with an American modeling agency. After a long international courtship, they decided to get married and soon had two adorable children.

At first, Charlotte gave up everything for her children, but after purchasing an estate in Virginia Beach, she gave in to her desires to return to the catwalk. Mitch found himself alone, trying desperately to raise their children and manage his business. He soon hired a nanny, and things seemed to work for a while.

Mitch and Charlotte both were busy that summer and decided to send the children, eleven and twelve, to California, to visit their grandparents. It was on this trip that their plane crashed in the Pacific Ocean as it made the circle along the coast preparing for landing.

Charlotte and Mitch's life was never the same after the loss of their children. Charlotte was now distant, and Mitch no longer knew how to reach her. He did know, however, that he loved her more than anything.

Mitch remained social and continued to try and get his business up and running. He didn't want to miss any potential business opportunities. When he met Hiwatha at a friend's party, Mitch was elated that they became instant friends. They started hanging out together, and finally, Hiwatha confided in him.

"Mitch, I don't want to be like these other boxers. They fight these hard fights, and all their money goes to the managers and promoters. I find that disgusting. I want to be my own manager. Will you help me?" Hiwatha asked.

From that day on, his trainer St. Claire Robinson, and Mitch were the only people Hiwatha trusted or would listen to. Hiwatha was hungry for knowledge. He took advice from Danton but researched all that he told him.

Their friendship grew as they became a team. It was a

beneficial partnership. Eventually, Hiwatha became Mitch's only client, and the association made both of them wealthy. With a little luck and a great deal along the way, they would become even richer.

Mitch was wise never to interfere with Hiwatha's training. It was clear he was merely the frontman and would assist Hiwatha with all negotiations and business.

"You advise me on the legal and monetary issues," Hiwatha told Mitch. "St. Claire and I will handle the training."

Mitch reflected on their partnership as the limousine driver opened his door. He was pleasantly surprised to see Antonio Rosanni waiting to shake his hand, "The man," himself.

Antonio appeared younger and looked more handsome than his pictures. He was evenly tanned, and his hair and mustache were trimmed perfectly. His hair was jet black, except for subtle graying at the temples. He had a very unapproachable aura that faded when he flashed his boyish smile. He was dressed in gold silk slacks and a short-sleeve white shirt. On his feet were leather thongs.

"Hello, Mr. Danton," Antonio said warmly. "Welcome to Oakridge. I hope you had a good flight."

"Glad to be here, Mr. Rosanni," replied Mitch. "The flight was as expected."

"Please call me Antonio," requested the master of the estate.

Antonio then began a guided tour of the spectacular estate. It had been in his family for a long time. After his father's death a few years earlier, his mother had decided to move back to Italy, leaving Antonio and his brother to run the family business.

Antonio obviously was proud of his family's success. He had a childlike glee and happiness about him as he went from room to room pointing out every renovation, from the hand-crafted furniture to the absolutely perfect water fountains that flowed into an indoor stream. He explained how it had taken him three years to redecorate his dream home. Mitch listened intently.

It was known throughout Hollywood that Antonio was a sports fanatic. He loved his two pro teams and was seen frequently at their games with an array of beautiful women.

Antonio was a driven and unrelenting mastermind in the movie business. He had inherited the Midas Touch". Few of his endeavors lost money.

It was Hiwatha who had met Antonio when he had just won his Olympic Gold medal. He always called Antonio a home run hitter and openly admired his lifestyle. Hiwatha hoped to be as successful and independent as the maestro one day. Now Hiwatha needed Antonio to promote the Fight of the Century. A plan he had been working on for almost a year.

As Mitch sat in the beautiful dining hall, being served a feast fit for a king, he was caught off guard when Antonio abruptly switched to the subject of the big showdown.

"How much will a fight between Hiwatha and this guy Magnificent make?" asked the movie mogul.

Before Mitch could answer, Antonio spoke again.

"You know if we could get a gross of eighty-million to maybe a hundred-million here in the States, it could be a monster."

Antonio paused to sip some champagne from his gold-and-diamond-encrusted goblet before continuing. "With international television, pay-per-view, and rebroadcast money, this could be exciting. I'm not so sure about the boxing business, but I know a good deal when I see one."

"No question about it," replied Mitch. "This is why Hiwatha sent me to see you. He doesn't trust any other promoter to handle a fight this big. Also, Hiwatha knows you can make the most money for everybody. He's not interested in a long-term promotional deal, and Hiwatha knows you would have no need for extended options."

"You know, boxing is a real dirty business," said Antonio. "It really sucks. I pay my performers, directors, writers, and everybody that works for me. This keeps them happy. I hear in boxing; this is not the case."

"I always liked Hiwatha," he continued. "He's not only fast with his hands but a quick thinker. He is without question the best thing that's happened to boxing since Ali."

Mitch knew Antonio had close ties with Vegas and that he also owned a sixty-thousand seat baseball stadium in Houston. His connections with the cable networks were vast. His top-notch publicity and promotional staff had what it would take to pull this off.

"If you don't mind me asking, how much is Shapiro offering you guys?"

"It doesn't matter," Mitch replied. "Hiwatha will never fight for him."

"I believe you, Mitch, but that's not what I hear about Mr. Orlando," responded Antonio. "I hear he's taken short money for his fighter with Shapiro before."

"That's true," responded Mitch.

"I'll tell you what Mitch. I think I can do something history-making here. I know that Hiwatha is not going fifty-fifty with Magnificent, no way shape or form," Antonio stated correctly.

"I'm prepared to make you this deal. I'll guarantee Wonderful Magnificent twenty-million and twenty-five million to Hiwatha. Depending on how well we do with pay-per-view, I'll give an eighty/twenty split of all pay-per-view money after eighty-five million. I'll let you work out the deal how Hiwatha and Magnificent will split the remaining forty percent. You won't get that deal anywhere else," Antonio said, looking directly at Mitch.

Thinking back to his conversation with Hiwatha, Mitch was shocked at just how close Antonio had come to predicting what the fight was worth."

"Man, this fight could be worth twenty-million to us in just the purse alone," Hiwatha estimated when last talking to Mitch. "I would guess a few more million with pay-per-view."

"To me, that sounds like a winner, Mr. Rosanni. I may as well tell you that I'm speaking for Mr. Orlando and Magnificent, too."

"Well, Mitch, I figured that," said Antonio. "It makes sense. This is the biggest attraction in boxing since the Hearns / Leonard bouts. You're welcome to stay at Oakridge for a few days so we can iron this out with my legal staff."

Mitch wondered why Antonio did not bitch or try to negotiate lower purses and percentages for the boxers.

"I know what you're thinking," said Antonio. "Why so easy? Well, Mitch, I'll tell you why. I can't lose on this deal. The whole world is talking about this fight. With a little luck, we can break all the records. I learned a long time ago, to strike while the iron is hot. Even people who like bridge and chess will pay to see this fight."

They both laughed in agreement. Mitch smelled a familiar scent in the air. It was the smell of money.

———◦《◦》◦———

Hiwatha's eyes scanned the computer screen. He steadily punched the computer keys to view his daily financial information. To him, this was serious business. Hiwatha had taken private tutorship to become computer savvy and learn how to handle his finances. It was paying off. He intently looked over his stock portfolio, real estate, bank accounts, and bonds. Hiwatha had managed to keep most of what his fists and endorsements had earned him.

Hiwatha was not only an athlete, but he was a businessman. He never missed the smallest detail when it came to his finances. He often corrected and reworded his own contracts before signing them. This even Mitch Danton admired. As Hiwatha studied the growth of his financial empire, the phone rang.

"Hi, Champ," Mitch said in an excited voice.

"What's up, man? Shoot me the details," was the straight forward reply from Hiwatha.

Hiwatha listened intently as Mitch explained the details of his meeting with Antonio. He could almost picture it in his mind. When Mitch finished, Hiwatha spoke.

"Look, this is just what I've been saying all along. We don't need Shapiro or Jackson. Antonio can take this fight to another level. Reach another market," Hiwatha said gloatingly.

"And let's be realistic," Hiwatha continued. "After this fight, there are no monster paydays out there. I'm looking over my books now, and I like what I see, but I'm going to like it better after this fight."

Before hanging up, Hiwatha reminded Mitch to make sure he was given star billing on all advertising and that on the night of the fight, he would enter the ring last. He also suggested that Mitch discusses with Antonio a double-header title bout featuring Magnificent and him, with separate opponents leading up to the showdown. No better way to fuel the public's appetite. Mitch listened carefully to his employer.

"And another thing," said the champion. "Don't screw yourself to death at Antonio's pad."

Hiwatha was laughing as he hung up the phone. Mitch was glad that Hiwatha was pleased with the deal.

Chapter 5

BROKEN PROMISES

Once again, Charleston was in a panic. He knew he could not dominate Theresa, more importantly, Charleston didn't realize at that very moment she was approaching his home. As he paced the living room floor, dressed in blue silk pajamas embroidered with his initials, Theresa was driving her Mercedes around the block.

Charleston felt the vibration of his cell phone going off for the second time. He rushed into his home office, quietly shutting the door. Charleston was almost frantic as he returned Theresa's call.

"Shit," he said into the receiver. "Where are you? What in the fuck is wrong with you?"

"You said you wanted to see me," Theresa responded as if she'd not heard a word of her lover's salty dialogue.

"I'm going to knock on your door, and then you're going to invite me in. I'm not going to continue our relationship this way. You say that you are my man, prove it. Look out your window," she teased.

Charleston was beside himself. The woman he loved was outside, tormenting him and unbeknownst to him; the woman who loved him was coming down the spiral staircase.

"Charleston," Danielle called from the hallway. "Is something wrong? Are you ok?"

Danielle knew her husband antics. She sensed Charleston was up to no good.

"No, nothing is wrong," he said nervously. "I was trying to find a letter in the office for Wonderful." Charleston lied for the hundredth time.

"No, man, I couldn't find it," he said, pretending to talk to his champion. "Call me in the morning." With that, Charleston hung up the phone.

If Danielle had only looked out her husband's window, she would have seen the cause of his obvious discomfort. As Charleston approached, Danielle looked into his eyes and remained silent. She knew he was lying but decided not to waste her time. It was best to pick your battles with Charleston. She turned and went back upstairs to her bedroom, securely, locking the door.

Since it was still early morning, Charleston rushed to get dressed, leaving a note on the counter informing Danielle he had a meeting with his trainers at the gym.

———◄(I)►———

Sometimes the boxers in the gym called them "crows," referring to the trainers who were always in a debate at the gym. They would sit, trading boxing stories while they waited for the boxers to begin training. This was a precarious lot. Most of them were yes men to Charleston, who did little or no work with his other champions. No one really knew Charleston only trained Magnificent. He was what they called in the trade a "showmen." Unfortunately, he would never share credit with anyone, especially his trainers.

Charleston had an insatiable lust for recognition and praise. That's why he would show up in the corner just before a televised fight. His trainers resented him for that but usually said nothing.

Most of the trainers were rather ordinary, but there was one who was indeed brilliant and gifted. He could effortlessly judge and decipher styles while summing up athletic potential in the blink of an eye. He was not much older than most of the boxers, but his knowledge of the sport placed him in another category.

Tony Francis had boxed some as an amateur. He had been decent, but his best sport was basketball. Francis had won a scholarship to college and was an excellent player. He could shoot and handle the ball well with both hands and was considered to be an all-around player.

One day Francis had an argument with his college coach over playing time. He did not start as a freshman or sophomore, even though Francis played as much as the team starters and often outperformed them. So naturally, his coach was surprised when he made "All-Conference" and was selected in the national small collegiate championships to the "All-Tournament" team.

Francis was frustrated over not starting. After another argument with his coach, he finally quit the team, left school and cursed basketball forever. He returned home to Chicago and resumed his communication studies.

Francis ultimately earned his degree from Northern Illinois University. He enjoyed working with children and eventually turned to his greatest love, boxing.

Francis was a diligent trainer and carefully counseled his boxers in offense, defense, footwork, balance, and counter-punching. These became the trademarks of his students.

Francis studied boxing as if he were earning a law degree. He read everything about the sport and recorded every fight shown on television until his library had grown to more than four thousand matches. He became not only an expert but a sought after historian of the sport.

He took great pleasure in challenging the other trainers' views about champions of the past. Francis scoffed at some of the past heroes such as Dempsey, Conn, and to a lesser degree, Joe Louis.

Francis had been a national debate champion in college and therefore, knew how to back up his arguments quite well with facts. This drove the other trainers into an immediate frenzy. They often argued loudly with him. To their amazement, Francis loved the art of debating, and by that alone, they could never win.

Even Charleston envied Francis' knowledge and presentation, rarely questioning his views. He knew Francis was a boxing honor student. Charleston was aware that Francis worshiped him as a son would a father. So fierce was his devotion to Charleston, Francis would have given his very life to protect him.

Francis primary role in Charleston's organization was to train and groom the amateur boxers. Under his leadership, they became a dominant team. Several of his fighters made the Olympic team winning gold medals, while others moved up the professional ranks, becoming champions.

Francis was quite handsome. He wore his single status proudly without being a woman-chaser. Due to his devotion to Charleston and his passion for boxing, Francis had lost the two great loves of his life. He did not smoke, drink, or hang out in bars living somewhat of a Spartan existence.

Eventually, Francis began to help Charleston with the professional side of the business. Aside from his duties as a trainer, he started picking opponents for the fighters, guiding their careers and traveling around the country, recruiting and signing talent to Charleston's stable. His tireless efforts brightened Charleston's future. Except for Wonderful Magnificent, no one else in boxing had contributed as much to Charleston's success.

Charleston was fully aware of this, but wouldn't fairly compensate Francis under any circumstances. Instead, he tried to use reverse psychology by bragging to everyone about what a great job Francis was doing. This caused a great torment within Francis. The stress caused him to pray nightly to God for guidance.

Francis slowly began to appear withdrawn. He became bitter watching all the talent he'd brought to Charleston become world champions. His pride was pushed to its limit. One-night Francis finally decided to go by Charleston's home to announce he was leaving.

"Charleston, you know I've filled your shelf with talent," said Francis. "All I've asked is to be fairly compensated, and you can't even do that."

"How dare you come to my home at this hour and tell me what you've done for me," said Charleston in anger. "My shelf is full because I made it that way. You will never take credit for that. The world knows who I am. No one has ever heard of you. So, don't try this fucked-up shit with me."

Francis tried to hold his composure as he responded but eventually began to raise his voice, not caring who heard him.

"You are a selfish bastard," he shouted. "Yes, you surely did fuck over me, but never again. When I am finished, the world will know who I am, and you will be exposed as the asshole you are. One day, not only your boxers but your wife and children will know the kind of man you are. You are lowlife scum, a cheat and the worse type of user. From this point on, I will be a thorn in your side."

With a sweep of his hand, Francis wiped Charleston's desk clean, sending the contents to the floor. Charleston jumped from his seat. He had never seen Francis behave in this manner and couldn't hide his shock. Charleston knew he had wronged Francis but was never going to admit it or share his wealth with anyone unless it was on his terms.

"Get out of my house, you broke motherfucker!" shouted Charleston. "I've taken care of you and carried your stupid ass all these years. No one else would have done that for you, punk."

Francis leaped across the desk and grabbed Charleston by the neck. They fell to the floor and began tussling. Danielle and her brother Troy ran into the room to stop the fight before someone got hurt.

"You two stop this at once!" screamed Danielle. "Please don't do this in my home, Francis. I know that he's wronged you, but please, don't settle it like this."

Charleston broke free, but Troy still held a tight grip on him, while Danielle pulled Francis into the hallway.

"Francis, it's okay," Danielle said in almost a whisper. "Call me in the morning. I will give you some money. I know what has been going on. I know."

She held Francis' face and gave him a kiss on the cheek as she wiped his tears. She could see he was a broken man. She thought of how many nights Francis had comforted her over the years while she cried over her husband's escapades. Francis had helped her through so many difficult situations. He had been a friend, and indeed like a son to her.

Danielle managed to get Francis out the door and returned to Charleston's office where he was now pacing back and forth, talking to Troy.

"That motherfuckers' got a lot of nerve coming in here and demanding money from me," said Charleston. "He's lost his mind. I'll make him pay for disrespecting my home."

"No, Charleston, it is you who have disrespected your home," said Danielle. "And it is you who will eventually pay. Francis is a good, decent, and trustworthy man. He has never done anything other than be kind to you, our children, and me. I am ashamed to see you act this way, and I'm ashamed today to be your wife. You will do nothing to harm Francis as long as I live. He has been like a son to me."

Danielle slammed the door to Charleston office and retreated to her bedroom, locking the door as usual. If nothing else she knew her husband. Danielle removed her checkbook from the dresser and wrote Francis a check for forty thousand dollars. This was far less than what Francis deserved, but it was all she could give him.

Charleston also kept Danielle on a tight rope. What she had managed to stash away over the years were rewards Charleston had given her after his big fights. Usually, it was ten thousand here, twenty thousand there, to buy jewelry and clothes for her and the children. Thinking about the future, Danielle made plans to financially protect herself. Several years earlier she began hiding money in an account of her own.

As Francis left town, he would forever be a changed man. He hated that his love, devotion, and unswerving loyalty had been spit on and flushed down the drain by his hero. Francis was bitter but knew that with the money Danielle had given him, added to the money he already saved, would at least allow him to start a new life somewhere else. This, of course, did not ease his pain.

Charleston tried to compensate for the loss of Francis. He hated to admit that it was a substantial loss to his business. He tried to fill the void by spending more time working at the gym and supporting his fighters at ringside.

This night, however, with good reason, Charleston had a look of grave horror etched on his face. His world lightweight champion, Tony Speaks was taking a beating from an Irishman named Ryan O'Kelly.

Charleston had taken the fight only because he thought O'Kelly was not a significant threat. Usually, Francis would have picked the opponent, but now Charleston had no one to rely on for this sweet science. As O'Kelly battered Speaks along the ropes, Charleston began to think about a previous conversation with Francis.

"O'Kelly is wrong for Speaks. He's got a chin made of iron, great stamina and O'Kelly is a non-stop punching machine. He's too rough for Speaks. I'm telling you, man, to find someone else," Francis had urged.

As Speaks flopped on his stool at the end of the tenth round, Charleston could see that his champion was a beaten man. Speaks' left eye was almost shut, and his right was not far behind. His nose bled profusely. Later, it would be discovered that it was broken.

"You've got to gamble, Tony," screamed a frustrated Charleston. "Back this man up and don't just sit down on your right hand. You've got to get this man out of here!"

Charleston hated to lose, and when his boxers did, he

would belittle them. Sometimes call them quitters or choke artists. He had no use for losers, and by the end of the twelfth round, Charleston had left Speaks' corner, aware of the impending decision. As the ring announcer said, "And the new lightweight champion of the world," Charleston was already down the aisle and headed for his hotel suite. Speaks watched in disbelief as Charleston vanished behind the black curtains.

———————⟨⟨⟩⟩———————

Speaks room was dark, still and silent, except for the sound of ice cubes being placed in a bucket to be wrapped in an ice pack. Solomon was filling the ice pack and bucket as he tended to his brother's wounds.

On the bed lay the former lightweight champion of the world. That evening Speaks had fought an undeniably tough opponent. Both eyes were slit, his nose broken and his ribs bore welts caused by the fierce infighting he had endured. His hands were swollen, especially his right. He had hurt O'Kelly several times during the fight, twice staggering him, but to no avail.

Since Speaks could barely see, Solomon slowly guided his hands and placed them in the ice bucket. Speaks winced in pain.

"Man, that hurts!" said the crestfallen champion.

His pain could have been eased by the nine-hundred-fifty-thousand-dollar purse, but Speaks knew a significant portion would go to Charleston. It had been several hours since the fight, and he still hadn't seen Charleston.

"Where is Charleston?" Speaks asked.

"I don't know," replied Solomon. "He split before they announced the decision."

"I fought my heart out," said Speaks proudly. "The man just beat me."

"Yes, you did, brother," replied Solomon. "You went out on your shield."

Through busted lips, Speaks' spat out, "Charleston is not right, man. I gave everything I had, and he walked out on me. Francis told him this was not a good fight for me. Without Francis to protect me, man, I'm not going to be able to stay with Charleston. He can't train me now and didn't train me before. Charleston is a damn fraud. I'll never fight for that bastard again."

Speaks laid his head on the pillow. He didn't want to risk falling asleep, so he began thinking of where to go and what to do when he left Charleston. Though loyalty is a noble virtue, sometimes it comes at a very high price.

Chapter 6

THE ODD MAN OUT

The news raced through the gym like a hot tip on a racehorse. Numwar Nasser was training at the gym today. It was true. The world's number one contender was definitely there to enter the lion's den.

The gym inhabitants were not usually star-struck. After all, so many champions had already been in their midst; but Numwar was the guy no one wanted to fight. Still, everyone wanted to confirm if he really was that good, and in this battleground den of boxing they would surely find out. It was known that sparring sessions in the Savoy gym were like wars. Many boxers had unwittingly left their best fights in this ring and not on television.

As Numwar, his trainer Oliver Xavier and Charleston walked through the double olive doors, at least twenty boxers and trainers were in some form of workout. There was a short but acknowledged silence. This greeting was usually reserved for champions, and it was even more pronounced for Magnificent. Then as quickly as they had fallen silent, they noisily went back to their workout.

As Numwar was led into the "regular" dressing room, he passed by a dark-skinned muscular fighter thunderously pounding the heavy bag. The guy looked to be at least a lightweight.

"Hey, Nasser!" shouted world-rated contender Maurice McFarland. "I've got the baddest left-hook in the world, and I can't wait to try it out on you."

Once inside the dressing room doors, Numwar spoke. "I box him last today," directing his gaze at Charleston.

"Don't worry, man," replied Charleston. "I've got plenty of dudes to box you."

Numwar took time to make sure his hand-wraps were perfect before entering the gym and beginning his thorough routine. He swiftly began to warm up and stretch, saving his shadowboxing for last.

Charleston directed Mr. Wright to get a couple of guys ready to spar. He made a point to tell him that McFarland would go into the ring last.

"Okay, baby, no problem," responded Wright.

All eyes were watching Numwar as he shadowboxed. He appeared to glide effortlessly across the blood-stained canvas of the ring. Almost like maple syrup pouring from a bottle.

With both hands in perfect synchronized combinations, Numwar shot his punches in short bursts. Hooks, jabs, uppercuts, and crosses. He was ready to spar.

Johnny Tillman eagerly climbed into the ring first.

Suddenly, the whole gym was on all four sides of the ring. It was standing room only.

Tillman was a young pro with a record of twelve wins, no losses, and ten knockouts. He was known to be a puncher. As Xavier applied the last smear of Vaseline to Numwar's unmarked face, pick, catch, pull, and parry were the instructions calmly spoken into his ear.

Tillman tried quickly to gain the respect of Numwar. He wanted to prove he was no chump. Numwar eased out to the center of the ring like a predator. He quickly sized up his opponent. A smooth shoulder fake here, with a nice feint there, he measured his man. Tillman started firing furiously.

"Go ahead and rumble," shouted one of the ring apron jocks.

Numwar blocked and parried all of Tillman's offensive attempts as he moved around the ring. He really didn't throw a punch of intent at Tillman but frustrated him as Tillman lost composure trying to land his shots.

Tillman still breathing heavy from the effort of his frequent misses finally exited the ring.

"He's smooth...real smooth," he told Charleston, who was looking on in uninterrupted concentration.

Now, it was McFarland's turn to spar. He got in the ring with an arrogant look on his face. He charged at Numwar firing punches in every direction. The noise level was at a fever pitch as the gym inhabitants shouted their own instructions. McFarland was wearing sixteen-ounce training gloves; still, everyone knew McFarland could get you out of there in a heartbeat. You would have thought Ali and Frazier were fighting.

Numwar remained calm as he moved and boxed. His instincts were like that of a snake easing up on his morning breakfast. This caused McFarland's punches to fall short.

Finally, Numwar felt he had studied McFarland's slugging style long enough. It was time to go to work and give McFarland a lesson in boxing etiquette.

Xavier began shouting from the corner of the apron, "Let's do it, my boy. Let's show...Let's go."

McFarland managed to throw a left-hook aimed at Numwar's chin. Instinctively Numwar caught the punch on the outside of his right glove. Before McFarland could blink, Numwar had countered with two flashing left-hooks that crashed right at the temple of McFarland, and a right that landed on his face. He instantly tasted blood in his nostrils.

McFarland tried to bring his right glove up to protect himself, but Numwar quickly exploded a left-hook to his liver. McFarland tried not to react to the blow until his right knee buckled slightly. Two more left jabs found his face as he tried to jab back. All he got for his efforts were a whistling right-hand counter, followed by a left hook to his chin.

"Look out!" hollered one of the Crows.

McFarland attempted to bull Numwar into the ropes as he fired a wicked left hook. Numwar effortlessly rolled underneath and landed a short side-right into McFarland's kidney, followed by another left hook to his liver.

The crowd knew Numwar was for real as he quickly

stepped around McFarland and punished him with a whistling left jab. Numwar feinted beautifully, and his opponent froze, allowing Numwar to paste McFarland with three unanswered left-jabs and a right-cross. He came back with another left-hook and right-cross-counter that not only knocked out McFarland's mouthpiece but twisted his headgear awkwardly around his face.

"Time...Time!" shouted Charleston from the ring apron. He had seen enough.

Charleston figured Numwar was good, now he had to get his arms around the fact that he was exceptional. Numwar had grace, fluidity, effortless punching, and a thinking man's brain. No, Numwar was not yet commercial, nor hailed by the masses, but he was definitely brilliant, and a dangerous scholar of the sweet science called boxing. He was one to be avoided at all cost.

Though Numwar was hoping he would get a considerable payday against Magnificent or Jordan, Charleston wanted to make sure he never got in the ring with his prize possession. In time, Charleston knew this would cost him his relationship with Numwar, but he didn't care. Money was more important.

Charleston reached in his shirt pocket for his cell phone to call Mitch. He wanted to tell him about Numwar's workout at the gym, but first, Charleston wanted an update on the negotiations. The call went to voicemail. Mitch was not only working on their promotional deal in Los Angeles, but he was also enjoying the other fringe benefits of his job.

As he strode into the pool area of Antonio's estate, Mitch had never seen women so beautiful. He had been faithful to Charlotte, so he'd forgotten how it felt to admire the beauty of another woman.

There were blondes, brunettes, redheads, Blacks, Asians, and Hispanics. Mitch looked on in amazement as he stood alongside the Olympic size swimming pool. He was openly staring at the women bodies when he heard Antonio's voice.

"Join us," said the host while being kissed and caressed by a quartet of beautiful women.

Mitch was already at a state of erection. After all, it had been a long time since Charlotte had slept next to him. He removed his clothing, and hurriedly accepted the invitation.

Before Mitch could get his footing in the pool, a young woman had her arms and legs firmly wrapped around him and was going in for the kill. Mitch tilted his head back, closed his eyes, and imagined he was in some type of sexual Shangri-La. Any thought of Charlotte quickly faded. His momentary need no longer allowed him to wonder where Charlotte was or what she was doing.

Charlotte lay awake in bed, thinking about her new lover, Roscoe. They had met six months earlier at a health club in Virginia Beach, and he had been servicing her sexual needs ever since. Charlotte enjoyed the way Roscoe made love to her. Though it was no secret Charlotte could hang with the best of them, Roscoe had her number and was running up the bill.

What Charlotte didn't realize is that the drugs Roscoe was introducing her to were clouding her judgment. She was slowly finding out what a real addiction was. Her sweet Roscoe was the epitome of the old school hustler, except his hustle was rich, lonely, married women.

Charlotte was now hooked on the drugs he was providing. She no longer cared if Mitch noticed the thousands of dollars missing from their bank accounts. At one point, no matter what was happening, Charlotte was home when Mitch was in town. Her attraction to Roscoe and the drugs were so strong, she was now missing in action, often lying to Mitch about her whereabouts.

Charlotte had become involved in kinky sex activities such as threesomes and even one or two women in front of Roscoe. She was at her lowest point, and Mitch hadn't even noticed. She resented the fact that boxing had become an outlet for his grief. For Charlotte, there was no end to her sorrow and pain. She had become a person with nothing to lose.

"Man, this bastard is on the cover again!" shouted a frustrated Wonderful Magnificent.

The object of his consternation was none other than "his

holiness" Hiwatha "Absolute" Jordan. It galled Wonderful to be second fiddle. Hiwatha's handsome face smiled out at him from the cover of a sports magazine. Never mind that he had just been on the cover of "Boxing World." Magnificent knew that until he defeated Hiwatha, he would never be recognized as the best.

Magnificent stormed out into his backyard. Not even the beauty of his majestic mansion could soothe his unabated anger. His "yes men," who were always there to do his bidding, moved from his presence. They knew it wouldn't be long before Magnificent lashed out at them.

Magnificent had an Elvis complex and patterned his lifestyle after the late rock idol. Like Elvis, he had bodyguards, a fleet of cars, closets full of clothes and a custom limo.

Magnificent truly loved his mother. Early on in his career, he brought her a well-furnished home. As time went on, he also made sure she had a driver as well.

Magnificent was basically a good guy, but with a dark side. Like the late rock star, Magnificent could be difficult. He kept a collection of guns and was an expert shooter. At one time he volunteered as a police officer and performed his duties conscientiously.

Magnificent also had a manager that he never questioned. Except over the past year, he had begun to take a closer look at his affairs. It was known that he had given fifty percent of himself to Charleston. Magnificent came to realize this was too steep. He finally confronted Charleston, demanding a seventy-thirty split, which he got.

Though his new deal was not without hassle, Magnificent was still proud of himself. He was now world champion, even if the other half of his world was ruled by Hiwatha "Absolute" Jordan.

Victory or not, Magnificent would still be considerably richer. He was on edge waiting to hear the results of Charleston's negotiations with Mitch.

————•《◉》•————

As Mitch sat in his first-class seat, flying above the clouds, he had every reason to smile. He'd just put the finishing touches on the biggest fight in history. The proposed meeting between the two undefeated middleweight champions was now a reality.

This could probably be the largest-grossing sporting event in history. Hiwatha stood to earn thirty million in one night if the Pay-Per-View projections were on target. Mitch knew that his ten percent would set him up for a really comfortable retirement.

With Magnificent standing to make twenty-million and a percentage of the pay-per-view after the promotional cut, Mitch knew that like it or not, Charleston's greedy ass would have to take the deal. It was merely an added bonus that both men would headline a doubleheader before the fight, each defending their respective titles against safe opponents.

After the doubleheader they would go on a twenty-day publicity tour, hitting all the major cities. Each boxer and his entourage would be flown from city to city in separate private jets. Hiwatha appeared nonchalant about the outcome of the financial windfall he stood to earn.

"Thirty-million is good, but look at what Antonio and his people will make," he pointed out to Mitch. "Everybody wants to see it. It's going to be a war, and I'm the general," bragged Hiwatha.

With Magnificent being no ordinary opponent, Mitch took the latter with a grain of salt. He knew Hiwatha would refer to his trainer St. Claire Robinson, who had trained him since childhood. Whatever St. Claire asked would be done. He would simply concentrate on working out the final business details with Magnificent's manager.

———◦《◉》◦———

Charleston had just hung up the phone and didn't know whether to be happy or upset. He and Mitch had come to terms, even though Charleston had questioned him every step of the way.

Charleston knew the deal was right. This would be one of Magnificent and his biggest paydays. Not a bad deal for a man who worshiped money. The problem was Charleston had to tell Magnificent his rival would possibly make millions more than him. For this reason, he kept Mitch up one night at a hotel in Los Angeles banging on his door every five minutes, trying to get more money.

"Never let them sleep, and the deal will be done by morning," Charleston was known to say.

Whether this really worked, Charleston never knew. As he drove his Mercedes over to Magnificent's mansion, Charleston was not thrilled with the deal but believed it was the best they could do. Neither Jackson nor Einstein would have given them more than ten million. Now with the possibility of making twenty-million or more on the fight, and another payday with the double-header, he hoped Magnificent wouldn't be too pissed off.

"It's me Charleston," he announced into the electronic speaker.

As the gate with Magnificent's initials carved in gold opened, Charleston slowly headed up the long tree-lined path to the door. Despite the humongous financial rewards, he was delivering, Charleston felt the meeting would still be awkward.

One of Magnificent's flunkies opened the door. He pointed Charleston toward the family room, which had an excellent view of the courtyard and pool area. Magnificent sat in a seat near the patio window, sipping a glass of fresh orange juice. He was still dressed in his midnight blue silk pajamas and appeared to be watching as the daylight began to peek through the clouds.

Charleston had no idea Magnificent was really watching one of his underlings make out on the patio with one of the gorgeous groupies from his impromptu wild party the previous night. Magnificent decided to invite several friends over for a get-together, but things had gotten a little out of hand, as they usually do when the fellas got together.

Before Charleston could take a seat, Magnificent spoke, "No use in sitting, man, unless you have some damn good news."

"As a matter of fact, I do," replied Charleston, who noticed the distracted look on Magnificent's face. "What the hell are you watching," Charleston asked as he saw the couple on the patio.

"How do you expect me to have a serious conversation with you if you're concentrating on this kind of shit? You can't afford to let this get in the way of our success on this fight."

"You got a lot of damn nerve trying to act holy in my house," responded Magnificent as he looked up at Charleston and raised his eyebrow. "You got more crap going on in your life than Victoria has secrets. But I will respect that we're doing business and spare you the entertainment."

Magnificent picked up the remote from the table and hit a button that closed the curtains leading to the patio. Charleston took a seat across from him and pulled a tablet from his briefcase that contained his notes.

"Now man, you have to hear me out completely before making any quick judgments about the situation," conveyed Charleston. "This package will set you up for life, and in the end, that's what I want you to focus on."

"Don't tell me what to focus on," snapped Magnificent. "I'm the one going into the ring, not you. This is my life, not yours. When you finish, I'll say whatever I want to say!"

Charleston started at the beginning, with his initial

meetings with Einstein and Jackson. That led to his meeting with Mitch in New York. He explained that he'd given Mitch time to work out a deal with Antonio Rosanni, who definitely had the best offer on the table. He then laid out the final proposal to Magnificent in detail, all the time stressing that he could probably get a few more minor things from Jackson and Einstein, but never what Antonio Rosanni was offering.

Magnificent lowered himself in his chair, placing his hands right below his chin then finally responded.

"Charleston I'm definitely not happy about the money. And they want me to enter the ring first. I, too, am a champion. I've worked hard for this. I'm tired of taking low when it comes to "Prince Charming," but I figured it would come to this. So, I am not surprised. I will accept the offer and challenge. However, I want it understood that when I win, it's my ballgame on the rematch, and I will enter the ring last."

"I will make sure that is known," replied Charleston, who was shocked that Magnificent had taken it so well.

Charleston was waiting for the real ball to drop, but to his surprise there was none. As he got up to leave, his ego took control. Of course, this is a perfect deal for him. He knows he can't make this kind of money anywhere else. He really should kiss my ass, but I know he's an ungrateful son-of-a-bitch.

It was late, and Mitch was heading home from his meeting with Hiwatha and St. Claire. It had been a while since he had seen Charlotte, and he had to admit she had been hard to reach these days. Still, Mitch was looking forward to seeing her. He wanted to tell her about the deal he had just inked with Antonio Rosanni.

As Mitch got closer to his house he noticed there were no lights on. Either Charlotte was asleep or not at home. Where could she be on a Tuesday night? Mitch began calling Charlotte's name as he flipped on the lights. He was looking forward to sleeping in his own bed with his wife.

Mitch had enjoyed himself in Los Angeles but felt guilty about his sexual escapades. That was out of character for him, and he repented profusely to God while mounting the stairs to their bedroom. Hopefully, Charlotte would not notice anything different about him.

To his surprise, Charlotte was nowhere in sight. Mitch quickly grabbed his cell phone and began dialing Charlotte's number. Some strange woman answered, and Mitch heard loud music and laughter in the background before the phone went dead. He quickly phoned again, and Charlotte picked up.

"Who was that and wherein the hell are you?" he asked in an angry voice.

"Oh sweetheart, you're back and finally concerned where I am," she said while taking another sip of her drink.

"What the hell is that supposed to mean?" he asked. "Whatever you are doing, I want you to get in your car and come home right now. This whole thing is getting a little out of control for me, and you sound drunk."

"Mitch, I will be there when I get there," Charlotte said defiantly as she hung up the phone.

Mitch called her back several times but got no answer, so reluctantly he headed downstairs to make himself a drink. He still needed to review several pending contracts in his office. He was still angry after his conversation with Charlotte. What was going on with her?

As Mitch placed his drink on the desk, he happened to look down at the wastebasket and noticed a torn bank statement sticking out from underneath other trash. Thinking that was odd, he grabbed pieces of it and began putting it back together. He knew Charlotte had never concerned herself with their bills or mail, so why now?

Mitch was able to make out the amounts on the bank statement. He could not believe his eyes. In a matter of a month, Charlotte had taken more than $80,000 from their account. What puzzled him most was the increments of ten-thousand here, twenty-thousand there. It made no sense to him. Even in her wildest shopping sprees, Charlotte didn't spend that kind of money.

Mitch went to the file cabinet and removed several other bank statements that he hadn't had a chance to look over since starting negotiations on the Jordan / Magnificent fight. Those bank statements bore the same type of activity, only in smaller amounts. Now he was pissed. Charlotte would definitely have to account for what she was doing with their money.

Mitch had worked hard over the past few years to secure a future for them, and he couldn't accept this type of behavior. Since the death of their children, he had put up and shut up far too long. This was beyond his loyalty and love for her. In the morning, his first stop would be the bank. He intended to close this account and anything else that had her name on it. Now Charlotte would have to go through him for any and all expenses.

With that, Mitch threw some clothing in a bag and decided to check into the nearest hotel. Though he longed for a night in his own bed, all of a sudden this did not feel like home. Charlotte had some explaining to do, and he wouldn't be back until she did.

Over the next few weeks, Mitch argued profusely with Charlotte about their lives and finances. Charlotte refused to give an inch. She cursed him to holy hell for cutting her off from the money and finally refused to speak to him. Until Charlotte could figure out her next move, she would have to settle for the eight thousand dollars Mitch promised her a month.

⸻ «(●)» ⸻

Hiwatha sat in his living room, stunned, holding the telephone to his ear. He could not believe Charlotte was on the other end. After all these years; she was threatening to tell Mitch about their affair if he did not pay her one-hundred thousand dollars.

"Charlotte, this must be some kind of joke," Hiwatha

retorted. "I can't believe you have the nerve to call me with this shit, knowing how much this would hurt Mitch."

"This is no joke," she said, confirming Hiwatha's worst fear. "Mitch has frozen our bank accounts and refuses to give me money."

"Why would he do that?" asked Hiwatha. "He's your husband for God's sake. Anyway, that's between you and him. You're married, and I want to stay out of it."

Charlotte began to shout into the phone. "You didn't say that when you were fucking me, did you?"

"If I knew you were married, I would never have laid a hand on you," Hiwatha responded in a curt voice. "There were many women I could have been with that night, but I thought you were someone special. Lord knows I was wrong."

"Sure, there were many women you could have been with, but this one, sweetheart, is going to cost you one-hundred thousand dollars," Charlotte replied coldly. "You damn athletes are all alike. You think you're God's precious gift to women. If you ask me, you're totally full of shit."

Hiwatha began shouting into the phone. "Trust me Charlotte, what I got from you was not worth seven cents, let alone a hundred thousand dollars. You are one evil bitch, but you don't know who you're messing with. Right now, you got me, so I'll play your game. To hurt Mitch now would allow you to destroy what we have worked so hard for."

Hiwatha put his hand to his head, "But what am I thinking...you already know that. So, let's do this...you low down dirty bitch! In the morning, I'm going to write your ass a check. Then I want you to explain to Mitch why I don't have two words to say to you again in life."

"I don't want a check," Charlotte countered. "Can't you get cash? I just told you, Mitch froze our accounts."

"Charlotte, with a one-hundred-thousand-dollar check from Hiwatha Jordan, any bank will open you a damn account. Also, if you ever choose to deny what you're doing today, let the record show what scum really looks like."

"Hiwatha, I don't care what you think," replied Charlotte. "What matters to me is that you give me the money. So, telling Mitch doesn't scare me as much as it does you."

Charlotte, you must think I'm stupid? Right now, you have the ups on me. And I believe you think you're going to ride me like a punk. That won't happen. You knock on my door or ring my house ever again, I will personally not only tell Mitch, but I will also make sure you never ask for anything else. This, I will always remember Charlotte. You can come by in the morning. I will leave the envelope on the entry table, and Ms. Reed will give it to you. Do not ask to speak or try to see me."

With that, Hiwatha slammed the phone down so hard on the table that he broke one of his favorite baseball collectible cases that held his autographed Hank Aaron ball. It had belonged to his late father and Hiwatha cherished it.

He quickly ran after the ball but fell to the floor while trying to prevent it from rolling under the couch. As he sat there holding the ball in his hand, he reflected on his conversation with Charlotte.

"Dad, how do things in life get so mixed up?" Hiwatha asked as he looked up at the Ceiling, almost expecting his father to answer.

"If I don't give Charlotte the money, it could mess up my relationship with Mitch. Though it goes against all my principles, I know that no man can understand his friend sleeping with his wife under any circumstances. Besides, we're working on one of the biggest paydays of my career. I can't let one-hundred grand interfere with that."

As Hiwatha spoke, something occurred to him. Why would Mitch freeze their accounts? What was going on? Had he found out about Charlotte's sexual escapes? With that, Hiwatha jumped up and grabbed his cell phone. Whatever was going on, his private detective buddy, Floyd Nash could find out.

Hiwatha often used Floyd's services to check out women or people who were trying to get close to him. They had been friends since High School. So, when Floyd left the police force and set up his own private investigator service in Virginia Beach, Hiwatha was more than happy to help him. He was also instrumental in getting Floyd other key clients. This somewhat indebted Floyd to him. As Floyd's voicemail picked up, Hiwatha waited to leave a message.

"Hey, Floyd, this is Hiwatha. I got a job for you. Come by the house this evening. This one is important to me, so it'll be money well spent."

Just as he ended the call, his phone rang again. Hiwatha

quickly answered. "Yes, ...who is this?" he asked in an aggravated tone.

"Why silly you, it's me, Caroline," came the voice on the other end. "I need to set up an interview with you and Riley Davis of the *Los Angeles News*. If I'm lucky and David Troy from the *Los Angeles Billboard News* calls me back, we can knock them both out fairly quickly. One catch, it might conflict with your training schedule."

Hiwatha listened intently as Caroline went on. She had no idea how much he had begun to look forward to her daily calls. Hell...even he was surprised that any woman could pique his curiosity. After all, he had dined and slept with some of the most beautiful women in the world; but right now, Caroline was just what he needed.

Hiwatha had gone to middle and high school with Caroline. As a young kid, he was friends with her brother Stevie. They grew up on the same street, but Hiwatha and Stevie became closer when they boxed in the amateurs together.

Back then, Hiwatha never paid Caroline any attention. To him, she never had what he called that "DO ME" appeal. He did remember her to be very intelligent and sweet, but Caroline wasn't in-crowd material. Instead, she was busy making the Honor Roll and running for class president.

Hiwatha was shocked when he saw her a couple of months earlier in Rosanni's office. The company she worked for had assigned her to do the public relations work for the fight.

Caroline Davis was no longer the plain Jane Hiwatha remembered. Her beauty was now breathtaking. In their youth, he hadn't noticed that she had gorgeous athletic legs. She also had a full set of lips that wrapped around a contagious smile. Though at this very moment another woman was upstairs in Hiwatha's bedroom, it was Caroline who was slowly becoming front and center in his life.

Hiwatha considered public relations to be the downside of his work. These days he looked forward to Caroline's daily calls to go over the publicity schedule. She was an excellent communicator, and her warmth always came across when she spoke. He could see why Antonio used her public relations firm.

Aside from her top-notch education from Yale University, she had received her master's degree in marketing from Northern Illinois University. Fortunately, she didn't come off as uppity. She remained that same girl he knew at Ridge Valley High.

Though Caroline had a crush on Hiwatha back in high school (like nearly all the other girls), she had no idea Hiwatha was now interested in her. He had been careful not to give off any signals. Hiwatha knew she was different from the groupies and starlets typically part of his life. Therefore, he was reluctant to move forward. A woman like that would always have questions.

"Hiwatha, are you listening to me?" Caroline asked with impatience. "I know this is something you don't like to do, but I really need this favor. Mr. Rosanni never hires us for his sporting projects, so I really need to do well on this one if we're going to see any others in the future."

"Is that what he told you?" asked Hiwatha. "Antonio is well aware that I don't interrupt my training for any reason."

"No...Hiwatha he did not come out and say that, but in business, your instincts tell you pretty quickly. Okay, let's take Mr. Rosanni off the table. Will you do it for me? Come on...we go back to Ridge Valley High. I'm the girl who sat behind you in Mrs. Allen's class and gave you the answers so you could pass the final. I'm not proud of that, but we both knew how important it was to your father that you passed that class."

"I know you're not going to go there with this," Hiwatha responded in laughter. He was actually happy to extend their conversation. For Caroline, he would definitely break his rule.

"You know what Caroline...if I do this, you'll have to take me to lunch when we get to Houston for the fight. That means you're paying."

"Is that all? You're on," she responded. "Besides, how much can you possibly eat before a fight?"

"Who said lunch was going to be before the fight? If you're paying, I'm going to make sure I'm ready to eat. You should know I'm a real expensive guy."

"Yeah, I hear you," she chuckled. "I'll make sure to bring my Platinum card."

With that, Caroline began talking about the press tour they completed the previous month. The time they spent together allowed Hiwatha to really get to know her. This time as a woman, and not the girl who lived down the street or sat behind him in math class.

Hiwatha and Caroline enjoyed every dinner and night they spent out dancing. They actually discovered they had a lot in common. Hiwatha loved her sense of humor and often found himself laughing uncontrollably at her jokes. One night he laughed so hard he fell to the floor holding his stomach pleading with her to stop talking.

Still, it felt good to spend time with someone that not only put him at ease but made him happy. With Caroline, he shared a history. More importantly, they both had their own memories and connection to his late Father Nathan. Something absent in all his previous relationships.

Hiwatha realized how good it felt to be with a woman who knew his Father. He enjoyed it when Caroline would tease him about something he did or said, then tell him, you're just like your Dad.

One night at dinner, Caroline told Hiwatha a couple of funny stories about his Father. He smiled when she threw in a few imitations of Nathan.

Caroline reminded Hiwatha of a favorite saying of his Father's. "No matter how many times you tell a lie, it will never be the truth." That stuck in his mind long after the dinner ended.

As time passed, Hiwatha became less guarded, allowing himself to be venerable in Caroline's presence. They talked long hours about old school friends, things they'd done as children, Hiwatha's heroic experience winning the Olympic Games, and Caroline's life after she went away to college.

Though Caroline spoke of her college boyfriend Lance to the point Hiwatha became irritated, he purposely did not mention any of his previous relationships with women. Hiwatha had begun to develop intimate feelings for Caroline, therefore, he was keeping all options on the table. Besides, Caroline was not oblivious to all the women that were gathered continuously around Hiwatha and Magnificent during the tour.

There were many nights Hiwatha thought of Caroline. One night he fantasized about knocking on her hotel room door but decided not to treat his childhood friend like a desperate groupie. There were enough women for that. Caroline was different, and Hiwatha knew it

⚊⚊⚊⚊«◉»⚊⚊⚊⚊

As Charlotte lay there in the bedroom of Roscoe's cramped apartment, she had sudden doubts about taking the money from Hiwatha. That soon faded as Charlotte listened to Roscoe, who couldn't believe she was able to pull it off.

"Baby, that was beautiful," he said, jumping up and down. "Now let's celebrate. I'm going to get you the best blow of your life. Maybe we can go away somewhere, and you can finally leave that stiff husband of yours."

In truth, that was the farthest thing from Roscoe's mind. He intended to bleed Charlotte and Mitch bank accounts dry. What he didn't know was that leaving Mitch was the furthest thing from Charlotte's mind. She had no intentions of leaving her husband, but the drugs were definitely becoming a problem. In her heart, she wanted to work things out with Mitch. Unfortunately, her marriage felt empty without her children whom she would give anything to have back in her life.

Charlotte could not stop blaming herself for having put them on that plane. Each day she relived what they must have gone through as the aircraft descended from the sky. Each moment she cried inside for not being there to comfort them.

As Roscoe carried on his dancing and singing for joy, Charlotte turned over and began to pray that she be released from the hell she was living in.

⸻ ⟨⦿⟩ ⸻

Hiwatha had just gotten back from his morning run when he heard the intercom from the front gate. He knew it was probably Charlotte, so he hurried to his room to change for the gym. Seeing her was the last thing he needed.

Hiwatha was surprised to see Victoria still stretched out on the bed. By now she should have left for the airport. This little relationship was getting a bit too cozy for his comfort.

"Shouldn't you be at the airport by now?" he asked. "I thought you needed to get back to New York to begin shooting your music video."

"I called this morning to make sure everything was still

on schedule. Unfortunately, the director told me the actor he'd hired had been in an accident. Since that was the scene he'd set up for today, they were going to regroup and prepare to shoot a different scene. It looks like we'll have to find someone else. By the way, wouldn't you enjoy being in a love scene with me? That would be so hot."

Hiwatha removed her arms from around his neck and turned to throw some gloves in his gym bag.

"I am not interested in being in no video, especially if I have to shoot a love scene."

"I thought you said you wanted to get into acting," Victoria replied while removing her robe to expose the tiny G-string panties she was wearing. "I thought you and I could get some practice in."

Hiwatha turned around and looked at her with near disgust on his face until he saw what she was wearing. There was no doubt Victoria Santiago was a beautiful woman, and she knew it.

Her parents, Edward and Maria Santiago had come to America from Cuba in the late 1950s. As performers themselves, they struggled for many years, hoping to achieve the American dream. With the birth of each of their children, that dream slowly faded. Their shining star became Victoria who began to sing before she could talk. It was no surprise to them when as a teenager she convinced her older brothers, Juan and Stepheno, to help her form a band.

It took some years of struggling and raw determination before Victoria was able to headline shows in Miami then

Diana Hicks Sherer

surrounding states. It was after a show in Atlanta that she was offered her first recording deal with a major label. That is a night Victoria will never forget.

After her first single release hit number one on the charts with two more to follow, the world opened their hearts to her. Now, after a string of hit songs, Victoria was standing face-to-face with the man she wanted desperately to give her heart to.

It was early May, and she had been carrying on a very passionate relationship with Hiwatha for almost a year. They had met through a mutual friend who had brought Hiwatha backstage to meet her after a sold-out holiday concert in Los Angeles.

To Hiwatha who didn't particularly care for starlet types, Victoria was a skilled bed partner. To Victoria, Hiwatha was the man of her dreams. Rich, good looking and with the grace to be on the cover of any magazine in America.

Victoria had fallen deeply in love with him. Her little lie about the video was her way of extending their time together. It made no difference that she was one of the most sought after faces in America. Victoria had her eyes set on being with Hiwatha.

"Listen Victoria, you look wonderful, but I have to get to the gym," explained Hiwatha. "I'm not messing with my training schedule. Ramiro will be back shortly to pick me up. That little deal we had yesterday is over until after the fight."

Hiwatha kneeled in front of her as she sat on the bed. "I will make it up to you when all this is over. Now go ahead and get on that flight. The last thing I need is to be tempted by your sweet ass."

"But I will miss you terribly," she teased. "Will you call to check up on me? You know how I like attention."

Hiwatha placed a kiss on her forehead and agreed to call. He was ready to end their time together. Suddenly he felt the vibration of his cell phone and looked at the number. It was Caroline making her usual daily follow-up.

"Hey, there, Lover Boy, I hope you're going to keep your promise to me. I arranged two interviews today for you. They shouldn't take too long. I gave both reporters the number to the gym. So, I need you to make sure you're available."

"I'll do that," Hiwatha said, throwing his gym bag over his shoulder.

Hiwatha was smiling while speaking to Caroline, and Victoria made a mental note that his mood had suddenly changed. As she pretended to look in the mirror, Victoria was still listening to his conversation. Hiwatha blew her one last kiss before leaving the room. Victoria's antenna went straight up. She didn't know who was on the other end of the phone, but Victoria's intuition told her it was not just business.

Chapter 7

THE SWEET SCENT OF MONEY

The Houston arena was sold to capacity. Caroline had done a beautiful job, and Antonio Rosanni was pleased. The doubleheader had turned out better than he and Mitch had anticipated.

The world was buzzing about the news of Hiwatha and Magnificent undisputed middleweight championship fight in October. Antonio was confident the unification bout would surpass all the other super fights. He was already set to make a sizable profit on the promotion in Houston.

On Saturday, Hiwatha would be defending his half of the title against Bryant Mitchell, who was a clever though light-punching, southpaw. He was rated number five in the world partly due to his promotional connection with Shapiro. Mitch and Antonio knew Mitchell had little chance against Hiwatha.

"I'm feeling good and looking good," Hiwatha told the press after his workout. "I'm ready for this fight."

It was true. Hiwatha had been sharp during training. It was

no secret in boxing circles that he already was training and preparing for his fight with Magnificent. Publicly, Hiwatha stated it would be no problem to defeat Magnificent. In private, he respected his rival's power and reluctantly admitted that Magnificent could box reasonably well.

———«()»———

As usual, Magnificent was upset that his title defense against Hector Mercedes was going on before Hiwatha's title defense against Mitchell. Truth be told, if Mitchell had no chance against Hiwatha, surely Mercedes had no right to walk into the ring with Magnificent. Curiously he had been given a world rating just three weeks before the bout. Even though his record was only four wins and two losses over the last year-and-a-half, this pretender had been ranked the number eighth contender in the world.

Charleston had no need to worry, but still, he was cautious. He was on the precipice of making a handsome fortune and would not consider taking the slightest chance. Magnificent's training had gone well. His instincts told him Magnificent was ready to quickly dismiss the pretender to his throne. Charleston was just a man of little faith.

Antonio would pay Magnificent 3.5 million for this title exercise and would shell out another 4 million to Hiwatha. This was a small tribute compared to the windfall he would make off the "showdown" between the two undefeated world titleholders.

At the urging of Mitch and Charleston, Antonio had

placed Numwar Nasser on the undercard. He was now curious to see the number one contender in action. It was no secret that he thought there might be another extravaganza between the winner of the "showdown" and this truly talented and deserving contender. Antonio was counting the minutes to fight time.

———————

Hiwatha and his entourage pushed through the doors of the Astro Village Hotel. They had completed their training for the day, and Hiwatha was ready to rest before eating his last meal.

"Hiwatha, over there at twelve o'clock!" shouted one of his cronies as he pointed to a woman sitting near the reception area of the lobby.

"Too bad you got a fight coming up because that is definitely play-time. I could ride that like a new car."

"The only riding you'll be doing in that car is in the backseat," responded Hiwatha as he noticed Caroline. She was wearing a powder blue suit that accented every curve, yet she still came off classy and professional. My kind of woman thought Hiwatha.

"Hold my gym bag," he said while shoving the bag into his underling's arm. "That happens to be a dear friend of mine."

Caroline looked up and noticed Hiwatha coming toward her. She was excited to see him and smiled as he came closer. Though Caroline knew her chances of being any more than a friend was slim, she was still happy to see him. As Hiwatha reached for her, Caroline stood to greet him.

"Well, don't you look handsome," she said as they embraced. "It looks like Virginia Beach really does agree with you."

"Not as much as that California sunshine agrees with you," Hiwatha responded as he kissed her cheek.

"You are a pleasant surprise, and you're definitely wearing that suit," he continued. "If I were your man, no way would you be sitting in the lobby of any hotel looking like that. I had to calm my boys down over there."

"Well, actually, I was waiting for Mr. Rosanni to come back from a meeting. You know how demanding he can be. Unfortunately, he's running late. So, I guess we'll have to meet later this evening. I'm just hoping it doesn't conflict with me picking up Stevie from the airport."

"Who the hell is Stevie?" Hiwatha asked jokingly. "I should've known a good-looking woman like you would have a man stashed somewhere."

"You know Stevie is my brother," she replied. "He decided to come to the fight. He can't wait to see you. I wish I were waiting for a man. That surely would make my day. There are so many beautiful women in Los Angeles; a girl just doesn't stand a chance."

"I don't believe that. A beautiful woman like you always has a chance. I'm not buying your poor-little-me routine."

Oblivious to Hiwatha's annoyance, Caroline switched the topic to her on-again-off-again relationship with Lance.

Just the guy Hiwatha had hoped floated out to sea.

"There was Lance, but you know that's been off and on since college. He wouldn't know a good woman if she fell from heaven and landed in his bed."

"Well, I don't feel sorry for Lance," replied Hiwatha. "If he can't find in you what any man with eyes can see, too bad."

"I guess you're right," Caroline stated as if she were having an AH-HA moment. "I shouldn't cry over spilled milk. Nobody likes the woman who's coming out of a screwed-up relationship."

"Caroline I'm not going to stand here and listen to your pity party over Lance. I'm going up to my room to get something to eat. You are welcome to join me. I can use the company. Maybe we can go over the interviews you have scheduled for me this week. But I do have one request."

Caroline looked up at Hiwatha with a look that said, I know you're not thinking of asking me to do anything but go over the schedule with you. Hiwatha noticed the look on her face and smiled. He grabbed Caroline by the arm and began pulling her towards the elevator.

"You know for a professional woman; you have a dirty mind. Do you think sex is the only thing men think about? I was actually going to request that you not bring up that jerk Lance to me ever again."

Caroline began playfully whispering Lance's name trying to annoy Hiwatha. When the elevator door opened, Hiwatha pushed her inside, stuck his VIP key in the slot and prayed the elevator would not stop until it reached the penthouse floor. He then turned and cornered Caroline up against the back of the elevator. He was standing so close she could feel his heartbeat.

"Caroline, it's about time you and I finally get on the same page," Hiwatha stated with a serious look on his face.

"I don't want to hear nothing else about Lance. For some reason, you're finding enjoyment in torturing me with this guy. By now you should have some idea I'm very interested in you."

"What are you talking about?" Caroline asked. "I thought we were going to your room to go over the publicity schedule. You look...,"

Before Caroline could utter another word, Hiwatha began passionately kissing her. His heart was now beating at a fast pace. What was it about this woman that made him feel this way?

The elevator doors finally opened, and Hiwatha was still kissing Caroline as he pulled her from the elevator. She pushed him back to straighten out her suit and hair.

"Okay, I admit that was a good speech and a pretty decent kiss, but can you tell me what's really going on here?" she asked in a confused voice. "Out of nowhere, you say these things to me, and just like that, you think our friendship and the professional relationship we have goes out the window. If my company knew I was carrying on with you like this, I'd be fired on the spot. Maybe it's not such a good idea that I go to your room."

"Maybe it's the best idea that you go to my room," responded Hiwatha. "I understand your desire to be professional. I'm not trying to stop you from doing your job. But there is something else going on between us, and I think you know it."

Caroline pulled her hand back from Hiwatha. She was suspicious of his intentions and felt he was trying to take advantage of her. This would inevitably compromise their friendship.

"Is this some kind of joke? Caroline asked. "There are dozens of women you can mess with and quite a few that you do. I'm far from blind. If you care so much about me, then don't get me caught up in that crap. Especially since we have to work together."

Caroline was standing face-to-face with Hiwatha. She looked directly in his eyes so there would be no misunderstanding.

"Hiwatha, you don't have to worry about the things that concern me as a woman. Nobody's ever going to place a derogatory label on you no matter how many women you choose to entertain. That's just how it goes when you're a man. Especially one in your position. For me, it's a different story, and you know it. I refuse to lose my job because you think you've got the right to piss and mark my tree. So, here's what I'm going to do. Stay cute, keep it professional, and pretend this never happened."

Caroline had no idea how sincere Hiwatha was. In fact, his intentions towards her were honorable. He couldn't say that about any woman. They were merely bed partners to him. After listening to Caroline' concerns, it was imperative Hiwatha didn't leave her with the wrong impression.

"I've thought about everything you're saying. I haven't done anything to make you think I don't respect you or the job you're trying to do. That's why I didn't want to approach you about this until after the fight," Hiwatha said seriously.

"I wouldn't have said anything today except it's been hard trying to conceal my feelings. Do you know that ever since I saw you in Antonio's office, I look forward to hearing from you? You have been the most real and definitely, the most refreshing person that has come into my life. I could shoot myself for being so shallow and not recognizing the person you were back then."

Caroline turned away from Hiwatha and pushed the elevator button. She wanted no part of this. She thought only of her career. Getting involved with Hiwatha could be very problematic.

"Hiwatha, you are an old friend and a client of Rosanni's. I can't just throw everything I've worked for away. You think because I broke up with Lance, I'm somehow free to become your bed partner."

"Caroline, that's really ridiculous. You know that's not what I just said to you. I'm standing here pouring my heart out to you, and you're acting like I'm trying to feed you some line of bullshit. I've been no less than a gentleman with you."

Hiwatha paused for a moment. "Though I don't believe I'm finally saying this, if you want all the women in my life gone, for you, they will disappear. You want my heart; you can have it. What I am saying is...."

When the elevator doors opened, Caroline jumped in. She had panicked and felt it best not to trust him, especially with her emotions. Hiwatha continued to hold the elevator door open as she spoke.

"To me, Hiwatha, trust is essential in a relationship. You know there's no room for that in your life. The only way a woman survives in your world is that she does her job, and at the end of the day, she goes home to her average Joe Blow husband who loves her."

Caroline stepped back to allow the elevator doors to close, but Hiwatha continued to hold them open with his hand. He was sorry that he'd offended her.

"Caroline, you will find that there is no guarantee that the average Joe Blow will love you. If that were the case, Lance would be standing here professing his love instead of me. Sooner or later, you're going to realize that men in my world fall in love and get their hearts broken just like everybody else."

With that, Hiwatha allowed the elevator doors to close. He stood there for a moment, wishing this whole scene hadn't happened. What was he thinking? Why didn't he wait? He had planned to tell Caroline how he felt after the fight in October. Life would be less complicated. He could have taken her away somewhere. He thought of going after her but didn't want to be bombarded by crowds without his entourage. He would have to wait and talk to her later.

The next morning, Hiwatha awoke to the sound of the telephone ringing near his bed. As he reached over to answer, he noticed it was five o'clock. He wasn't scheduled to be up until six-thirty. He grabbed a pillow to put over his head. Sleep was all he needed right now. He and St. Claire had stayed up late, watching tapes and going over their strategy for Saturday night. Hiwatha had every intention of walking away with the victory.

His cell phone rang again. After a long sigh, he reached down beside his bed to answer it. He could see that it was Victoria.

"Hello," he said with irritation in his voice. "Somebody better be dying if you're waking me up this early."

"Hi, sweetheart. I haven't heard from you," was the reply from the other end.

Hiwatha was not happy to hear Victoria's voice. He knew this situation could be a problem for him after his conversation with Caroline.

"Vicky, why would you wake me at this hour?"

"I'm calling because you didn't answer your phone last night, and you made no attempt to call me back."

Victoria was trying to remain calm. She had missed Hiwatha and needed to hear his voice. Whether he wanted to accept it, Victoria had fallen in love. Now she wanted to make sure no other woman was sitting ringside at his fight.

It was time the world knew about their relationship.

"Hiwatha, you know I'm coming there on Friday for the fight. So, tell me how I'm going to get tickets? You promised a month ago that you would have Mitch arrange a room."

"Victoria, maybe this isn't a good idea," Hiwatha said hesitantly.

Victoria had a bad temper, and Hiwatha knew this would definitely start an argument. This was one of the reasons he maintained a distance between them.

"What in the hell do you mean?" asked Victoria in a heated tone. "What kind of game are you playing? Do you know how difficult it was for me to rearrange my schedule to be there?"

"I know, and I'm sorry," he said apologetically. "It's important that I win this fight. I don't want to be distracted. I have to look good if we're going to have a successful promotion going into the fight with Magnificent."

"Hiwatha, that's bullshit, and you know it. Am I important to you or not? Because that's what this is about."

"Vicky, this has nothing to do with how important you are to me. This is about what I'm trying to do here."

"Do you think I'm stupid or something?" she said, cutting him off. "Just tell me who the little bimbo is? I'm smart enough to know when there is another woman in the picture. So, just level with me and don't waste my time."

Hiwatha wanted to tell her about Caroline. He didn't want to risk Caroline seeing him with Victoria after the confession he'd given her. He needed to convince Victoria not to come. But how could he do that without pissing her off?

As crazy as it sounds, Hiwatha was not ready to let Victoria go. With Caroline in California and Victoria frequently traveling, for a short time, he could still make the situation work. Hiwatha wanted to keep Victoria around because Caroline, though worth it, was a long-term project. He paused to think through his options.

"Okay, Vicky, let's do this. I'll have Mitch arrange everything for you. But you must promise me you will not try an see me until after the fight. If I lay eyes on your fine ass before that, it will make me weak. You know how much I enjoy making love to you."

Victoria smiled as she turned to look in her dressing room mirror. For her, that was a satisfactory answer. As long as she was in the same vicinity as Hiwatha, nothing else mattered. Victoria couldn't wait to get off the phone and call Mitch. She was determined to block all entrances and exits when it came to Hiwatha.

⸺⸺《(I)》⸺⸺

Theresa Tarver was staying at a hotel down the street from the Astro Village Hotel. She was steaming mad with Charleston. Not only did Danielle show up sooner than expected, Charleston had not come by to see her in a couple of days.

She was now throwing her clothes in a suitcase, not caring where they landed. How could Charleston fly her to Houston then treat her like a second-class piece of ass? This

Theresa could not take.

Charleston had sent one of his underlings to give her some money as if that was going to appease her. Theresa wanted out of Houston, and hopefully out of Charleston's life. It had been two years, and that was enough time to waste on a relationship going nowhere. Her cell phone rang, and Theresa ran into the living room to answer it.

"Hello," she said in a salty voice.

"Hey, baby," replied Charleston. "I know you're mad at me, but it's been crazy over here. I haven't been able to getaway. Magnificent has several interviews scheduled this morning and I still need to attend the press conference."

"Charleston, I don't give a shit," she retorted. "You brought me here so you could be with me, and I'm sitting over here by myself."

"Baby...I had no idea Danielle was coming before Friday. She has never done that."

"Well, I'm leaving on the next flight out of here. Don't try to call me, and definitely, do not try to see me now or ever. I am through with you. You hear me! I am...through!"

"Theresa, baby, I understand if you want to leave. Right now, there's nothing I can do that would please you, but I will make it up to you."

"Don't worry, Charleston. At this point, you've already done enough." With that, she clicked off her phone.

Charleston stood in the lobby of the hotel, wondering what he should do. He was in double trouble. With Danielle there, he was locked in. No way could he explain not coming back to the hotel at night. His wife had not said anything, but Charleston felt she may suspect he was having an affair.

For now, Charleston had to play it cool. He couldn't afford a divorce from Danielle, nor did he have intentions on giving up Theresa. Charleston sent another one of his underlings over to the hotel where Theresa was staying. He needed to make sure she got to the airport safely, and the gesture would let Theresa know he was still thinking of her.

Chapter 8

DOUBLE TROUBLE

Hiwatha began to prepare for his morning run. It was no use trying to go back to sleep. He rang Ramiro's room to tell him he'd be running early today. Maybe it was best since the pre-fight press conference was this afternoon.

As he dressed, Hiwatha thought about Caroline. He had not seen her for two days. It was apparent she was avoiding him. When he called her cell or left a message in her room, it was Dale Rice, her assistant, who responded.

Hiwatha found it refreshing. He hadn't chased a woman in a long time. He found it amusing that Caroline was able to turn the tables. Despite his healthy appetite for beautiful women, her actions were only making him want her more.

———⟫⟪⟪⟫———

Caroline was seated at the reception table, listening to Dale read off her messages. She waved him on as he read several calls from Hiwatha. Dale, who would do almost anything to climb the corporate ladder, was taking note of Caroline's disposition towards Hiwatha.

"What's going on with you two?" he asked. "I'm trying to help the poor guy out, but he only wants to talk with you. There's nothing else I can do."

"Oh...you know how these celebrities are," Caroline responded as she tried to redirect Dales snooping. "You do everything for them, and nothing is good enough. He thinks he's too good to deal with you, but I have a lot on my plate handling the publicity for this event. I tried to tell him you, too, were a consummate professional and on some things, you could be of great help."

"Well, thanks for your vote of confidence. I did try to assure Hiwatha I could help, but he was pretty clear he wanted you. So, I think you'll have to deal with Hiwatha, and I'm going to assist Magnificent. He's nicer, anyway."

Caroline agreed and instructed Dale to continue reading their agenda for the day. She would have to deal with Hiwatha soon enough. Right now, the podium and signage needed to be in place for the press conference. She also had Magnificent scheduled for several interviews before the start of the conference, and she needed to make sure Rosanni's right-hand man, Stan Goldstein, attended the organizational meeting with the Boxing Commission.

Caroline had no time to deal with her growing emotions for Hiwatha. The thought of their previous conversation scared her. Although she couldn't deny the kiss was one for the memory book, there was no way she would allow

Hiwatha to use her.

Caroline looked up from the press table as the media began to scramble when Hiwatha entered the room. This guy knows how to make an entrance she thought to herself. It didn't hurt that Hiwatha was dressed to the nines in a tailored suit. You had to give it to him, he was classy.

At the first glimpse of Caroline, Hiwatha felt a lump growing in his throat. Though reporters were trying to get his attention, his eyes remained fixed on Caroline as he stopped to do an interview. She was looking even more beautiful than he could remember.

Caroline caught his gaze and quickly dropped her head, pretending to work on a press release. She got a funny feeling in the pit of her stomach as she tried to mask the flood of emotions that rushed through her.

Hiwatha abruptly cut his interview short with a reporter to make his way over to Caroline. To avoid a lengthy conversation, when Hiwatha started to speak, she grabbed his arm and led him towards the stage.

"If I don't get you on the stage, we'll never get this press conference started on time."

"Why are you avoiding me?" Hiwatha asked with his sexiest smile. "Do you really think I'm going to let you off the hook so easily?"

"Hiwatha, we cannot have this conversation right now. Besides, you already know why I'm avoiding you."

That didn't faze Hiwatha. He continued his pursuit. "Then when can we have this conversation?" he persisted.

"I have no intentions of shutting up until you agree to meet with me and listen to what I have to say."

"Can we do this after the fight?" she asked. "You should dispose of Mitchell pretty quickly and come out without a scratch."

Hiwatha smiled. He was amused by her comment. Though he was sure of his win against Mitchell, what made Caroline so sure? Since when had she become a boxing expert? Still, he was not going to allow her bad attitude to deter him from his mission. He continued to push. If nothing else he was going to get a date.

"If you're going to put me off until after the fight, then I'll see you for lunch Sunday before I leave."

"That won't be good for me. I have an early flight," Caroline snapped.

"Well, change it. After all, I am an important client. Besides, you promised to take me to lunch when we got to Houston. Just in case anyone asks, there's your professional excuse."

Hiwatha felt his emotions rise as he looked down at Caroline. He put his hand on her shoulder, then whispered in her ear.

"Caroline, if for one moment you consider blowing me off, I swear I'll grab this microphone and tell the world I'm in love with you."

Caroline reached over and quickly put her hand over the microphone. She had no intentions of being embarrassed in front of a room of reporters.

"You wouldn't dare do that to me," she pleaded.

"Try me," replied Hiwatha.

Caroline looked at him with irritation. Why was he pushing the envelope with her? There were many women this man could be bothering. Why her? Lord give me the strength she thought to herself.

Hiwatha knew he was breaking down Caroline's last line of defense. Now all he needed was the final confirmation.

"OK, I'll have lunch with you," she reluctantly replied.

"Good, make sure your ready eleven o'clock sharp. Now smile, I'm not exactly the worst guy you can fall in love with."

"No, but you are the most annoying. Now please sit down so we can get this press conference over with."

Hiwatha watched her walk away as he took a seat next to St. Claire and Mitch. He leaned over and whispered into Mitch's ear.

"You know, I'm going to marry that woman one day."

"Yeah and I'm going to be president of the United States," responded Mitch as he thought of the numerous women, he'd previously seen in Hiwatha's company.

As a matter of fact, he had his travel agent arranging to fly Victoria to Houston. In Mitch's mind, Hiwatha was headed for double trouble.

Caroline was awakened Friday morning by her assistant Dale. He was having an issue with one of the undercard fight camps. Apparently, they had not gotten their room per diem, and their manager was upset. This was not an issue Caroline would typically handle. Her role had expanded since working with Rosanni. He trusted her to get things done to his liking.

"Can't you find Rolando and let him take care of this? He was given the cash to settle this with each of the camps upon arrival."

Caroline was irritated by the lack of professionalism. She didn't need anything else to ruin her morning. She had been up until 2:00 a.m. piecing together a lot of the final documentation Rosanni needed.

"I'll find him, Caroline. Hopefully, that asshole didn't spend the money."

Caroline ignored Dale's last comment. She knew all about tying up loose ends. As she prepared to shower, her thoughts reflected on her conversation with Hiwatha. Could this gorgeous hunk of man really be digging his hometown girl or just trying to score points? She needed to figure that out before it went too far.

Caroline was heavily in debt due to her school loans. She liked her job and could not afford to be out of work for any reason. There was also her mom to think about. Since the onset of her illness two years ago, she hadn't been able to work. Caroline and her brother Stevie were her sole providers.

Stevie handled the day-to-day care since moving back home two-years earlier. Caroline was thankful for that. Right now, she wasn't willing to rock the boat for anyone.

Not even handsome and talented Hiwatha. Though she had to admit, he was wearing down her resistance. If Hiwatha could make love even remotely close to that kiss he put on her lips, she was in trouble.

Her only solution was to try an avoid him as much as possible. Unfortunately, that would also mean avoiding the beautiful friendship they had renewed. How she enjoyed talking to him. They could laugh for hours over the silliest things, especially their childhood memories. Hiwatha knew how to make her feel special.

A sudden knock at the door startled Caroline and brought her back to reality. She quickly grabbed a robe from the back of the bathroom door to see who now needed her. As she opened the door, a valet stood there, holding two dozen roses.

"Good morning, Ms. Davis. These are for you," he said softly.

"Thank you," replied Caroline. "Hold on while I get you a tip."

She re-emerged quickly with a ten-dollar bill. She couldn't wait to see who the flowers were from. There was a part of her that hoped they were from Lance. Maybe he had second thoughts about their break-up. That would be just what she needed to get out of the clinches of Hiwatha. She quickly opened the card.

Dear Caroline,
    I meant what I said to you the other day by the

elevator and also what I said to you at the press conference. It was entirely from my heart. With that said, I do respect and understand your feelings about the professional side of the situation. Just don't lose sight of the fact that you and I were friends before it became professional. With that in mind, know that there is no mountain you can fall from that I won't be there to catch you. Regardless of the outcome of the fight on Saturday, well or injured, our lunch date stands. I'll be at your door by 11:00 a.m.

Hiwatha Jordan

Caroline stood by the window with her hands covering her mouth. Hiwatha was coming after her, and there would be no ducking him, especially with the fight on the schedule for October. She had to decide quickly how she was going to proceed.

——⟨⟨◉⟩⟩——

Victoria was pacing the floor. Her makeup artist had not arrived, and it was already noon. She was anxious to make a grand entrance at the weigh-in by three O'clock. She hadn't seen Hiwatha since she arrived last night. Victoria definitely wanted all eyes and cameras on her at the weigh-in.

She missed Hiwatha terribly and was annoyed that he seemed distracted lately. With her own stardom on the rise, she couldn't get enough attention. She gloated at the sight of her face plastered on billboards and magazine covers all over the country. Her single was Number One on the Billboard charts, followed by her new release. Who could ask for more? Now she was pulling out all the stops for Hiwatha. After this weekend, everyone would know they were an item.

—— ((•)) ——

Hiwatha sat near his room window, half-listening to St. Claire critique yesterday's workout. Hiwatha already understood what he had to do. This was settled in his mind. He would quickly dispose of his opponent, who he couldn't dispose of was Victoria. She had been calling his room since her arrival. He could only manage brief conversations with her. Hiwatha felt it was time to get rid of Victoria before the press got wind of their relationship.

Since the start of their affair, Hiwatha had been careful not to be too public. He knew time was not on his side. There was no way Victoria after a year would allow their relationship to remain private.

She was a beautiful, sexy woman, but not what Hiwatha wanted in a wife or as the mother of his children. She was much too Hollywood to play that role in his life. Though he had to admit, she was arm-jewelry and the best sex a man could ask for.

Thanks to Mitch, Victoria and her friend Elan were on a shopping spree. The plan was for them not to get back to the hotel until after the weigh-in. The last thing he needed was for those two and Caroline to cross paths.

How stupid of him to confess his feelings to Caroline so soon. He wanted to make sure everything was perfect before entering her life. After all, she'd been through with Lance, this was his opportunity to be her knight in shining armor.

Women like Victoria move on to the next man willing to feed their ego. Caroline was different. She still believed in honesty, trust, and loyalty. While Caroline is worried about her professional reputation, Victoria is busy plotting her next headline.

As Hiwatha began listening to St. Claire, his thoughts quickly moved to the upcoming weigh-in. He would have to start getting ready to leave his suite and head to the auditorium. There would be a horde of reporters and fans he would have to contend with upon arrival.

———————— «(◉)» ————————

As Hiwatha strode into the crowded room, he was quickly blinded by flashlights going off in his face. He tried to stay in the middle of his entourage as they made their way to the stage. The room was filled to capacity with screaming fans, reporters, and camera crews. He was relieved when Caroline appeared and guided him to the backstage area.

Hiwatha stopped briefly to acknowledge Wonderful Magnificent and his entourage. Magnificent was in great shape and recognized him in return. Hiwatha knew it was all for the cameras. It was no secret that Magnificent and

Charleston hated sharing the division with him. Like it or not, he was Hiwatha "Absolute" Jordan, one of the best in boxing.

Hiwatha continued to follow Caroline so he could quickly meet with the doctor and sign the necessary paperwork. He acknowledged Mitch and St. Claire as he passed the table holding the gloves. They were both carefully examining them for approval.

Hiwatha could barely focus on what the doctor was saying. He could not take his eyes off Caroline. They had not spoken since the press conference, and Hiwatha wondered if she'd received the flowers. For the tenth time, he felt utterly vulnerable. He wanted to hold Caroline close to him instead of keeping up his pretentious performance.

"Come on, Hiwatha. I guess it's time to get on the scale," Caroline said as she grabbed his hand. "Just in case I don't see you before the fight tomorrow, good luck. I'll be cheering for you."

The noise from the theater was so loud, Hiwatha had to bend down to speak in her ear. "Did you get my flowers?"

"Yes, they were beautiful."

Hiwatha stared attentively at Caroline. Then without thinking, he grabbed her shoulders and kissed her on the forehead.

"Eleven o'clock sharp. Don't forget."

Hiwatha turned and walked toward the black curtains leading to the front of the stage. As he pulled the curtains back to get a better view of the audience, his jaw dropped as he caught a glimpse of Victoria standing in the center of a group of reporters holding court.

When the crowd began to chant Hiwatha's name, Victoria instantly began fanning the reporters away like flies at a picnic. She started moving in the direction of the stage. Hiwatha's only advantage was that he was on stage and Victoria was still pushing through the crowd beneath him.

He was relieved to see Mitch grab Victoria's hand to re-direct her attention away from the stage. Some shopping spree Hiwatha thought, as he caught her eye and waved. She blew a kiss while half-focusing on what Mitch was saying.

"Look, Victoria, you're going to have to give us a min-ute here. We have to go live with the weigh-in in about five minutes. Why don't you let one of Hiwatha's guys take you into the VIP area? I will make sure Hiwatha meet you there."

"Mitch, I'm not going anywhere," Victoria said firmly. "I want to watch my man do his thing. That's what this is all about. Hiwatha supports my career, I support his. What you can do is have one of your guys find me a seat."

"Suit yourself," Mitch responded in irritation. "I got busi-ness to take care of."

Mitch motioned for one of the security guards to as-sist her then made his way back to the stage. Hiwatha gave him one of those "what the hell is she doing here" looks as Mitch approached. Mitch raised his shoulders and shook his head. He pointed directly at Hiwatha.

"Just like you can't control her, neither can I."

The announcer started to calm the crowd as the television crew gave him the signal. Hiwatha and his opponent were scheduled to weigh in first.

As Hiwatha stripped down to his briefs, the crowd went wild. His nakedness was not lost on Caroline, who was surveying every inch of his body. Never had she seen a body so symmetrically put together. She held her hand to her mouth in embarrassment, at the mere thoughts running through her mind. Caroline had just become Hiwatha's number one fan.

———«(❂)»———

The Houston arena was rocking. Though this doubleheader was just a warm-up, the stadium was filled to capacity. Everyone wanted to be a part of the excitement. It was known that Hiwatha "Absolute" Jordan and Wonderful Magnificent would be battling for the undisputed middleweight championship of the world. With Antonio and Mitch being the driving force behind the promotion, this unification bout would surpass all other "super fights," In fact, they were already in the black.

Tonight, Hiwatha would be defending his half of the title against number-five-rated Bryant Mitchell. His rating was mainly due to his promotional connection with Shapiro. To boxing insiders, it was no secret that this clever, light-punching southpaw had no chance against Hiwatha Jordan.

"I'm feeling good, and as usual I look good," the champion told the press after his final workout.

Hiwatha looked sharp and was in great shape. No one knew that better than Magnificent, who was now leaving his dressing room headed for the ring. His demeanor was calm. He was surrounded by Charleston, two other trainers and his entourage of hangers-on. He was ready to do the job. He walked casually down the dimly-lit stairwell. Several police officers were waiting to greet him and his handlers.

"Just follow us, champ," said officer Taylor. "We're here to lead you into the ring. Remember, after the fight is over, we'll take you back to your dressing room and then to the press conference.

Upon seeing Magnificent, the crowd erupted, as this was the first big fight Texas had seen. The fans were ready to see him go to work. The closer Magnificent got to the ring, the louder the crowd roared. The police officers had to push the fans back and clear the aisle as they approached ringside.

"Look out!" they repeatedly shouted to clustering fans.

After the lengthy introductions by the announcer, who had to be reminded that traditionally the champion is introduced last, it was time to get to fist city.

Hector Mercedes looked as if he had no chance. He was dressed in red velvet boxing shoes and red trunks. He looked like a man who had a meeting with the Internal Revenue Service.

Magnificent was resplendent in white satin trunks trimmed in gold that bore his name in gold lettering. He wore white boxing shoes complete with gold tassels. His upper body looked impressive under the hot ring lights. One of the announcers at ringside remarked that Magnificent looked like a light-heavyweight. At the first bell, Magnificent glided out to the center of the ring like a predator.

Mercedes was a dark Mexican with a thick mustache. His eyes were opened wide. He seemed to be intent on not getting hit early. He tried a few tentative jabs, all of which fell short.

Like a tailor measuring a client for a fitting, Magnificent was sizing up his unworthy opponent. By mid-round, he had seen enough. Swiftly working behind his punishing left jab, Magnificent snapped his opponent's head back with two heavy jabs. This caused Hector to blink. Then another jab found its mark, followed by a whistling straight right-hand.

The crowd erupted in cheers. Hector buckled and began staggering. Magnificent saw his opportunity and pinned him in the corner with a thudding right to the kidney and a short right-hand to his jaw. This nearly embalmed the hopelessly outclassed and over-matched pretender. He was saved by the bell.

In Mercedes, corner, his trainer was frantically speaking Spanish, trying to revive his man as best he could. In truth, the fight should have been stopped.

In Magnificent's corner, Charleston spoke to his champion directly. "Look, man, just dress him up with the jab and then nail him with a right hand. We don't have time for this bullshit. Let's go home, the party's over."

With that, Magnificent got off his stool at the bell for the second round. It was time to finish the job. A double-jab followed by a double-left-hook nearly left Mercedes for dead. Magnificent then landed a crushing left-hook, right-hand, left-hook combination to the chin of his challenger.

As Mercedes hit the canvas, the referee did not bother to count. It would be close to a minute before Mercedes moved. The crowd roared with approval as they gave Magnificent a standing ovation.

Hector Mercedes earned all of his two-hundred-thousand dollars. His jaw was shattered in two places, and he would pass blood for a week. Hector also had to endure a lengthy operation to piece his left jaw back together. He would fade into obscurity as quickly as he had been pulled from it.

———⸺«(●)»⸻———

Hiwatha was in his dressing room, watching the fight on a television monitor. Magnificent's performance had not been lost on him or his team. Hiwatha tried to downplay the situation, as he began to shadowbox in his underwear.

"He looked okay," he commented.

If Hiwatha was impressed, he didn't show it. He moved about lightly on his feet and soon had broken a light sweat. He finally sat down to allow St. Claire to begin taping his hands. Soon he would complete the long walk to the ring.

———⸺«(●)»⸻———

It was the first round, and the crowd was shouting Hiwatha's name. He was in the ring with Bryant Mitchell who was trying to show off with his southpaw style and slickness. He was not fighting to win the title, but to make Hiwatha look bad. The champion had been able to counter the slick lefty, but Hiwatha had been countered as well. At the end of round seven Hiwatha was leading on all cards, but his trainer St. Claire was not pleased.

"Get busy with your left hand! You've already hit him on the chin, he can take it. Now let that left-hook to the body go. Then work back up on top with both hands!"

At the bell, Hiwatha became more purposeful. He worked behind his jab and found his prey with cracking left-hooks to the body and head. The combatants had a lively exchange before Mitchell landed a left-cross and a slapping right-hook. Hiwatha countered with three blistering left-hooks and another right-hand on the chin.

Mitchell was now bleeding from the nose and had a nick in the corner of his left eyebrow. By the middle of the tenth round, Mitchell was being hurt by the champion. A hard-jab and straight right-hand found him off guard. He clenched the champion, but Hiwatha was relentless and refused to let Mitchell rest. He pursued him to the ropes with a ripping right-uppercut followed by a left hook to the body. Mitchell wobbled. Another straight right, followed by a double left hook put Mitchell on the deck.

The crowd roared and stomped their feet. This had been a fierce battle. When Mitchell hit the canvas, Hiwatha raced to the neutral corner and climbed the ring ropes.

As the count reached "eight," Mitchell gamely climbed to his feet. The referee looked into his eyes and asked: "Are you all right?" Mitchell did not speak.

With that, the referee waved his hands, and the bout was over. There was pure bedlam all around. Hiwatha ran to ring center and did a complete somersault, landing on his feet. This had turned out to be a tough fight. It required boxing artistry at its best.

Mitch, who had just entered the ring, grabbed Hiwatha to congratulate him. He had been sitting ringside with Antonio holding his breath. Also, sitting ringside was Magnificent, watching his rival up close and personal.

"Hiwatha looked good, but he took too many shots," Magnificent told the announcer working ringside.

"Shut up, chump!" screamed a leering Hiwatha from the ring. "Since when you start talking?"

The announcer was caught off guard by Hiwatha's un-sportsmanlike like behavior.

"I'm going to take this chump into deep water and drown him!" screamed the heavily breathing victor. "You don't want to mess with me. I'm going to kick your Windy City ass," he shouted while pointing at Magnificent.

"Hiwatha!" shouted Magnificent, trying to regain his attention. He was now seething, but Hiwatha had turned away and would not answer. The stage was set for the two superstars to collide.

Chapter 9

IN THE NAME OF LOVE

Hiwatha had not slept. He would typically wine down slowly after a fight and eventually rest the next day. This Sunday would have been no different, except Caroline was on the menu. He had argued most of the night with Victoria about their relationship. She felt it was going nowhere, and Hiwatha had earned another battle wound by saying, "And it never will."

Hiwatha was so annoyed with Victoria's starlet performance; he almost ended the relationship. Instead, he decided to change gears and make peace with Victoria. In truth, Hiwatha was unwilling to compromise sleeping with her that night or any other night. After all, Caroline still lived in California. Though he was hoping for the best, she was hard to read.

"Call me selfish," he rationalized, "but as long as I can have my cake and eat it too, then please, Heavenly Father, keep baking them."

With the help of Mitch and his entourage, Hiwatha was

careful over the weekend to keep his distance from Victoria in public. He knew she would have loved to get a picture with the two of them together in one of the popular gossip magazines. Thankfully after the fight Mitch had given Victoria the key to Hiwatha's suite along with a note. After reading the note she quickly headed for the exit.

Hiwatha checked his watch. It was time to collect his prize from downstairs. Caroline would have to be awake by now. Hiwatha had arranged for a limo to take them to an upscale restaurant nearby.

The restaurant, Ivery's Place, had become a hot spot in Houston if you wanted some down-home soul food. Hiwatha often stopped there when he was in town. The owner was a former sports agent and still held many connections with top athletes. He was known to be an excellent cook and hosted the best entertainment parties. Besides, he had a private room in the restaurant for celebrities. This morning Ivery was cooking one of Hiwatha's favorites, shrimp and grits.

As promised, Hiwatha was knocking on Caroline's door at eleven-o'clock sharp. He was surprised when her brother Stevie opened the door. He was surprised when Caroline's brother opened the door. Stevie immediately grabbed Hiwatha to give him a big home-boy welcome.

"Man, you looked good last night," conveyed Stevie. "Thanks to Caroline, I'm finally getting to see you after all these years. I can't believe how famous you've become."

"I'm still cool, man. Don't believe the hype," replied

Hiwatha. "I forgot Caroline told me you were coming to the fight. It's good to see you, man. I hear you're back in Brooklyn."

"Two years now," replied Stevie. "My wife and I split up, and I was tired of those Southern women. They started to give the brother a hard time. We men think we can handle more than one, but that shit's not easy."

"Tell me about it," responded Hiwatha. "I still don't know if I'm coming or going. What I have figured out, is they got something we need."

The two slapped hands and began laughing in agreement. Stevie flopped down in the chair he'd placed in front of the television and started flipping channels on the remote.

"Where is that sister of yours? Hiwatha asked, looking at his watch. "We have a reservation for lunch."

"Caroline should be back in about five minutes," responded Stevie. "She had to give that Rosanni dude some paperwork. Where you headed for lunch?"

"A buddy of mine has a spot nearby."

"Do you mind if a new friend and I join you?"

"No problem, if you don't mine Caroline sitting with me at another table. No offense, but I have some private business, I want to talk to her about."

"I don't have a problem with that, my brother. My little sister can handle herself. It's you, I'm worried about."

"Stevie, it's just business," Hiwatha replied in a defensive tone.

"Business, my ass! You up here just a little too early after a fight, my brother. Only a very interested dude would do that."

"Okay, you got me. I'm checking for Caroline's fine ass. What can I say; we're all grown, right?"

Stevie turned to look at Hiwatha. "I say you treat her right or our friendship will stay a thing of the past. No offense, but that's what I say to any brother checking for Caroline's fine ass."

"Man, you will never change, but I respect that. I would be the same way if she were my sister. Let me put you at ease. I really care for Caroline beyond her physical assets, which I had not seen or touched. We are friends first and foremost. That will stay the same, whether we can develop a relationship or not."

"That's good to know. I'm glad we had an opportunity to talk. By the way, did Caroline tell you our mother was ill?"

"No, she didn't mention that," responded Hiwatha. "Is it serious?" He asked in concern.

"Well, she's had all types of crazy things going on since they diagnosed her as diabetic a few years ago. That eventually progressed to something else, and so on. I'm surprised Caroline didn't tell you."

"I am sorry to hear that," Hiwatha conveyed sincerely. "When I come back through Brooklyn next week, I'd like to stop by and see her."

"Oh, she'd love that, Hiwatha. You know my mom always thought you could do no wrong. She watches every one of your fights. Hollering at the T.V., that's my friend Nathan's boy."

The two old friends passed the time laughing about old school memories, their football days and the time they spent in amateur boxing. Stevie brought Hiwatha up to speed on some of their childhood friends, like who was now married, divorced or had children.

When Caroline returned from her meeting, she looked radiant as usual in her skin-tight jeans and white blouse. She immediately began apologizing to Hiwatha for being late.

"Hey, baby, it's okay. Stevie and I were just catching up on old times. When you're ready, which I hope is soon, I'll call downstairs for the car."

"Yes. Just give me a few minutes to freshen up."

"What more could you do to such a beautiful face? Stevie and I are hungry."

"Who said Stevie was going," Caroline asked while giving Stevie an annoying look. "I thought you had a flight to catch."

"Mind your business, woman. I met someone. She's definitely worth the delay. As a matter of fact, I'm going to return her call right now." Stevie searched his bag for the room number.

Hiwatha picked up the morning paper from the coffee table to see if there were any articles on the fight. As he flipped through the pages, it occurred to him that this was the first time he wasn't front and center in a woman's life. Under other circumstances, he would have been annoyed, but today he was just a hometown guy getting ready to enjoy lunch with two childhood friends.

Maybe that was part of his attraction to Caroline. She had no problem treating him like the average guy and saying what she truly felt. To her, Hiwatha was merely a guy on the block trying to get her attention.

Caroline emerged from the bedroom refreshed and ready to go. Hiwatha looked up and smiled. How simple she looked in her baseball cap and jeans. Caroline wasn't willing to pretend to work just a little bit for his attention. Somehow that was still very sexy to Hiwatha.

Stevie's date arrived, and the four of them headed down the hall to the service elevator. Hiwatha grabbed Caroline's hand. From this moment on, he wanted it perfectly clear to Caroline that he intended to be front and center in her life. The professional concerns he would leave for Mitch and Antonio to work out.

———◦((◦))◦———

Numwar Nasser was signing autographs in the lobby of the Astro Village hotel.

"Man, you looked great," gushed a fan. "I've followed your career since you won the Commonwealth Games."

Numwar smiled. He had put on a good show in Houston knocking out "Schoolboy" Pat Farmer by the sixth round. He boxed him in a smooth, calculating style. This allowed Numwar to dismantle Farmer with five and six shot combinations highlighted by ripping left-hooks to the liver and right-hands to the spleen and kidneys.

Diana Hicks Sherer

Numwar's right-hand to the spleen, thrown in a short uppercut fashion was so devastating that Farmer spat out his mouthpiece and collapsed to the canvas. The Mexican fans, who enjoyed watching a skilled body-puncher at work, gave him a standing ovation.

Numwar took a seat ringside after his bout to study Magnificent and Jordan at work. He felt Magnificent was a swift, hard puncher with an exceptional finish. To Numwar, he was still beatable.

He acknowledged that Hiwatha was an incredible athlete, skilled in many areas of the sport, especially defensively. In his eyes, he too had a style that could be beaten.

"I will box Hiwatha and use my ability to counter-punch," he told his trainer Oliver Xavier. "I will be patient and wear him down with body shots."

"Son, I think they both would be a handful of trouble," Xavier laughed. "But you got the goods to handle them both."

They looked at one another and shared a heartfelt laugh.

<hr />

Antonio Rosanni was happy and with good reason. "You know, Mitch, we are running way ahead of schedule. We're in the black already on the big fight and even made some decent money off the double-header."

Though Mitch had sweated through Hiwatha's title bout, he was pleased that his superstar knew how to bring the curtain down.

"When do we start the tour?" Mitch asked Antonio.

"In a month. I've already planned the press conferences for New York, Chicago, and Los Angeles. New York will be our last stop. I'll make sure that Hiwatha and Magnificent travel by private jet. That way we can quickly get in and out of each city. This fight will be hyped like none other. I've got them set up to do the whole talk show circuit, and also several guest appearances on major television shows. I'll contact you about shooting the television and print ads."

Before leaving for the airport, they began putting the final touches on minor details.

"Your money has already been wired into your account," Rosanni said while leading Mitch to the door of his suite.

————))((((●)))((————

The match-up between Magnificent and Hiwatha was a press agent's dream. Caroline couldn't have been more pleased. Hiwatha was indeed the media darling and definitely popular beyond the sports pages and headlines. He was the most talked-about boxer since the days of a young Cassius Marcellus Clay. All the top sports magazines had done features on him, and even the women who had no interest in sports were drawn to his charisma. He was undoubtedly a blessing to the sport of boxing.

On the other hand, Magnificent was merely a great fighter. He was attractive because of the atomic power lodged in his right fist. Though Magnificent was good with his left, the right-hand was his bazooka. Caroline wished he was as eloquent as Hiwatha, but he was still able to hold his own. If there were any issues, Charleston typically stepped in to speak with the press. Though this appeared to be okay with Magnificent in public, privately it was a sore spot in their relationship. He blamed Charleston and not himself for this shortcoming. He had just finished cursing Charleston profusely over the whole deal, but in reality, it was he who had the complex about his speech.

As Magnificent's plane landed in New York City, the final stop on their tour, he felt that a victory over Hiwatha would make the difference in money, prestige, and recognition. Magnificent was aware of how far he'd come but understood how much further he needed to go.

"Please look over here, fellas!" shouted a photographer from the Times.

Magnificent and Hiwatha were dressed to perfection and standing face-to-face in boxing stances. The room was filled to capacity with reporters. Flashbulbs popped from every direction.

"Hold still, guys. One more! That's it! Beautiful!" shouted the row of photographers.

"I'm going to give this man a lesson in boxing," said Hiwatha as he looked sternly at Magnificent. "I owe it to the public to defeat this man and I shall."

Magnificent was not intimidated. He looked directly at Hiwatha when he replied. "I've been waiting a long time for you. You've ducked me long enough. I'm going to win, but first, I'm going to punish you."

The press was hanging on every word as they watched the exchange between the fighters get more heated. Finally, several handlers stepped in to quash any potential blows.

"I am pleased to bring these two great champions together," said Antonio.

"I'm sure that come October sixteenth the whole world will witness a spectacular boxing event."

With that, the crowd moved over to the lavish spread of food and drink. Antonio's staff had made this a first-class tour.

⸻ ⸱⟨⟨◉⟩⟩⸱ ⸻

Caroline was now exhausted. The tour had provided her and Hiwatha an opportunity to spend quality time together. They had fallen deeply in love, spending most nights together. Their lovemaking was passionate. Caroline knew Hiwatha had to start his rigorous training schedule in Virginia Beach. Mitch and St. Claire would make sure of that. She, too, had work to complete on the fight. How on earth would they part tomorrow?

As Caroline turned the key in her room door, she felt a sense of sadness overwhelm her. She loved Hiwatha with all her heart. When she turned the light on in her suite, sitting at the dinner table, practically naked, waiting for her was Hiwatha. He hit play on his iPod, and soft music began to play through the Bluetooth speakers. He stood up as she rushed over to be in his arms.

"OK, this is beautiful. You really know how to win a girls heart."

"Anything for you, sweetheart. I wanted our last night to be special."

They continued to embrace as Hiwatha kissed her. He was indeed in love with Caroline. His father would have been very happy for them.

"Caroline, I am so in love with you. I don't know what to say. The thought of us being apart does not sit well with me. I need you in my life. I can't believe I've been all over the world only to find someone who was half a block away."

"I love you too," responded Caroline. "More than I have ever loved anybody. I no longer care who knows. I've been so sad today knowing that I have to leave you. How can I do this? You have to help me. I've fallen for you, and I am so scared I'm going to wake up and find it's not real."

Hiwatha picked Caroline up and headed for the bedroom. "I hope you're not hungry," he stated. "I just lost my appetite. Is that real enough for you?" Caroline smiled warmly. "I think I can take care of that."

<hr />

The next day Hiwatha headed to the airport a changed man. As he looked out the airplane window in silence, he reflected on the press tour, and the time he'd spent with Caroline. He purposely tuned out Mitch and St. Claire chatter.

Victoria had been on a ten-city concert tour, promoting her new album. Though he had spoken to her numerous times, Hiwatha knew there was no way he could continue their relationship. Not after holding Caroline. It was too different. She had sparked something deep within him. He actually could see himself starting each day with her next to him.

Hiwatha now saw the distance between them as a real problem. He was ready to tell Victoria goodbye. She was due to be in Virginia Beach tomorrow evening. Hiwatha would definitely have to end the relationship before Caroline found out.

He decided that after the fight, he would ask Caroline to marry him. There was no reason for them to live apart. He'd already gotten Stevie and her mother's blessing the week before. Hiwatha had contacted Mrs. Davis to find out if she'd received his fifty-thousand-dollar check from Mitch. He had asked both of them not to tell Caroline about the money or his plans to marry her.

When Stevie informed him of how hard Caroline had been working to keep things afloat for the family, Hiwatha decided to take care of her school loans. There was no way the woman he loved would be burdened. He made sure that Mitch took care of everything. This included making sure that Mrs. Davis got the medical assistance she needed. He was less worried about Caroline's future. He was going to make sure that was secure.

⸻ ((◊)) ⸻

Charleston knew he was weak for Theresa. At times he loved her more than life itself. When they made love, Charleston felt like he was transformed to another time and place. He was lying in bed with his eyes glued to his lover. They were staying in the presidential suite of the Beverly Hills hotel. Charleston looked at the naked sleeping form beside him and realized Theresa had wrapped herself around his life as quickly as she had wrapped her legs around his back the night before.

Her kiss to him was like a dream, and her lovemaking outstanding. Her passion knew no limits. Charleston couldn't bear to be away from her. He had done all he could to possess Theresa. There had been trips to Florida, Vegas, and New York. He called her several times a day and would curse when she did not immediately respond.

Charleston had become addicted to Theresa's beauty and class. He knew other influential men wanted Theresa. He hated that she was educated and in the public eye. These thoughts at times drove him into an uncontrollable jealous rage.

With other women, Charleston could easily have his way. Nice dinners, dancing, and maybe a quick nightcap, except making love to Theresa was just as important as making money to Charleston.

Though Charleston loved Danielle, he no longer slept with her. He wanted the superstar type of woman, and Theresa was it. He would never admit it, but he was pussy-poisoned.

All of this tormented Charleston because he was slowly losing control of Theresa and Danielle. He was also losing control of Magnificent. There was a time when his word was law with the champion, but Magnificent had become truly savvy when it came to his career. He was discovering his manager's weaknesses and started putting unreasonable demands on him.

Charleston had blown deals and accepted less money, which had eroded his credibility not only with Magnificent but within boxing circles. Their first contract of fifty-fifty was now coming back to haunt him.

Charleston had a star complex and couldn't accept that Magnificent was less dependent upon him. He had kept himself out front and didn't understand that the main objective of a manager and trainer should be to build up his fighter.

Charleston continued to lay there, thinking. Soon he would not only have to deal with Magnificent but his situation with Theresa and Danielle.

———— ((O)) ————

Hiwatha had just returned home from playing a few rounds of golf with Mitch. He was set to start training the next day. He hit the button on his answering machine, and Caroline's voice came through the speaker, wishing him a beautiful day. Before Hiwatha could pick up the phone to call Caroline back, Victoria's message began to play.

"Hiwatha, my flight has landed. I thought you would be here or send a car. I left my flight information with Mitch yesterday. Never mind, I'll just get a limo. See you soon, baby."

Hiwatha would have dismissed the message, except he knew what was about to happen. There was no way he was going to get out of dealing with Victoria's hot temper. The sooner, the better was his thinking.

It wasn't long before Victoria arrived. As Hiwatha watched the driver remove her luggage from the back of the limo, he knew she had far too many bags for the short stay he had planned.

"Hey, baby," she cooed as she dropped her carry-on bag at the door. "I missed you so much."

Hiwatha stared at Victoria as she opened her coat to reveal the lace teddy she was wearing. On any other day, he would have been excited. Her body was gorgeous, and Hiwatha couldn't deny it. No other man could resist this level of temptation. He played it cool and greeted her with a chill in his voice. When Victoria tried to kiss him, Hiwatha removed her arms from around his neck.

Victoria sensed something was wrong. She stepped back and placed her hands on her hips. Hiwatha saw a familiar look in her eyes. Trouble was about to start.

"What's the matter with you," she asked, lowering her eyes in disapproval. "I don't like it when you act this way. Now, I don't care how you treat those other women in the street, but I'm not one of your groupies."

"Vicky, I have never treated you like a groupie, so don't go there. You might as well take your hands off your hips and settle down. I've just got other things on my mind."

Victoria reached for him again. Though Hiwatha was in a

bad mood, she was happy to see him. She put a smile on her face and began rubbing her body up against him.

"I'm sorry baby. I just wanted a better homecoming."

Hiwatha stepped back. He didn't want her to get comfortable, at least not tonight. He had thrown many women out, and today would be no different. By the end of the evening, Hiwatha wanted Victoria out of his life.

"Let's get something straight. This is not your home." His tone was direct and cut straight to the point.

Hiwatha removed her arms again from around his neck. He braced himself for the worst. They had a passionate relationship, never seeing eye-to-eye on anything but sex. So, the look on her face that spelled trouble didn't matter. He was prepared. She took off her earrings and threw them in a bowl on the entrance table.

"Okay, tell me just what the hell is going on? I've been calling your black ass since yesterday, and lately, you've been acting strange when I do see you. I show up at the airport, and you're not there. I get to your door practically half-naked, and you've got the nerve to treat me like this."

She reached up to slap him, but Hiwatha quickly grabbed Victoria's hand and continued to hold it tightly as he spoke through clenched teeth.

"I don't hit women, but don't you ever raise your hand to me again. I'm not your valet, and I'm definitely not one of those punks in your videos." He dropped her hand and walked into his Study.

"Now have a seat. And it doesn't matter which one. I

need to seriously talk to you, but first, can I get you something to drink?"

"No, I don't need a drink," Victoria answered in anger. "What I need to know is what the fuck is wrong with you?"

Hiwatha shouted loudly for Ms. Reed. He was annoyed and unable to hide it from Victoria. In his own way, Hiwatha did care for her; she just wasn't the woman he wanted to marry. To make his point, he needed to soften his approach and try to handle the situation more delicately. He changed his tone as he again called for his maid, Ms. Reed, to get them both something to drink.

As Hiwatha turned back to face Victoria, she jumped up from her chair. No way was she going to sit down and tolerate Hiwatha's behavior. She had planned to spend some quality time with him. Before getting to know Hiwatha, she had inquired about him for over a year. It was no accident that his friend brought him backstage to meet her. Now they were together, and he was the man she loved. Didn't that mean anything to him?

She had come today to make peace, lay her cards on the table. This was her constant thought while on tour. Though Victoria had spent time with her old boyfriend Phil Ross, she missed Hiwatha. That is when she decided to go all the way with Hiwatha and told Phil about their relationship. In Victoria's heart, no man compared to Hiwatha. The thought of losing him was absolutely the last thing on her mind. She lowered her voice to almost a plea. She was wondering whether someone had told him about Phil.

"This is insane, Hiwatha. Why are we fighting?"

"I don't know," responded Hiwatha. "I really wanted to have a decent conversation for once. Not all this tension that's always between us. Now all of a sudden, I am annoyed to hell with your starlet bullshit. I think we need to end this relationship. This is going nowhere, and you know it. I am no more than great sex to you, and quite frankly, I need more than that from a woman."

Victoria's heart stopped. What was he saying? It couldn't be over? What gave him the right? Doesn't he know who I am? He's stupid if he thinks I'm going to get out of his life so easily. Her anger at this moment knew no limits.

"Just like that, you think it's over!" Victoria shouted with venom in her voice. "Who in the hell do you think you're dealing with? I'm not interested in playing games with you. One minute you're calling me crying, Vicky I need you. Vicky, I miss you. The next minute you come up with this shit. You son-of-a-bitch, I should kick your black ass for letting me get on a plane and waste my time coming here. You could have told me this bullshit over the phone. I'm not stupid. I know this is about some other bitch."

"There is no other bitch. I have no room in my life for more than one bitch."

Victoria slowly turned her head around as if she were in a scene from the horror movie Exorcist. She looked at Hiwatha as if her ticket meter had run out of time. No, this man is not calling me a bitch. Does he think he'll live to repeat it?

Victoria threw her hands up in the air, then walked over to Hiwatha's golf bag and grabbed one of his golf clubs. She then proceeded to break everything in sight, starting with his glass coffee table. What she didn't break Victoria threw at Hiwatha as he ducked out of the room. This girl had a set of well-oiled pipes and was now crying and screaming as if she wanted the whole world to hear. She was devastated and ready to even the score.

"Come back here, you low-life piece of shit," she shouted through her tears. "Nobody talks to me this way. I will kill your sorry ass," Victoria screamed into the Foyer as she smashed the mirror above the fireplace.

"Bring your black ass back in here before I torch this matha-fucking house with you, your crazy ass butler and cross-eyed maid in it. My family has killed trash like you for less than the cost of a bullet. Who in the hell, do you think you're fucking with?"

Hiwatha continued up the staircase to his bedroom, never looking back. He could hear glass breaking and things being thrown all over the Study. One item, then another came whistling out of the Study with such force they spattered all over the Foyer.

As Hiwatha passed Ms. Reed on the stairwell, he instructed her to call the security guards at the front gate. He knew Vicky was capable of keeping her promise to burn his house down. He was sure that last sound of glass breaking was the picture window behind his desk.

"I want Vicky out of my house," he calmly conveyed to

Ms. Reed. "Have security take her and all her bags back to the airport. If that doesn't work, call Mitch and have him set her up in a hotel until she cools off. Either way, get her out of here before she tries to burn the house down."

With that, Hiwatha locked the door to his bedroom and dialed Caroline's number.

Chapter 10

THE GAMES PEOPLE PLAY

Hiwatha woke up the next morning not ready to face the day. He was tired after talking to Caroline all night. He had stayed in his bedroom after Victoria left. He wanted to sleep longer but was curious to see the disaster she'd left for him downstairs.

He splashed cold water over his face before grabbing a bathrobe and slippers from the front of the bed. As Hiwatha turned the corner to head downstairs, he saw his butler Franklin pretending to dust one of the tables in the hallway.

"I see you had a pretty rough night boss," Franklin stated in a slightly disapproving tone. "I know you pay me the big bucks, but what on earth happened here yesterday?"

Franklin rubbed his bald head in confusion, then continued. "Now I'm pretty sure there was no tornado in the neighborhood last night. What I do know is there must have been some evil spirits floating around in that Study. Some really evil ones. The kind that comes back from the dead because you stole something from them. You need to see it for yourself, boss."

"I thought you would have started cleaning that up by now," Hiwatha responded. "Since you say I pay you the big bucks."

"Now I try to keep this place clean," responded Franklin. "Work my ass off for you. But that pile of shit you got downstairs is beyond understanding."

"Well, it still needs to be cleaned up," responded Hiwatha.

"No...No...No...No...No I can't clean that up. That's like asking me to clean the U.S. Congress and Senate of parasites," Franklin stated while waving his duster in the air.

Hiwatha looked at Franklin and began laughing at his spirited performance. He got a kick out of how Franklin vocally phased his words. In another life, he could have definitely been a successful comedian.

Hiwatha liked the idea that Franklin took good care of him. Almost as if he was a close relative or uncle. Hiwatha suspected there was definitely serious cleanup work to be done, but he was having fun messing with Franklin.

"Oh, that room is going to get cleaned up, and you're going to help me," Hiwatha stated as he snatched the duster from Franklin's hand.

"Well, we'll see about that after you go check out the damage," Franklin stated as he snatched the duster back from Hiwatha. "I'm too old for this, foolishness. Young people like drama. When will you learn beautiful women have ugly problems."

Hiwatha smiled at Franklin and started down the stairs to his Study. Victoria had done some severe damage to his property. From the initial assessment she'd broken the picture window behind his desk, pulled the curtains down from all the windows, shattered the glass coffee table and mirror over the fireplace, trashed his office, threw his laptop out the window and smashed his Father's glass cabinet containing his baseball collection. Baseballs were everywhere.

Hiwatha was furious but consoled by the fact Victoria was no longer in his life. He moved to the center of the room and stood amid the aftermath wondering how such a tiny woman could do so much damage. Yeah, Franklin was right, that was an evil spirit.

———————«(◦)»———————

Magnificent was glad the publicity tour was over. He was planning to relax before going into training. He was tired, but not ready to sleep.

His underlings had arranged earlier for two beautiful women to join him at his mansion that evening. One of his walking tax shelters entered the room to inform him the women had arrived.

"Send them in," Magnificent responded happily.

The two women stepped into his bedroom. Both were picture perfect and blessed with distinct physical gifts. One was dark bronze, and the other had a burnished gold complexion.

"Hello, ladies," laughed Magnificent as he greeted them.

They smiled and laughed easily with the champion. After taking a swim, the two women enjoyed the sauna before returning to Magnificent's room. In seconds they stripped and jumped in bed with the champion. They were there to receive his undivided attention. To their dismay, his focus suddenly moved to the real void, he was trying to fill.

Magnificent had broken off his relationship with his long-time girlfriend Wendy Thomas months earlier. She had been there for him off and on since they met through a mutual friend in Atlanta.

After dating for a few years, she moved to Chicago a year ago and finally began to press Magnificent for a commitment. He was reluctant to come in out of the rain or change his lifestyle to accommodate their relationship.

Magnificent did genuinely care for Wendy, but he often struggled in the area of emotional intimacy or any association with a woman that required his commitment.

Magnificent found himself confiding in her about the things in his life that bothered him. It was Wendy who recommended he take speech therapy so he could gain more control over his career. She encouraged him to look more closely at his finances, and his relationship to Charleston whom she felt was using Magnificent. For this reason, she did not trust Charleston.

Magnificent began to slowly listen to her advice and hired a lawyer to look at his contract but didn't credit any of the changes taking place within him to Wendy. Instead, he was dismissive towards her. This, along with his acts of unfaithfulness, became the reasons Wendy finally ended their relationship.

Though he missed her, his pride wouldn't allow him to call. Instead, he tried to fill the void by hiding behind his celebrity, other women, and his ego. He was using the benefits of his wealth to disguise his loneliness. Unfortunately, the painful tears that result from self-afflicted wounds are the ones the world never sees.

For Magnificent, it was easier to put his personal life aside to focus on becoming the undisputed champion in the middleweight division. He would have to dispose of Hiwatha Jordan, then the pretender to the throne, Numwar Nasser. Boxing fans eventually would demand someone credible fight, Nasser. It was a test Magnificent, nor Hiwatha really wanted.

———————◦《◦》◦———————

Numwar was restless, edgy and in a sour mood. "When will I get my turn at the middleweight title?" he asked Oliver Xavier.

"Look, Numwar, calm down," Oliver pleaded. "After Magnificent and Jordan get it on, one of them will have to fight you. The public will demand it."

Numwar continued to pace the floor. He was restless by nature. "You know all I want is to be champion of the world. I don't want to die in some damn gym like a lot of fighters. They just never get a chance at the title."

Numwar was a habitual searcher. He was dying inside. Oliver had advised him before about his feelings toward Charleston. It was strange that he so readily signed Numwar. Oliver was concerned as to why. He was aware that Charleston could easily stretch or not tell the truth.

Numwar was the most dangerous contender in the world. He knew Charleston had never seen such a dedicated boxer. Some thought he was better than Magnificent and Jordan. Oliver hoped in his heart Numwar would get a chance to prove it. He was the type of boxer managers and trainers dreamed of, unless, of course, they had a boxer that had to fight him. Oliver knew Charleston had Magnificent.

Numwar trained six days a week, including holidays. He got upset when he couldn't spar. He was a scientific boxer that always studied his craft. At times Numwar would pound the heavy bag with just his left hand. He diligently practiced and polished his feints.

Rosanni, who was working his own plan behind the scenes, had scheduled Nasser to fight on the undercard of the big "showdown in October. He thought the exposure would be great. Numwar was happy with anything that would bring him closer to his shot at the title. He prayed that Magnificent or Jordan would give him a chance.

Rosanni had been watching very closely. He wanted to capitalize on the current level of talent in the middleweight division. His family had been in other areas of sports for many years, and he could see the trend happening in boxing.

Since the late fifties and early sixties, the other major sports like baseball, basketball, and football had opened up to minority athletes. Many of the talented athletes who would have chosen boxing as their profession opted to showcase their talent in other sports. This was beginning to severely water down the heavier weight classes in boxing, thus making the sport less competitive. Boxing would be forced to look for talent in the lower weight classes.

Rosanni wanted to be on the cutting edge by continuing to recruit and promote talented boxers. To accomplish this, he needed a great talent scout. He also was thinking of Mitch as being his front man at some point. With his hectic schedule, Rosanni would not be able to devote the kind of time needed to accomplish his goal. He planned to talk to Mitch after the fight.

"You really took care of business, Mitch," Hiwatha said after his workout. "Now, all I have to do is kick this chump's ass."

"I am glad you're pleased," replied Mitch. "This fight will make you filthy rich. Besides, it could potentially put you in a class by yourself."

Hiwatha knew he had reached a different stage in his career. Though the money would be astronomical, the risk was gigantic. So far, his training was going well. He felt confident in his abilities. He didn't want Mitch or Antonio to worry.

"Mitch, just let Antonio know that I'll arrive in Las Vegas ten days before the fight. You guys arrange everything, so I can keep up my training schedule."

Hiwatha was trying to put Mitch at ease, but privately Hiwatha knew this fight would be difficult. He was sure that Magnificent and Charleston felt the same way, except Charleston, had other issues besides the big fight.

———««•»»———

"You always lie to me. Anytime I ask you something, you lie."

Danielle Orlando was talking to her husband on the telephone. She was utterly frustrated with their marriage. Once again, Charleston was making a lame excuse from over 2,000 miles away.

"I'm not lying," countered Charleston. "I know you are with someone," she replied. "You don't have to come home," Danielle stated in anger. "I am sick of you and our marriage."

"Baby, I've got to finish this deal, and then I'll be home," Charleston responded.

While Charleston was speaking to his wife, Theresa had just finished showering. She and Charleston were vacationing in Los Angeles. They had plans to have dinner then attend a comedy show in West Hollywood. As he listened to Danielle, Charleston was staring greedily at Theresa, who was getting dressed for the evening. Her scent was driving him wild.

"Look, Danielle, I'll talk to you when I get back. I'm not going to fight with you," replied Charleston as he hung up on his wife.

"Who was that," asked Theresa.

"Oh, that was just Wonderful, up to his usual shit," Charleston stated as he sat back and lit his cigarette.

———— ⸺«◉»⸺ ————

Danielle never missed a Sunday at church. She was a God-fearing woman who found solace in her religion. She knew her faith was being severely tested. It was apparent her husband was serious about another woman.

Charleston's past indiscretions were minor compared to this. He now found excuses to stay out of town. So numerous were his affairs, she no longer wanted to sleep with him. At one time, he was her one true love, but now, having acquired fame and money, he had deserted her intimately. In her eyes, he had become a male whore.

For a long time, it was common knowledge that Charleston was a playboy; but now something stronger had taken hold of him. Not only could Danielle hear it in his voice, but she could also see it in his eyes.

Danielle still loved Charleston, but no more as a husband or lover. On several occasions, he tried to talk his way back into their bedroom. Danielle knew he only wanted to control her. As she kneeled and prayed to God for answers, she had no idea that nearby, in an upper-class neighborhood, lived her husband's mistress.

———— ⸺«◉»⸺ ————

After buying a house for Theresa, Charleston helped her decorate it. She had photos of them throughout the house. One photo was taken in Las Vegas with Theresa's favorite entertainer.

Theresa knew their relationship was explosive in and out of bed. She would tell her girlfriends that she was leaving Charleston but never did.

Although Theresa earned a six-figure income, Charleston had spent lavishly on her. Now Theresa wanted to secure her future by becoming the next Mrs. Charleston Orlando.

They often argued about his wife. Charleston would lie and tell Theresa to be patient. Soon he would leave Danielle. In a fit of anger one night, Theresa even threatened to kill Danielle. She had grown tired of riding the bench.

Theresa hated going to social functions alone or with Charleston's hired help. When she became depressed, shopping was her outlet. She enjoyed spending Charleston money, often flying to Toronto and going on weekend shopping sprees.

Theresa knew Charleston was weak for her. She too loved sex and did not like sleeping alone. At first, Theresa thought his possessiveness was attractive. Now she wanted to turn the tables and take control. She had begun to curse Charleston without mercy. Then, with no warning, Theresa would ignore him and not receive his calls. Charleston would have to beg her to make love.

Theresa's phone was ringing beside the bed. She knew it was Charleston before answering.

"Hey, baby. I was thinking about you. Can you meet me at the 1940 Chop House for dinner?" he asked.

"No, I'm too tired," she replied. "I really don't feel like being out tonight. Why don't you come by when you're finished?"

"Okay, I'll see you later," he responded.

Theresa suspected he would come soon, and thirty minutes later, Charleston turned the key in her door. He waited for Theresa to go into the shower before trying to check her voicemail.

Theresa knew Charleston wanted to make love, but tonight she planned to insist that he get a divorce.

"Look, after the fight I'll take care of it," Charleston pleaded. "I promise I'm gonna speak with Danielle. I know that I've put you through a lot, but I'm going to make you happy. I love you. You know, I do."

Charleston searched her face for a reaction. He was lying and hoped she couldn't see through his bullshit. Theresa looked at Charleston with an eye of an irate bill collector. Charleston slid down next to her on the sofa and continued his smooth talk. He wanted to get pass this conversation and into the bedroom, but Theresa was not buying it. She jumped up and began fussing profusely at Charleston.

"You don't love me, and I know it," she shouted. "I've been your woman long enough. I'm not some groupie you just fuck and come back to when you feel like it."

Her eyes were flashing, and Charleston was becoming uncomfortable. He could see that this was going to be a long night. The lovemaking just might not be worth it.

"You make me hide here in this house," shouted Theresa. "Don't go here, don't go there. I'm coming over. Shit, we make love on a schedule, and I'm tired of it. I'm not going to wait for, your can't-tell-the-truth ass anymore."

Charleston took a deep breath. He was no longer in love with Danielle but still had concerns about leaving his children. He loved himself too much to have his private life splashed across the front pages.

Charleston sat quietly, knowing he'd abused his wife and clearly the one woman he considered his dream girl. He was annoyed that Theresa was causing him to seriously evaluate himself.

"Goddammit, don't do this to me!" Charleston screamed. "Just give me some time. I told you that after the fight I will get a damn divorce. Back up off me. I promise I'll take care of it."

"Well, I don't believe you. I am not going to wait for you forever. You have until after the fight. That is all the time I'm giving you. Now get out of my damn house."

Charleston didn't really want to leave, but getting laid tonight was undoubtedly out of the question. He grabbed his cell phone and keys from the table and quickly made his exit. He had a big payday coming up, and Charleston was unwilling to let anything get in the way of Magnificent's victory over Hiwatha "Absolute" Jordan.

Hiwatha was tired, and his body was full of sweat. His heartbeat like that of a drum. He had run four miles and finished off with four forty-yard sprints. He had been joined by six sparring partners, three trainers, and a driver.

"I've got a long way to go," he spoke loudly. "But I'm

going to be on time when I undo "Mr. Pitiful."

Hiwatha enjoyed belittling his opponents. He felt he was a better class of person than other athletes in his profession.

When he was finished for the day, they returned to the gym. St. Claire helped Hiwatha out of his wet clothes. He immediately rubbed him down and helped stretch his muscles. One of his entourage gathered his clothes to be washed.

"You're not too tight, that's good," St. Claire said cheerily. "This leg of training is always the hardest, but you look stupendous."

Hiwatha was silent. Training felt like a prison without Caroline, and even Victoria, whom he had discarded. He wondered whether all the running, the brutal exercise, the strict diet, the torturous sparring sessions, and the abstention from sex was really worth it. Actually, the abstaining from sex thing he believed was old school and purely psychological. He had grown to hate training but knew he must sacrifice. His reputation and millions were at stake. For that, he would stay in jail a little longer.

His routine was now set. He was up at 5:30 a.m. to run, breakfast at nine with two poached eggs, fruit, and juice. Then he would read the papers and rest until one o'clock before going to the gym at two o'clock where he worked on his game plan.

Some days he would spar eight four-minute rounds, then hit the heavy bag, jump rope and proceed to do a series of brutal exercises to strengthen his neck, abdomen, back, and shoulders. Then he would hit the speed bag.

St. Claire knew Hiwatha well. Overworking him wasn't necessary with the monumental task ahead. So, St. Claire varied the amount of sparring and running daily until he could see Hiwatha's form taking hold. Then he would cut the sparring back to no more than four or five rounds, telling the sparring partners to go all out while trying to simulate the style of Magnificent.

St. Claire was a thoughtful man that never missed a trick inside the ring. Yelling at his fighters was not in the rule book. He preferred treating them with care and respect.

St. Claire was a short, stout man with a sandy complexion. He had a bald head and wore a medium mustache. You could see that at one time, St. Claire was relatively handsome.

Unlike many trainers who stepped in to work with the finished product, St. Claire liked developing boxers from scratch. Earlier in his career, he worked part-time for the park and recreation department, grooming young fighters.

He was a master strategist that really loved boxing, the skill, the movement, and the one-on-one competition. St. Claire could pick out the slightest flaws of an opponent and instruct his charge to capitalize on those mistakes.

He knew Hiwatha was gifted from the moment they met. St. Claire nurtured and taught him not only boxing but self-confidence. He loved him like a son.

Yes, Mitch was the lawyer and adviser, but Hiwatha would never enter the ring without St. Claire in his corner. He trusted his judgment completely.

St. Claire was not like Charleston. He enjoyed being in the background. His goal was not to out-shine the fighter. For this reason, the press unknowingly thought of him as a lesser trainer than Charleston.

St. Claire had a lot of respect for Magnificent as an athlete, but none for Charleston as a trainer. He, too, was looking forward to the showdown. This would give him a chance to finally confront his rival.

"Time," St. Claire called out as he hit the ring apron.

Hiwatha eased to the center of the ring. His sparring partner was a tall light-heavyweight named Willie Wise. He was a journeyman who was relatively swift on his feet with a quick right-hand. Hiwatha feinted his man and glided effortlessly about the ring. St. Claire's eyes never left him for a second.

"Work with your jab a little more!" he shouted.

Finally, West tried to get his jab working, but Hiwatha blocked it and countered with a jab of his own. He had been working on this maneuver since the first day of training. Now he was beginning to use this weapon at will.

Once, twice, three times, he snapped his jab into the face of Wise without return. He slipped and parried all of West's offensive attempts. Hiwatha was working almost exclusively with his left hand. He was trying to neutralize the "bazooka" right-hand of Magnificent.

"Nice, real nice," cooed St. Claire. "Let's hook off the jab now."

St. Claire was expertly spreading Albolene on the

unmarked face of Hiwatha. He rinsed off his mouthpiece, placed it in position, and then put his hands on each side of Hiwatha's rib cage while waiting for him to take at least three deep breaths. Lastly, he tugged the upper edge of his sparring gloves to be sure they were snug before Hiwatha got back in the ring.

"Time," he called once again.

St. Claire was pleased with what he saw but knew they still had a long way to go before securing the victory.

"How's he looking?" asked Mitch who was speaking to St. Claire by phone.

"Looking good," responded St. Claire.

Mitch never doubted him. He knew how valuable St. Claire was to Hiwatha. Mitch took care of his business expertly and trusted St. Claire would do the same. He was aware of how hard Hiwatha could be to work with, but knew St. Claire could always bring out the best in him.

"Hiwatha knows this is going to be a war. He is taking care of business and leaving nothing to chance," conveyed St. Claire.

"I know this is not only a money-making event but a war," said the worried lawyer. "Look, I'll call you once a week. If anything comes up that you don't like, call me. And please don't tell the champ we talked, okay?"

"Don't worry. Hiwatha will be ok, come fight night," replied St. Claire as ended the call.

It didn't matter Mitch was worried. The money situation was right. The press coverage and publicity had been great. Everything seemed perfect, but there was something wrong, and he couldn't put his finger on it.

————— ((○)) —————

Victoria sat across from her best friend, Elan Escavez. The two had decided to get out of the recording studio and enjoy lunch in an upscale Manhattan restaurant. Victoria asked for a booth in the back so they would have privacy. Today, she needed her friends' shoulder to cry on. She had recently begun filming the dance scenes for her upcoming video release. Her "Love to Dance" single was a hit on the pop charts, but due to her hectic calendar, the video production was off schedule, like the rest of her life.

It seemed everything was urgent or just plain screwed up. To make matters worse, last week, Victoria had fainted at rehearsal and was taken to the hospital. Not only did she have to deal with the onslaught of reporters, but her doctor had informed her that she was two-and-a-half months pregnant. This was news she was not prepared for. She also knew this was news Hiwatha didn't want to hear.

Victoria hadn't spoken to Hiwatha since he'd thrown her out of his house a month earlier. There was also the issue of explaining the circumstances to her agent and publicist. She was Catholic, so for her, abortion was not an option. Depending upon Hiwatha's reaction, she may have to consider the impact of the pregnancy on her career.

Victoria discussed the possibility with Elan of telling her ex-boyfriend, Phil Ross, that the baby was his. Phil had spent time with her on the road in June before starting training for the upcoming football season. She knew Phil would take her back in a heartbeat. The truth was, based on the precise timeline given by the doctor, the baby was definitely Hiwatha's.

"Vicky, I've listened to you over and over," conveyed Elan. "Regardless of how afraid you may be, remember your pregnancy is nine months, but your baby will be with you forever. Do not lie now, because you will have to live with that. Hiwatha is a wealthy man who was not forced to do anything, especially sleep with you."

Elan knew Victoria would have to deal with the consequences, but she was unwilling to let Hiwatha off so quickly. She didn't care how Hiwatha felt. His options were either to marry Victoria and be a father to his child or write the damn check each month. It was just that simple.

"Elan, I just don't know how to tell him," Vicky said, putting her head down. "Hiwatha made it clear he wants nothing to do with me. You should have been there. He treated me like trash dropped on his doorstep. No one has ever done that to me. I had planned never to speak to him again."

Elan leaned across the table and gave her friend one of those looks that questioned whether she was indeed an idiot.

"Let me understand something. Did you say you had plans?"

"Yes! Why should I see Hiwatha ever again?" Victoria rationalized.

"Vicky, God's plan is always bigger than ours. You have

to trust in Him. One day you may not have your career, but you will always have your baby. When we were kids, you dreamed of being rich and famous. Now you are. You have enough to be this child's mother. Look at me. You pay me peanuts to be your stylist, but I somehow still can afford to take care of my daughter. Is my man around? Hell, no!"

The two shared a quick laugh.

"I pay you peanuts?" replied Vicky. "I don't call paying you a six-figure salary, peanuts."

"And I don't call saying that Phil Ross is the father of your baby is the right thing to do."

"Then, what is the right thing to do, because my hormones are all out of whack. I'm sinking fast over here."

Victoria pushed her food away and began crying.

"I'm serious, Elan. I am in love with Hiwatha. The only reason I'm sitting here with you and not on his doorstep is the one ounce of pride, I have left. Trust me, I want this child, but I want Hiwatha too. I don't see how this works without having him in my life."

Elan reached across the table and grabbed Victoria's hand to comfort her. She knew how much Victoria loved Hiwatha, but Elan didn't understand why she had taken a chance being with Phil. That relationship had ended a year ago. Victoria stated at the time he was not worth it. Regardless, Elan was going to stand by her friend.

"Whatever you decide, remember I'm your best friend. I'll be here for you, come hell or high water. You know, ride or die. There's just one thing that puzzles me. Why did you sleep with Phil if you're so in love with Hiwatha?"

"Closure, Elan. Phil and I never had true closure in our relationship. So, spending that time together gave us a chance to emotionally have some finality. So, the sex was for old time sake."

"Let's just say I hope you never have to explain that to Hiwatha."

"Can we get back to figuring out a way to tell him about the baby?" Victoria asked with an annoyed tone.

"Why do you have to tell him?" asked Elan.

"I'm not following you," responded Victoria. "If I don't tell him, how will he know?"

"That's why you pay your sweet-ass publicist the big bucks. If she leaks the story, Hiwatha will have to come to you."

Victoria's eyes opened wide. She knew Hiwatha hated controversial publicity. Anything that messed with his ego or image was like kryptonite. Still, leaking the story sounded like a good idea. Victoria just didn't need it to come from her. Sitting there, pregnant was not helping her relationship, either. At least this could get her off his doorstep and back into the driver's seat. Maybe she could convince Elan to do it. It was known that they were close friends, and she would be believable.

"Well, I'm not calling Veronica to ask her to do this," Victoria paused as she went in for the kill. "But you, Elan, could call as a concerned friend. I know two reporters who would eat this story alive. This is the kind of shit that makes or breaks careers. You know Hiwatha has this big fight coming up. This is as good a time as any to bring his ass down a peg or two. He'll regret the day he ever messed over Victoria Santiago."

Victoria sat back in her seat and smiled as she pretended to wipe her tears beneath the napkin. Elan thought for a moment then nodded her head in approval.

Chapter 11

THE PRICE OF GLORY

"Ninety-eight, ninety-nine, one-hundred," said Charleston as he counted Magnificent's sit-ups. "Great, that was good, really good."

Magnificent quickly got off the exercise table determined to get through the day. He was purposeful with his training. After getting down on all fours, he waited ten seconds before starting several sets of push-ups.

The team had been training for weeks. The anticipation and pressure to perform were stretching everyone to their limits.

As Magnificent conducted his daily exercises, he would listen to music on his iPod to stay focused. When certain songs would play, Magnificent found himself thinking of Wendy. Though he downplayed his feelings, Magnificent had come to realize that Wendy provided a foundation, which kept him grounded in reality. Through their relationship, he'd learned so much about himself.

After completing his exercises, Magnificent stood while

his handlers quickly moved toward him and prepared to towel him off.

"Looking good, Champ," said Alan Newton.

Newton was a well-kept seventy-year-old, who served as a trainer and "yes man" to Charleston. Other trainers in the gym disliked him, but Magnificent thought of him as a good guy. Outside of Tony Francis, Newton was the only trainer in Magnificent's favor.

How Magnificent missed Francis. He wanted to find out what happened between him and Charleston, so he asked one of his close confidants to locate Francis. After the fight, he would settle the score with Charleston about his career, Francis and Speaks. This and his relationship with Wendy weighed heavily on his mind as he strolled into the hot shower.

"Say, Newt. Get my towel ready, please. I won't be long today."

As Magnificent toweled off, he heard Charleston coming toward the showers in a good mood.

"You're boxing good now, baby. I know that chump is going to try and surprise you, but you're going to box him. Put some wood on his ass."

"Yeah, I'll do that," Magnificent replied, putting on his warm-up suit.

Magnificent looked suspiciously at Charleston. There was definitely another purpose for his visit.

"Look, man, a guy from Sports Daily will be with us for dinner. They're doing a story on the fight."

"That's all fine and good, but I'm getting tired of these damn interviews."

Magnificent was frustrated. He wanted to think only about his opponent and the sex he was missing. He stood in front of the gym and waited for his driver to take him back to the hotel. He wanted to rest before going to dinner. The promotional responsibility had been challenging to manage while training. He instructed the driver to turn up the volume on the radio as the smooth old school sounds of Marvin Gaye's hit "Inner City Blues" blared across the airways. He loved rap music, but there was nothing like a good oldie that captured the heart and soul of a time gone by. The radio station began running a promotional spot about the upcoming fight. After the introduction, Hiwatha's voice came blaring through the speakers.

"I'm going to destroy him mentally and physically. He can't beat me," Hiwatha's voice resonated in the car. "I feel you've been ducking me. I've shared the spotlight too long. Now I'm going to eliminate you once and for all. Don't miss the showdown!"

As Magnificent listened to the commercial, he had to admit it was exciting. This fight would surely bring him out of the overwhelming shadow of Hiwatha. Then Rosanni and Mitch would have to come to him.

———◉———

Antonio was thrilled about the financial results. Usually, he was too busy to get involved in the day-to-day business or tying up loose ends.

"Mitch, the pay-per-view has gone through the roof.," Antonio said with excitement.

Mitch agreed. This was definitely the largest-grossing fight in boxing history. He was thankful that Hiwatha had gotten Antonio involved. It was a smart move.

"It looks like a monster, all right," replied Mitch. "I don't think we could have done this without you. Sure, we could have had an enormous payday, but nothing of this magnitude."

"I'm hearing that Hiwatha is looking good," said Antonio. "But you know this Wonderful can fight. I have a lot of respect for Hiwatha. He brought boxing back to its glory days. I just think he's in deep water with this one. So, I expect a real fight, but honestly, as a businessman, I don't care who wins."

Mitch hung onto Antonio's words. He knew this fight could rival Ali-Frazier, Graziano-Zale, Dempsey-Tunney, Robinson–LaMotta or Louis-Schmeling. All of these fighters met in the prime of their careers. Yes, Mitch understood the risk.

Hiwatha was considered the best fighter in the world. Boxing fans knew this, but Mitch still found himself admitting that Magnificent was capable of challenging Hiwatha's position. They were both superb athletes who would stop at nothing to secure victory, especially against each other. This would indeed be a battle between two highly-skilled, young, undefeated champions.

Mitch felt from the moment he'd met Hiwatha that the champ was born under a shooting star. Mitch himself had grown rich in his association. This he was thankful for and had told Hiwatha on numerous occasions.

Mitch cared deeply for Hiwatha. He worked to protect him from unscrupulous promoters and managers. In this respect, Mitch was like St. Claire. Right now, he felt a need to pray that Hiwatha would prevail over Magnificent. Then maybe retirement would be an option.

———⚫———

St. Claire was doing two things he loved, watching a tape of Magnificent's fight, and cooking dinner for Hiwatha. There would be broiled fish, salad, pasta, spinach, fruit, and iced tea. Hiwatha loved when St. Claire cooked for him. It was one of his unique talents.

While St. Claire was preparing dinner, he was shouting at the television. "He loves to sucker you in and make you reach for him. Then he explodes with the right hand," he shouted.

St. Claire had been watching this tape since the start of training. He was desperate to exploit every mistake Magnificent made by turning over every stone. His summation was that Magnificent was a great counter-puncher, but had weaknesses. He was still not a finished boxer.

Hiwatha, on the other hand, was extraordinary and capable of comprehending any lesson St. Claire wanted to teach. As a youngster, St. Claire knew Hiwatha was gifted with speed and reflexes seldom seen.

With the image of Magnificent looming, St. Claire thought back to the year Hiwatha won the gold medal and Magnificent was the "Amateur Boxer of the Year." Even when Hiwatha was becoming the shining star, he kept hearing about this new kid from Chicago.

Unlike most trainers, St. Claire was fair, especially when it came to assessing talent. Magnificent would be a tough nut to crack and a difficult fight for Hiwatha. Though Hiwatha was faster, Magnificent had the height and reach, therefore was only a half-step behind.

St. Claire, while still working on his strategy, walked toward the Study and gently knocked on the door. "Champ, your food is ready. You need to finish up and come eat while it's hot."

Hiwatha closed his computer for the night. He knew this was the start of their strategy session.

⸺«❍»⸺

"Thirty seconds," shouted Charleston as Magnificent pounded the heavy bag. Thudding lefts and rights sounded off like basketballs being slammed off the walls of an empty gym. His punches were straight and delivered with snap and leverage on each blow.

"Time," shouted Charleston.

With that, Magnificent's handlers were upon him, removing his gloves, toweling him off and handing him his water bottle.

"Man, I'm tired," complained the weary champion. "You guys have worked me today."

Magnificent had boxed five blistering four-minute rounds and completed another four on the heavy bag. His body was reaching the point of automatic pilot, giving him anything he asked.

Magnificent was still not pleased. Some things still needed to be sharpened. Without a second thought, he quickly began a series of punishing exercises.

Charleston saw his champion getting better each day. His sparring had been so excellent that he was considering giving him a day off. Magnificent was landing searing left-jabs. Most importantly, his defense and left-hook were looking exceptionally well.

No matter how good Magnificent looked, Charleston still worried that neither of the two champions could afford to leave anything to chance.

———»«◉»«———

As Charleston headed back to the hotel, Theresa Tarver was on his mind. As her voice mail greeting ended, he could hardly wait to leave a message.

"I want you to fly out here tomorrow if you can. I need you to stay with me for a couple of days," Charleston pleaded.

He hoped Theresa wasn't still mad about Danielle. Being faithful did not matter to Charleston. In his mind, he took care of Danielle, Theresa, and his other women. This entitled him to do as he pleased. While he was calling Theresa, he was actually on a date with a dancer he'd met at a strip club. She was just his groupie type; beautiful and dumb.

Charleston excused himself from the table as his cell phone rang. It was Theresa, confirming she would come for the weekend. He agreed to take care of the flight arrangements in the morning. It was best to spend this time with Theresa since he had no intentions on her attending the fight. To keep up his image as a family man, only Danielle was entitled to sit with him ringside.

⎯⎯⎯⎯⎯⎯»⟨⟨◆⟩⟩«⎯⎯⎯

Antonio and Mitch had underestimated how quickly the promotion would captivate the public's imagination. Antonio had to admit, Hiwatha had the foresight to capitalize on a ripe market. Mitch himself was in awe of how calm Hiwatha was when he laid out their promotional strategy.

This was not the case with Charleston and Magnificent. Charleston just happened to have a boxer who was dominant in the sport. He had done little to contribute to the promotion, and his ego was suffering for it.

Hiwatha and Mitch had made him a "take it or leave it" offer. If he'd been a better negotiator, he could have gotten Magnificent another three or four million. As Magnificent was beginning to discover, Charleston was all show. When it came to sitting across the table from the mega-powers, he usually came up short.

Now his private life was beginning to become more public. He partied often and was seen around town regularly at all the hotspots, drinking and hanging out with groupies. He had become loose with his money and found himself at times, having to borrow from several not-so-upstanding individuals.

He'd sold the interest in several of his boxers to pay a few outstanding debts. He overextended himself foolishly. Many in his organization had begun to resent him. He continued to keep favor with ass-kissers and not those that served him faithfully.

His previous father-and-son relationship with Magnificent had changed. After several meetings with his lawyers, Magnificent reduced Charleston's fifty-percent take to a more reasonable thirty-percent. To make up the difference, Charleston was hoping that this super-fight would solve all his problems. In public, he strutted around like a marine drill sergeant; only privately did he worry. He desperately needed Magnificent to win.

——————⟫⟪⟪⟪⟫⟪——————

"Enough! Time!" shouted St. Claire. Hiwatha dropped his hands and moved to the corner of the ring. His sparring for the day was over. St. Claire began toweling him off as one of his assistants removed his gloves, mouthpiece, headgear, and protective cup. Hiwatha remained oblivious to those working to free his equipment.

As he swiftly moved to the speed bag, his thoughts were on Caroline. As he rattled the speed bag non-stop for six minutes, he thought of the time they'd spent together on the press tour. Soon the fight would be over, and he would propose. He then heard St. Claire call "Time" signaling him to move quickly to his daily exercise routine.

There was a boundless grace to his movements as he jumped rope. He kept repeating to himself as St. Claire counted, "Soon, this will be over, and I'll be the undisputed middleweight champion of the world."

After his workout, Hiwatha was toweled off from head to toe. St. Claire's eyes never left him. There were only two weeks before the fight. From his vantage point, Hiwatha was prepared both physically and mentally. He also knew, so was Magnificent.

St. Claire was expecting a real war. He was concerned about compensating for the difference in their size and reach and finally spoke to Hiwatha as he helped him out of his wet clothes to shower.

"From here on out we will be reducing the workouts and start sharpening up. You're looking good. Damn good."

Hiwatha felt he was close to his peak condition and spoke in a matter-of-fact voice.

"Don't worry man. I'll take care of business when it's time."

Still, St. Claire was resolute about working on their strategy. He was a meticulous trainer who left nothing to chance. They were preparing for the greatest contest ever between two middleweights. It was essential to stay focused. He prayed, Hiwatha understood. Soon he would be in the ring with a fighter that in any other era could be considered one of the greatest ever.

Hiwatha was no fool. As he lay in his bed, looking up at the ceiling, his muscles told him he had trained hard. Even after a warm bath, he still ached.

The grounds of Hiwatha's estate had been transformed into a training facility. The previous summer, he decided to build a four-bedroom guest house and gym near his lake to accommodate his trainer and sparring partners.

His gym was small and modest, intentionally giving the look and feel of the places he'd trained as a child. On the walls hung photographs of his favorite sports heroes, such as Jackie Robinson, Ezzard Charles, Muhammad Ali, Hank Aaron and his nemesis Sugar Ray Robinson.

As a fighter, Hiwatha admired Robinson and was in awe of his hand speed and grace. As a child when he learned Robinson had won the middleweight title five times, he was in disbelief. He began studying his style and reading everything about his life. Although the necessary items and equipment for training were in his gym, it wouldn't have felt like home without a picture of Ray Robinson.

During the winter, Hiwatha and St. Claire had held two youth camps. Hiwatha always said that one day he would find another Hiwatha Jordan and make them a champion. With just the money from endorsements alone, it would soon be time to consider making his exit.

Hiwatha was fortunate to make more money out of the ring than in. Yes, it was time for him to get married and move on.

The next day, Caroline was due to fly in and hold a work-out session for the press. Though this was against Hiwatha's better judgment, Caroline had been very convincing. She had arranged for several key reporters from the New York, Philadelphia, and D.C. area to fly in and take a look at Hiwatha's progress.

He knew in his heart; this was indeed the woman for him. Who else could get him to break all his rules? Caroline also shared fond memories of Hiwatha's father, the only man, and person Hiwatha truly loved.

Thank God he did not remember the day his mother abandoned him. Who in their right mind would leave a two-year-old at their father's front door in the heart of winter? This is a question his mother has never been able to answer since reappearing in his life six years ago.

She didn't have the guts to come near him while his father Nathan was alive. Now, Hiwatha paid her to stay away. This may be a sore spot for his two younger brothers, Kyle and Vincent, but they would say nothing long as Hiwatha continued to pay for their college education. Their new found lifestyle was a far-cry from the inner-city housing projects.

In good conscious Hiwatha couldn't allow his family to stay there and keep his media darling image. Surely someone would eventually question his integrity. He didn't want to raise questions about his past?

Hiwatha asked Mitch to help him purchase a beautiful home (that he never visited) in Baltimore, Maryland for his family, set up a college fund with expenses for his brother's education and a monthly check for his mother. Now on Mother's Day, she can have bragging rights among her friends and the few reporters that will listen. "Hiwatha Jordan is my son!"

Hiwatha still says quietly to himself, "Big fucking deal. You were never a mother to me." He clutched his pillow and vowed never to abandon his children. When he finally married Caroline, it would be for keeps. That would be the beginning of a new life for him and the inevitable end of an impressive and successful career in boxing.

"Leave on a high note, and I will always hear your song playing," his Dad once told him. "Well, Dad if you're listening, the orchestra is warming up, and your son is preparing for the "Fight of the Century.""

———— »«⦿»« ————

Caroline rushed around her apartment that overlooked Wilshire Boulevard in Los Angeles. She loved the Westwood area and was looking forward to Hiwatha visiting her after the fight. She had already made a list of events and things they could enjoy together. How she missed him. Soon the fight would be over, and Hiwatha would have some free time to recuperate. The distance between them had added to their bond, but Hiwatha was too handsome to leave dangling in mid-air. After all, he was a man with needs that too many women were in line to fulfill. Though Caroline didn't want to appear insecure, it was difficult.

In a matter of hours, Caroline would be landing in

Virginia Beach. Nothing in her closet seemed to fit the occasion. This was the part of dressing women hated. She finally settled on a pair of black slacks with a cute pink blouse that complimented her skin tone.

Time was not on her side. The cab would be there shortly to take her to the airport. She checked and sealed the small box she needed for the private press workout and placed it at the bottom of her luggage cart.

As Caroline jumped into the cab, her cell phone rang. It was Dale from the office, confirming the press list. She was happy to hear that all of the key players would be there. She leaned forward and told the driver to step on it. She was not about to miss her flight.

———«()»———

Mitch threw his luggage across the bed of his hotel room. Living this way was not what he wanted. His relationship with Charlotte had deteriorated to almost nothing. Most of the time, he had no clue where she was, what she was doing, and, he was afraid to admit, didn't know with whom.

Mitch was exhausted with the travel and the amount of work needed on the fight. How he wished for Charlotte to comfort him. At these times, Mitch felt the pain of losing his children. He grabbed his cell phone from his belt to check in with Hiwatha. Training should be over by now. On the second ring, Hiwatha's butler Franklin answered the phone.

"Good afternoon," he said in a calm voice. "You've reached the Jordan residence."

"Hey, Franklin, is Hiwatha around? This is Mitch."

"Sure, Mr. Danton. Can you hold one moment while I ring his room?"

Hiwatha picked up the phone next to his bed and asked Franklin to put the call through. "Hey, Mitch, you're back sooner than I expected. Did everything go all right in L.A.?"

"Yeah, I took care of everything we discussed yesterday, but Magnificent and Charleston are still bitching about little details."

"Well, you know Charleston is trying to save face," responded Hiwatha. "He knows the money is short, but that's on him. I think the shit is funny myself."

"Has Caroline arrived yet? Antonio had some papers he wanted me to sign, but I had to rush to the airport. He said he'd send them with Caroline."

"No, my baby is running a little late. I sent my driver to pick her up from the airport. It shouldn't be long before she gets here. I'll let her know to call you. Are you still coming to the workout tomorrow?"

"It wouldn't be a press day without me," Mitch said jokingly.

"Yeah, I guess you're right," Hiwatha replied, as he looked out the window at the driver pulling up. "Well, man, I got to go. Caroline just got here, so later."

Hiwatha raced down the stairs. Though he was not looking forward to the press day, he was excited to see Caroline. She could barely get in the door before he was all over her. She laughed while giving him a big hug. The two stood there, embracing for what seemed like an eternity.

"I missed you so much, Caroline. I love you."

"I love you too, sweetheart. I'm sure we'll make the best of every moment."

"You're right," Hiwatha answered as he pulled her into the dining room. "Franklin, lights please," he said, clapping his hands together.

Before leaving for the evening, Hiwatha had asked St. Claire to prepare dinner for Caroline, complete with candlelight. Franklin remained in the kitchen, having an evening cocktail while waiting for Hiawatha's signal to serve dinner. As usual, he was jamming to the sounds of his old school music and acting as the nights Dee Jay.

"Oh baby, this is beautiful," Caroline said with surprise. "I can't believe you did this for me."

Hiwatha whispered in her ear as he grabbed her close. "I'm going to do a lot more for you. You just wait and see. I'm so happy to see you."

Caroline suddenly released herself from Hiwatha's embrace and started turning in circles. "Oh, that's my song playing right there," she cooed while snapping her fingers and moving her head back and forth to the rhythm. "Turn that up," Caroline shouted to Franklin as she began swaying left and right with her hands in the air. "I am feeling real sexy tonight. Can't you feel it?"

Caroline grabbed Hiwatha's hand and pulled him towards her as she danced in front of him.

"You know my father loved this song," Hiwatha said as

he started to dance with her.

They both began laughing while moving to the rhythm of the music. As the sounds of a Gladys Knight oldie Midnight Train to Georgia filled the room, they found themselves suspended in time. It wasn't long before they were singing along. Caroline took the lead as Hiwatha started acting as one of her backup Pips.

As the evening went on, they kept dancing and singing as Franklin kept playing one oldie after another. On occasion, he would throw in a popular dance song hoping to tire the two of them out.

Franklin was getting a kick out of seeing Hiwatha so relaxed and happy. It wasn't long before Franklin got his wish and the two took a seat on the sofa near the table. For a minute, Hiwatha and Caroline simply gazed at one another.

Hiwatha began thinking about their future together. He pulled Caroline close to him.

"I promise I'll never leave you, Caroline," he confessed. "Please don't let anything cause you to lose faith in us. I've done a lot of things in the past that I'm not proud of, but I want our life together to be different. I hope you know that."

"Yes, I do. We both have been young and foolish, but I do like the sound of us. You and me. Like Bonnie and Clyde. To infinity and beyond."

"Yeah, that sounds about right," Hiwatha stated in agreement. "You and me with about ten kids out back by the Lake. Me on the grill and you rushing from the house with some cold Ice Tea."

Caroline almost choked. "Earth to Hiwatha. Ten children! I see you got jokes tonight."

"Maybe, but you must admit we could have fun trying."

"Don't be teasing me. You know I'm only ten minutes from crazy over you. Especially since you claim to be on lockdown."

"Baby, that's just a myth. Besides they're all kinds of ways to be intimate. Don't you agree?"

"I think I'm following you," Caroline stated as she watched Franklin putting the food on the table. "Now when are you going to feed me? That food is looking awfully delicious," she said while making her way to the table.

"Well, how about I spoon-feed you tonight," Hiwatha playfully stated as he sat down next to her and grabbed a spoon. "Now open those sexy lips."

"Wow! No man has ever spoon-fed me before."

Hiwatha looked intently at Caroline as he held the spoon to her lips.

"No man has ever loved you the way I do."

Chapter 12

THE DOUBLE CROSS

Caroline had gone over every detail for the press workout. The bus carrying the reporters from the airport was due to arrive shortly.

Hiwatha had completed his morning run, showered, eaten breakfast, and had finally come downstairs. He looked relaxed in his white warm-up suit and sneakers. Caroline was going over the catering instructions with the staff. She took a deep breath as she watched Hiwatha walk into the room.

There would be about ten to twenty members of the press. Caroline and Mitch would host the event. The media would first grab a bite to eat then take the short walk down to the lake where Hiwatha, St. Claire and his sparring partners were training.

"Hey, baby. You really look sexy this morning," Hiwatha said as he stood behind Caroline. "Your man anywhere around, cause if he is, I'm gonna have to disappoint him today. You shouldn't be walking around here showing those gorgeous legs."

"You just get yourself down to the gym, Mr. Jordan," Caroline responded as she spun out of his embrace. "I will surely protect myself. You're lucky I didn't creep down the hall and wrap these legs around you last night."

Hiwatha laughed as he saw the look on his staff's face. "Caroline, your embarrassing my staff. Keep that up, and I won't be able to invite you here anymore."

Hiwatha's butler Franklin stuck his head in the room. "Miss. Davis, your guests have arrived."

"Thanks, Franklin," she replied.

Hiwatha turned to Caroline. "I'm out of here. Ring my cell before you and Mitch head down to the gym."

As Hiwatha slipped through the patio doors, Caroline headed to the Foyer to greet the press. Mitch was already there shaking hands.

"Welcome, everyone," Mitch said with a smile. "I hope the ride was comfortable. I'm glad all of you could make it. Please follow Caroline into the dining area."

The press was obviously hungry after the long ride from the airport. They wasted no time sampling the array of dishes prepared by the chef. Once lunch and the small pleasantries were over, everyone headed down to the gym.

Hiwatha and St. Claire were already in the ring, working on several combinations. The photographers began snapping pictures, while the camera crew's set up their equipment.

Hiwatha moved quickly to the speed bag before finishing up with his daily drill of exercises. One of his handlers came over and began toweling him off. St. Claire handed him a water bottle while Hiwatha worked to calm his breathing. He was reluctantly preparing for his day with the press.

Caroline came over to guide Hiwatha to a chair near the ring. The press immediately began shooting questions from every direction. Hiwatha remained poised. He knew the drill all too well. As the reporters continued to ask questions, Hiwatha was firing back on all cylinders. He wanted to move this session along as quickly as possible.

"Hiwatha, is there any truth to the rumor that Victoria Santiago is expecting your child, and if so, have you made any plans to marry," asked Tom Tally of the New York Daily Chronicle?

The crowd of reporters fell silent as they watched the look on Hiwatha's face change from relaxed to utter annoyance. It was apparent to everyone he was caught off guard by Tally's question.

Mitch put his head in his hands, and Caroline dropped the stack of publicity photos on the floor, then began scrambling to pick them up.

Tom now knew his question surprised Hiwatha. He quickly placed the microphone right under Hiwatha's mouth to hear his answer. Hiwatha looked up as the Daily Chronicle photographer snapped his picture.

"Victoria Santiago is as pregnant by me as you are, Mr. Tally. Don't you think that would be a better question for her boyfriend, Phil Ross?"

"It would be, except that's not what's coming out of her

camp. According to a very close source, they're confident you are the father," Tally replied with a smirk.

"Well, I vehemently deny any allegations, and that's all I'm going to say on the subject. Now if everyone is here to talk about the fight, let's talk, but if you're here to discuss rumors, this show has just ended."

Hiwatha gave Tally a look that could silence a tiger. Tally stepped back as Caroline immediately stood between them.

"If everyone is ready, we can begin one-on-one interviews. Who's set up," Caroline asked, trying to diffuse the situation.

Bob Rice with WNN Sports raised his hand. "We're ready over here, Caroline. It shouldn't take more than five or ten minutes."

Hiwatha moved quickly through the crowd of reporters and took a seat in front of the camera beside Bob Rice while Caroline made a bee-line over to Tom Tally. Hiwatha was annoyed that he didn't know what they were saying. Most of all, he hated not being in control of the situation.

"Tom, what was that line of questioning?" Caroline asked. "I've never known you to get involved in the rumor mill. The Chronicle is a little more respectable. That's more for the gossip rags."

"No, Caroline, I have a daily boxing column. Anything relevant to my audience is important to me. Victoria Santiago is one of the hottest young stars in America. She's on every magazine from rumor rag to respectable. If Victoria is pregnant by Hiwatha Jordan, the proposed "King of Boxing," then that's news."

"You didn't say she said anything. You said that you heard it from another source."

"Caroline, for your information, Victoria fainted on the set of her video production and was rushed to the hospital," explained Tally. "Her camp initially said it was exhaustion, but I got a call from a very reliable source who works closely with her. She claimed to have spent the day consoling Victoria because she didn't know how to break the news to Hiwatha."

"I see," responded Caroline. "So, Victoria decided you would be a better person to break the news. Sounds like a publicity stunt to me."

"No, it sounds like we're still in the business of selling papers," Tally said in a matter of fact manner. "That's what it's all about. Isn't that why you flew me here today? So, who's using who?"

Tally grabbed his bag and stuffed his recorder inside. He motioned to his photographer to begin vacating the premises.

"Look, I'll be out front, waiting on the bus to go back to the airport. My job is finished here for the day. Take care, Miss Davis."

Hiwatha watched out the corner of his eye as Tom Tally left. He knew the consequences were not in his favor. Though the remaining press had not asked any further questions about Victoria, Hiwatha expected their footage and comments would be altered to incorporate his response.

He was sure Victoria had orchestrated everything. Now he wanted to know if she was really pregnant, and was it his?

———————•((•))•———————

The press workout ended on schedule. Hiwatha grabbed his gym bag and hurried out the door in silence. He was not going to prolong the embarrassment. Caroline rushed out behind him.

"Wait up, Hiwatha!" she shouted. "I need to speak with you!"

Hiwatha paused a moment to allow Caroline to catch up to him. He was still fuming over the issue with Victoria.

"Caroline, I need you to get Victoria Santiago on the phone for me immediately."

Hiwatha's tone sounded like a direct order, and he acted as though there was no relationship between them. Caroline suddenly stopped in her tracks.

"I know you're not telling me to call Victoria about this shit," Caroline responded.

"Are you or are you not being paid to be my publicist?" Hiwatha asked directly.

"I'm your publicist, but I'm also supposed to be someone special in your life."

"Well, you're still special, but today I need the publicist I'm paying for."

"Correction, Mr. Rosanni is paying for my services."

"I don't give a damn who's paying. I need you as my publicist to help me clear this situation up immediately."

Caroline stood still in disbelief, desperately trying to understand why Hiwatha was being so disrespectful towards her.

"You know what? I think you need to get Mitch to help you. I'm catching the next flight out of here."

"I don't think so," replied Hiwatha. "Not tonight, anyway. You'll be here as long as I need you, Ms. Professional. Now that's compliments of Mr. Rosanni."

"You've lost your damn mind," Caroline stated in anger. "You don't own me. You must be crazy."

Hiwatha became more irritated. The only thing on his mind was erasing what had happened in the press workout. Hiwatha loathed the thought of dealing with Caroline right now on an emotional level.

"Caroline, you wanted to play ball in the big leagues. Suck it up and let's get down to business. I need the publicist in you to squash this story by morning."

Caroline, in irritation, stepped back, hit pause on the conversation to take a good look at Hiwatha. Angry couldn't describe what she was feeling. One thing for sure, she definitely intended to stand her ground.

"You get down to business! I'm going to make sure the press gets back on the bus then to the airport. You and your baby momma, Ms. Victoria Santiago, can go to hell. And that's a direct order from your former publicist."

"Wait, Caroline! Hold up, baby," Hiwatha pleaded as he grabbed her arm. "Don't leave. I didn't mean to say those things. I'm just upset this happened, especially in front of you."

Caroline turned around to face Hiwatha. She was so

close; Hiwatha could feel her breathing heavily. He had underestimated this woman. Caroline appeared ready to go toe-to-toe with him if necessary. Hiwatha took a step backward. After Victoria vandalized his Study, he wasn't about to say what a woman wouldn't do.

"Is this your child?" Caroline asked in anger.

Hiwatha looked directly at Caroline. He decided not to lie or try to favorably position the truth. This was the woman he eventually wanted to spend his life with; therefore, honesty was essential.

"Honestly, Caroline, I really don't know," Hiwatha said with uncertainty.

"I don't believe this is happening," Caroline said as her eyes filled with tears. "Last night you asked me to believe in us. Now today you want me to get on the phone and speak with one of your women whom you can't say for certain is not pregnant by you. Do you see how ridiculous this is? By the elevator in Houston, I gave you an out. I told you I wanted to keep our relationship professional and remain friends. You're the one who pursued this relationship."

"Yes, I did, because I fell in love with you," he answered in a sincere voice. "I promise you I have not been involved with Victoria since you and I spent that time together on the press tour. I came home and broke it off with her because I wanted us to have a real chance to build a life together. It has taken me a long time to find someone I genuinely love. So yes, I'm upset and afraid this could mess things up between us."

"Why should I believe you," she snapped.

"Because I'm asking you to stand by me and confront the first real test of our relationship. If we can't get through this together, there is no way we can get married. This kind of shit happens all the time in my world. You know how many women claim to be pregnant by wealthy and famous men."

"First of all, who said I want to marry your damn ass," Caroline responded in anger. "I'm not interested in marrying a man with whom I have to live with the constant fear of infidelity. You might have gotten me to sign up for this bullshit this time, but next time I'm reading the fine print."

Hiwatha started to reach for her but noticed Mitch approaching with a few members of the press. He handed Caroline a towel from his pocket to wipe her eyes.

"Look, Caroline, go ahead and help Mitch take care of the press. I'll see you back at the house. We can finish talking, then."

"Don't count on it," Caroline said under her breath.

Hiwatha turned quickly and began rushing towards the house. He wanted to get in touch with Floyd Nash who had pictures of Victoria and Phil Ross. He'd anticipated possible problems with Victoria and had Floyd follow her while she was on tour.

Floyd had kept Hiwatha abreast of their relationship. Though he hoped he'd never have to use the pictures, Victoria was forcing his hand.

"Hey, Floyd. Man, I'm glad I reached you. I was hoping you were in town."

"Yeah, I got back last night," he responded in a crusty voice.

"Dig this, Victoria leaked to the press that she's pregnant," Hiwatha stated in a nervous and hurried tone.

"No, shit, man! Is she pointing the finger at you?"

"Of course, she is. I had a press day at the gym, and the guy from the New York Daily Chronicle popped the question in front of the entire room of reporters. You know by morning they'll have a field day with this story. I think Vicky is trying to get back at me for breaking it off with her. She knows I got this fight coming up. Women know just when to screw with your life."

"You obviously intend to do something about it, or you wouldn't be calling me. You know I got the photos of Victoria and that football guy," Floyd replied gloatingly.

"Yeah, I need to get those photos to Antonio immediately. Can you take care of it?" he asked and prayed at the same time.

"Yeah, just text the info, and I'll take care of it right away."

"You're the best man. I'll let Antonio know you're sending them. Can you also stop by? I need to talk to you. Bring the pictures with you. I'd like to take a look at them."

"No problem," responded Floyd. "I'll see you around six-o'clock. I need to get dressed."

Hiwatha hung up the phone and quickly dialed Antonio. He was embarrassed to bother him with this, but Caroline would not be a good confidant right now. For the sake of their relationship, he decided to leave her out of it.

Mitch entered the Study to inform Hiwatha that Caroline and the press had boarded the bus headed for the airport. Hiwatha leaned back in his chair. This could not be good. Caroline leaving without speaking to him, could only mean the worst. He'd hoped for a chance to clear things up face-to-face.

As Antonio answered his phone, Hiwatha took a deep breath before proceeding to tell him about the press day. It wouldn't be long before the story would break. He had faith Antonio's publicity machine would squash it by morning.

———◦«◦»◦———

Numwar was sitting with his trainer, Xavier, watching the evening entertainment news. He laughed at the reports concerning Victoria and Hiwatha.

"That's just what that goody-two-shoes chump gets," Numwar said with glee. "All I know is I better get my shot at the title. I'm ready to kick his ass. Make him regret the day he heard of Numwar Nasser."

Numwar sat back in his chair, wondering if he would ever get an opportunity to fight for the title. He was just as good as Jordan and Magnificent. In his heart, the reality loomed that it would be a long road to the title. No manager really wanted to put their fighter in the ring with him. Sure, Charleston had placed him on the "Showdown" undercard, but Numwar already was having his doubts about their alignment.

Numwar was setting the gym on fire. Xavier had confirmed he was getting better each day. Numwar simply wanted to be known as the best in the world. Charleston had promised him a title bout after Jordan / Magnificent fight. All the world governing bodies had him rated as the number one contender. In his eyes, he was the uncrowned champion.

"I will not die in anybody's gym!" he shouted to Xavier. "I will not do it! I've got to get my shot!"

"Don't worry so much," Xavier replied, trying to calm his spirit. "It will come. Soon they will not be able to duck you."

Xavier knew Numwar had two strikes against him. He was not American, and until recently, he hadn't gotten much publicity. Numwar was a superb fighter with exceptional skills, but he was simply too good for other managers to risk their prospects, contenders, and champions against.

Xavier prayed that things would work out because he didn't want Numwar's talent to die in the gym. Xavier knew Antonio was pleased with Numwar's performance in Houston. So, he had been careful to nurture that relationship.

Xavier felt Antonio was a man of his word. He had already placed letters of credit to all parties connected with the promotion. Ninety-five percent of the pay-per-view projections had come through. It was estimated that they would reach more than one-hundred-eighty million in sales.

The other promoters in the sport were not happy to be cut out of the biggest promotion in boxing history by an outsider. How long would it be before every champion would be ringing Antonio's doorbell?

This amused Antonio. He hated boxing managers and didn't feel they earned their money. At least he promoted and protected his movie stars. In some cases, he gave them percentages of the film's gross profit. In boxing, they always worked to keep the fighters profit down.

Although Antonio had a lot of respect for Mitch, he respected Hiwatha even more for calling his own shots. On the other hand, he detested Charleston and felt he was cheap and unworthy of running a great fighter like Magnificent's career. He winced when he thought of how Charleston was accepting under-the-table deals from Shapiro in exchange for lower purses for his boxers. Thankfully due to Magnificent's marketability, he was able to still make a lot of money, but not the money he would have made with better representation.

Antonio had heard the rumors of Charleston's borrowing money from underworld figures. This was the dirty side of boxing. This was one of the reasons he was skeptical about furthering his business ventures in the sport. His instincts were telling him the financial rewards could be in his best interest. If he moved forward, the best option would be to align himself with a protégé to handle the day-to-day dealings. The problem was he didn't need the money, so his motivations were different.

As Antonio sat on his Patio having lunch, he was looking at the daily entertainment report on television. He had arranged for his public relations team to deflect the stories being aired about Hiwatha and Victoria's relationship. They were now showing pictures of Victoria and Phil Ross, kissing on the beach in Miami, holding hands at dinner and dancing at a club in New York. How happy they looked together. It was becoming evident that the public sentiment was with Hiwatha. By the time Antonio was finished, Victoria would look like a complete fool.

———◦《◦》◦———

Victoria sat up in the bed as she heard the news reports blaring from the television. She was stunned to see the pictures of her and Phil Ross showing on the screen. She shouted in anger at the TV when they showed a picture of Hiwatha at a charity event with a group of children. Her night of glory was over as quickly as it had appeared.

Victoria and Elan had been up the night before watching the reports of her affair with Hiwatha on various stations. Victoria thought she had him, but as usual, Hiwatha was one step ahead.

Victoria checked her cell phone and noticed that Phil had left several messages. She couldn't call him back until she'd made up her mind whether to lie or tell him the truth. She wanted to talk to Elan before she swallowed her pride and contacted Hiwatha.

What a mess, she thought. Here I am, pregnant with my first child, and it's a nightmare. She grabbed her cell phone, and reluctantly made Hiwatha her first call. She was prepared to leave a message but was surprised when Hiwatha began to speak.

"Well hello Vicky," he said calmly. "What can I do for you this afternoon? You finished playing with my life?"

"Hiwatha, I need you to know that these stories they're running aren't true."

"What? You're not pregnant?" he asked.

"Yes, I am pregnant, but it's not Phil's child. Don't believe what you are hearing."

"You were with him?" Hiwatha asked not necessarily confirming. "I think they got that much right. Unless you mean, I shouldn't believe what I'm seeing."

"I was with you, so don't get this twisted."

"You're the one who seems to have this twisted. To my surprise, I'm not the only guy you've been sleeping with. I guess shit happens, right?"

"Don't you dare try and make this sound like I'm some kind of a whore," she said in anger.

"It's okay for you to sleep with whomever you want, but I can't. That's bullshit! You're a hypocritical son-of-a-bitch."

"Vicky, I don't appreciate standing in some sperm donor line-up to prove that I am the father of your child."

"Hiwatha, I spoke with my doctor. I know this is your child."

"Vicky, I want confirmation. I definitely need a paternity test. Until I know for sure, I will do nothing. I personally think you're doing this to get back at me. I guess, trashing, my house wasn't enough damage for you."

"Please don't say that. I'm genuinely sorry for the way

we parted, but I wouldn't lie to you about something as serious as this."

"Then, are you lying to Phil?" he asked directly. "What are you telling him? Or did you decide to hedge your bets on me first? Either way, I'm not amused at having my reputation and personal life aired in public."

"So, you think I want my personal life on the news?" she shouted. "I have a career, too. You're not the only one in this relationship with fans."

"Vicky, I'm not stupid. I know you went to the media. That was always what you wanted. You like having your name on the front page. That's precisely why we can never work. I don't need that type of shit in my life. As you said, this is pretty serious. If it's true, why didn't you come to me privately?"

"How can you say that?" she asked with tears in her voice. "I wanted to call you, but I was afraid to after leaving you the way I did. I do love you, Hiwatha. I've loved you from the moment I laid eyes on you. I definitely didn't plan for it to work out like this. What do I need to do to make things right between us? I was hoping that after all we've shared you'd at least be more understanding."

"Understanding! You can't be serious."

"Hiwatha, I am serious. This is no time to be playing games. I'm trying to have an honest conversation with you. I believe I deserve another chance. I am pregnant with your child. Doesn't that mean anything to you?"

"Vicky, this will never work," he replied coldly. "I don't

feel the same way about you, and I don't have any intentions of continuing a relationship with you. If this is my child, I will help you take care of it, and of course, I will want to be a part of their life. If I find out it isn't mine, I want you to go on with your life, and we can pretend this never happened. That is the understanding I want to have with you."

Victoria began screaming into the phone. She was hurt, humiliated, and embarrassed. She could not believe how cold he was towards her. As manipulative as she had been, she did love Hiwatha. She finally threw her cell phone across the room and fell to her knees in tears. She knew it was over. The baby made no difference to him. She was now pregnant and without a shadow-of-doubt alone. What was she going to do? She cried for hours before calling Elan.

———————◦《●》◦———————

Charleston sat in his suite, cursing at Theresa. She was not moved by his verbal explosion.

"I will not be looking at your wife sitting ringside while I'm watching the fight from some damn bleacher," she shouted.

Charleston trembled with rage as he tried to control himself. Their arguments were becoming more explosive, and neither of them could walk away from the affair. Instead, they worked to manipulate one another.

"Goddammit, I don't know why you keep giving me grief," Charleston shouted into the phone. "I've spent a small fortune on your ass, and you have the nerve to treat me like this."

"And how do you treat me, Charleston? I love you, too. You keep telling me you're getting a divorce. When? It's been more than two years, and I've put my life on hold for your ass. And you keep telling one lie after another."

"I've got to go," he said in surrender. "I don't need this shit right now."

"Don't try and get off the phone," Theresa shouted. You always run from the truth."

For once Charleston was silent. He listened for a moment to what he felt was abuse. He definitely couldn't see his own faults. Theresa was talking to a man without a heart. Charleston finally hung up the phone without warning.

⸻))(()((⸻

Hiwatha had finished his training and decided to try Caroline again. She was not answering his calls. This was beginning to get awkward since they still needed to work together. Now she had her minion Dale calling. Hiwatha had already hung up on him at least three times. He thought Caroline would eventually call, but no such luck. Again, he got her voicemail.

"Look, baby. This is getting a little ridiculous. You have to talk to me at some point. I understand you're mad, but I think we need to talk about this. I'm running out of ways to tell you I'm sorry. I hope you got the flowers I sent. If I don't hear from you soon, I will simply resort to other measures. You know how creative I can be."

Caroline was looking at her caller I.D. She was not giving in. No way was she going to be a fool. Her brother Stevie was not in agreement. He had been pleading with her to call Hiwatha.

"Caroline, you don't work through a relationship in silence," Stevie pleaded. "The guy obviously cares for you, or he wouldn't be calling to work things out. You know how these women are."

"Stevie, please, I'm no fool! That woman did not get pregnant by herself. He even admitted to being in a relationship with her."

"So, what, he had a relationship with her. He still wants to be with you. You also had a relationship with Lance."

"That's different. Lance and I had already broken up. Besides, I'm not asking him to forgive me for being pregnant by Lance."

"Well ok, there are a few strings attached, but it's not something you two can't work out. The circumstances may be complicated right now, but I believe Hiwatha is telling you the truth. My advice is to give him a chance to make it right."

"I'll think about it. Now get off my phone. I know it's time for you to take Mom to the doctor. I'll deal with Hiwatha when I'm ready."

"Check you later, Sis. Just, don't screw this up. And don't make him wait too long. Call him."

Magnificent held his final sparring session. He appeared sharp. His boxing was purposeful and his punching power impressive. He usually didn't punish his sparring partners, but now they were painfully earning their wages.

In his final workouts, Magnificent's rough edges needed tuning. He was definitely looking more like his name, shinning in all phases of his training. Charleston and his other minions had done all they could to assure victory.

Now Charleston had begun to openly question the heart of Hiwatha on television and in print. He was basking in the glow of late-night television and appeared on several prominent stations. Though Charleston was not the attraction, he worked hard to be more visible than his fighters.

After a workout session, Hiwatha, who was being interviewed by one of the country's top newspapers, finally responded.

"Charleston Orlando is all show and talks too much. You hardly hear Wonderful say anything. It's like a robot with an actor in his corner. Maybe Charleston should consider moving to Hollywood or Broadway. Boxing is for real men. And as for me, not having any heart, I will soon have an opportunity to show him personally."

When Charleston read Hiwatha's response in the paper, he was furious. His ego couldn't take public scrutiny. He turned back to his desk and began trying to fill his list of ticket requests. This was no small feat. He had negotiated and purchased nearly sixty tickets. They were mostly cheap seats for his trainers and other boxers in the gym. He kept his ringside tickets for his high roller friends and to those whom he was in debt.

He knew the money from this fight could put him in good standing, especially with the IRS. Unfortunately, he would always need a small fortune to cover his lifestyle. He was not only reckless but also required the constant roar of the crowd.

————«(●)»————

Magnificent lay in bed trying to backtrack. He was taking care of all the small details, such as tickets and hotel rooms for his friends and family. It was a pain, but he wanted their support the night of the fight. Magnificent had been in the shadow of Hiwatha for a long time and felt this fight would solidify his status in boxing history.

Unlike Charleston, he was honest in his assessment of Hiwatha's talent. He understood Hiwatha could move, punch, box, and defend equally. So, Magnificent prepared daily and was cautious not to miss the slightest detail.

————«(●)»————

Hiwatha had arrived in Las Vegas, and so far, it seemed everything was going as planned. He stopped at his favorite restaurant to enjoy some pasta with his entourage. Things would get hectic as the week progressed, starting with the press conference on Wednesday. Dale was waiting in the lobby of the hotel upon his arrival to give him his itinerary.

Caroline made sure she was not present. Instead, she was in her room, still avoiding Hiwatha. Not willing to play her game, Hiwatha made a scene and refused to deal with Dale. He threw the itinerary back at him and insisted that he find Caroline.

Dale finally had enough and complained to Antonio Rosanni. It wasn't long before Antonio called Caroline to his suite.

"Caroline, what is this I hear that you are refusing to work with Hiwatha," he asked, knowing the answer. "I hope you realize I pay your firm handsomely. So, I expect my business to be handled and the fighters to be taken care of."

"I apologize. I was busy handling other things, so I asked Dale to assist me," she responded. "It won't happen again."

"Don't play games with me, Caroline," he said in a stern voice. "I know the situation between you and Hiwatha. Under normal circumstances, I would have replaced you, but out of respect for Hiwatha, I did not get involved. Now you have included me," Antonio said with irritation in his voice.

"Mr. Rosanni I'm really sorry," Caroline replied.

"Let me remind you that I expect you to put your personal feelings aside," Antonio continued. "Hiwatha has top billing on this promotion. I want you and your staff to provide his team with whatever they need to make this promotion a success. I'm not interested in your emotional problems. Have I made myself clear?"

"Yes, Mr. Rosanni, I'm clear. I will check in with Mr.

Jordan right away."

"And, you will stay checked in with Mr. Jordan for the duration of this promotion."

Caroline stood to leave the suite. She was embarrassed that Antonio had to speak with her, especially about her lack of professionalism. Letting her emotions interfere with handling business was a rookie mistake.

Caroline called Dale on his cell phone to get Hiwatha's room number. It was time to talk to him in person. If the baby is Hiwatha's, could she live with Victoria being part of their life? She took a deep breath and made the long walk down the corridor to his suite.

A young Mexican man named Ramiro opened the door. Caroline responded to his greeting while surveying the living room of the suite. Things were terribly quiet for this time of day. She finally asked Ramiro if Hiwatha was there. Hearing her voice, Hiwatha appeared in the doorway of his bedroom. Caroline's heart nearly stopped at the sight of him.

"Well, you do exist," Hiwatha said as if he was surprised. "Not sure why I had to raise such a fuss."

"I was thinking the same thing," Caroline replied as she laid her notebook on the counter.

Hiwatha looked over at his assistant Ramiro, then asked him to leave the suite. He motioned to Caroline to take a seat next to him on the sofa. Wanting to keep her distance, she decided to take the chair opposite him. They made idle conversation for a while until Hiwatha felt comfortable enough to bring up the subject of their relationship.

"It's good to see you," he spoke with a smile on his face. "I've missed you. I was hoping we could take some time to resolve the issue between us? I feel terrible about the situation. I could have handled it better. You didn't deserve this, and the timing couldn't have been worse. Just tell me what I need to do to make things right between us."

Caroline suddenly felt resentful towards him as she thought of her conversation with Antonio. She decided not to give an inch. In truth, Caroline was not ready to make a decision. Professionally she needed to work with Hiwatha. Personally, Caroline was not sure how to continue their relationship. If only she could roll back the tape to that moment by the elevator. She would have followed her intuition.

"Look, I just want to do my job and get this fight over with. Then you can go back to your happy little life, and I can go back to mine. Maybe at some point, even be friends again."

"Unfortunately, my happy little life doesn't exist without you," responded Hiwatha. "As I've stated, I'm in love with you. So, whatever needs to be done in order for us to get pass this, I am willing to do. I understand the circumstances, but I cannot change what has happened. I apologize for hurting you, and I'm still willing to stand by everything I've promised you."

"That's just not possible. I don't want to be involved in this mess between you and Victoria. We were friends and should have stayed friends. You knew how important this project was to me. Being one of your many women was not part of the deal. I just left Mr. Rosanni's suite, and he's not too happy with me."

"I will take care of that," Hiwatha said calmly. "I will take full responsibility. You've done nothing wrong."

"Oh, yes, I have. I've allowed myself to get involved with you. It's impacting my better judgment and my ability to be professional. If I hadn't gotten involved with you, I would have stayed and handled the situation after your press workout. I would have been there to greet your camp. I should have given you the topnotch service you deserve as a client of Rosanni. You can't accept responsibility for that. So, you need to step back and let me do my job. At least give me until the end of the promotion. We can talk about our relationship then. Now, do you need anything, Mr. Jordan? Is there something my staff or I can do for you?"

"Caroline cut the dramatic bullshit," Hiwatha said, trying to control his anger. "You can't just dictate how we're going to handle our relationship. This decision should be between two people who love each other. I already told you I ended the relationship with Victoria. I'm not in love with her. I am in love with you."

"If you love me, then you will back off and let me do my job? That's all I'm asking. Can't I ask something of love, too?"

"Do you really want me to back off?" Hiwatha asked, not wanting to hear the answer. "I thought what we have between us was special to you."

"Special! I don't call another woman having your baby special. I think the only thing special is your inability to grasp that. So yes, back off."

Hiwatha put his head in his hands for a moment. He felt himself becoming impatient with Caroline. The conversation was going in the wrong direction. There was no way he could walk into the ring with this on his mind. He had no other choice, but to concede.

Although in his heart he wanted her blessing and support, the fact was, he wasn't going to get it. He was becoming visibly angry. He had tried for weeks to speak with her. Now he could no longer deal with her rejection.

"Okay, I will back off," he replied as he got up from the sofa in defeat. "Have it your way. I have to concentrate on the fight. I don't need to get all messed up in the head over you. Obviously, you are unwilling to compromise. So, tell you what, you don't have to see or speak to me until you're ready. Your handy-man, Dale can take it from here."

Hiwatha walked into his bedroom and slammed the door. He was hurt but tried to keep his composure and focus on his victory over Magnificent. He stood and listened through the door as Caroline spoke.

"Hiwatha, I'm sorry. Please forgive me. Eventually, things will work out. Just make sure you're prepared for the fight. I don't want to see you get hurt."

Hiwatha snatched open the door starling Caroline. She stepped back, recognizing the look of anger on his face.

"What the hell do you care if I get hurt? You're too damn

busy worrying about your job. You keep talking about making a good impression on your boss rather than working things out between us," Hiwatha shouted as he banged his fist on the counter.

"Don't you know I can afford to buy your company and your so-called boss three times over? Do you really understand what I'm offering you? I'm tired of pouring my heart out to you. I was honest with you about the situation with Vicky. What more do you want from me? I'm talking about you and me having a life together, and you insist on throwing this professional bullshit in my face. I think it's a good idea you stay out of my life until you're ready to talk to me about that. I refuse to continue playing these stupid mind games with you. I love you, but you need to grow up, be a real woman, and deal with me like I'm a real man who's trying to spend his life with you. Until you're ready to do that, I have nothing to say to you."

Caroline started to speak, but Hiwatha put his hand up to silence her. He then walked to the door of his suite and opened it. Caroline stood there for a moment in disbelief, wondering what to do. Hiwatha had never been this upset with her. As he began to motion for her to get out, she finally grabbed her notebook from the counter to leave. When the door slammed behind her, the consequences of her actions were not clear.

Chapter 13

THE SHOW-DOWN

The day of the weigh-in was chaotic. Media from all over the world were in Las Vegas to see the unification title bout. You would have thought it was the Olympics. Even though the two champions appeared calm, you could sense the tension.

Magnificent entered the backstage area flanked by Charleston and his brother Davis. He wore a black warm-up suit trimmed in red. It was complemented by his favorite red jogging shoes with white shoe strings. The undercard fighters had already weighed in. Now it was Magnificent's turn to hit the scale. Two doctors stood nearby to take the physicals of both middleweight champions.

When Magnificent stripped to get on the scale, the crowd in the ballroom of the Hollywood Grand Theater became engulfed in a mass of hot lights as they roared in approval. They all pressed forward to get a closer look.

The announcer stepped to the microphone. "Please, can you settle down for a moment?" he asked the audience.

"We'd like to start the Weigh-In. I want to thank all of you for coming. First up the WBI champion Wonderful Magnificent then the WBF champion Hiwatha "Absolute" Jordan."

Hiwatha was standing stage left wearing an eggshell-white jogging suit, trimmed in silver with white shower shoes. A gold chain adorned with a simple gold cross glistened at his neck. Mitch chatted in his ear, and his words brought a smile to the champion's lips. St. Claire stood alongside them with a stern look on his face.

Flashbulbs popped as the live camera feed rolled. Magnificent stepped on the scale, wearing only briefs. To the crowded room, Magnificent was definitely not "Mr. Pitiful', as Hiwatha had often referred to him. He was cut and defined like a bodybuilder, but without the bulk. His shoulders and back could have been those of a man close to two hundred pounds. It seemed impossible that Magnificent could weigh less than one-hundred-sixty pounds. He looked like a full-fledged light heavyweight at one-hundred-seventy-five pounds.

Magnificent's arms were developed, and his muscles were elongated. His chest and stomach just rippled. The women in attendance screamed at the sight of such a specimen.

"Wonderful Magnificent weighs one-hundred and fifty-nine-and-three quarter pounds," said the boxing commissioner as the crowd gave their applause. Charleston handed Magnificent a small cup of orange juice as he stepped off the scale. As Magnificent finished his physical, he took time to address the fans in attendance.

"I feel great, and I'm ready to unify the title. I am confident that all in attendance will witness the greatest fight ever."

Several reporters followed Magnificent as he swiftly left the theater determined to have little contact with his rival.

Hiwatha quickly removed the necklace from around his neck, stripped down to his briefs and stepped on the scale. St. Claire peered nervously over his right shoulder. He knew his champion looked like a model for a perfect body ad. His chest, shoulders, and calves were well developed. He was not as defined as Magnificent, but was still a specimen to behold. Hiwatha held up his arms and flexed his muscles while looking over at Caroline, standing near the edge of the stage. She caught his gaze and quickly looked away.

The announcer once again addressed the audience as Hiwatha stepped off the scale.

"Ladies and gentlemen, Hiwatha "Absolute" Jordan weighs in at one-hundred and sixty pounds."

The crowd began cheering as Hiwatha stepped off the scale. He quickly dressed as his entourage stood nearby. He looked impatiently at St. Claire.

"I'm glad this is over. I am starving."

"Yes, but you still need to address the crowd. Go ahead and get that over with," replied St. Claire.

Hiwatha walked over and grabbed the microphone from the announcer who was in mid-sentence. It was evident that he was impatient.

"I am the greatest boxer in the world, and I will prove it to you tomorrow night," Hiwatha shouted to the crowd.

With that, Hiwatha and St. Claire quickly left the theater. For this fight, the two champions were being heavily guarded. Bodyguards were posted outside both their suites with a couple of police officers down the hall.

In Hiwatha's suite, St. Claire prepared a hearty dinner for his champion. After the meal, Hiwatha decided to take a well-guarded walk with his friend Floyd Nash and St. Claire before retiring to bed. The fight weighed heavily on his mind.

St. Claire never left Hiwatha's side. He had sat near him as he ate. They walked together, and while Hiwatha slept, St. Claire sat and read the newspaper next to his bed. He made sure Hiwatha didn't leave his sight.

Other than the small conversations Hiwatha had with St. Claire or Floyd, he remained silent the day of the fight. He had his last snack three hours before fight time. Now he sat near a window in his suite, looking down at the Las Vegas Strip. Hiwatha had done everything possible to prepare physically. Now he was mentally getting into his zone. Mitch Danton spoke briefly with him before leaving the suite to take care of some last-minute details.

<hr />

Everyone connected to the fighters was nervous. Charleston steadily paced the floor and stayed on his cell phone tying up loose ends before Numwar Nasser entered the ring against Don Caffery.

"Hands up and take your time," Oliver Xavier whispered into the ear of Numwar who was bouncing up and down, testing his shoes against the canvas. From the ring, he could see the crowd was growing steadily. Before the night's main event, the arena would be sold out, and the worldwide pay-per-view would do history-making numbers.

Xavier knew his man was ready to go to work. In the opposite corner was vaunted left-hook artist Don Caffery, a rough, tough brawler from England. He was the current British champion with a record of thirty-seven wins, five losses, and two draws. He was rated "Number Five" in the world and was reputed to be a puncher who had knocked out twenty-six men. Caffery was a square-jawed man with flaming red hair. His solid black boxing trunks with a red stripe made his hair seem even redder.

The first-round bell sounded. Numwar eased out of his corner while Caffery came out bombing, throwing punches from every angle before grazing Numwar's chin with a right hand then hitting him below the belt with a left hook. Caffery was showing no respect for the uncrowned champion. Numwar had to slip, roll, block and parry the punches of his robust and determined opponent.

Caffery continued his mission as a non-stop punching machine, stunning and wobbling Numwar with a quick right-hand and left-hook combination to the head. Numwar immediately clinched. The crowd was roaring in approval for the Englishman. At the bell, Caffery was clearly the crowd favorite and the winner of the round. Xavier had Numwar on the stool as soon as the bell rang.

"Listen, Numwar," Xavier spoke as if in a library. "This guy's going to burn out. Start getting your distance with the jab and counter. Stay off the ropes and make this guy lunge after you. Then punish this bum with every blow."

Numwar listened intently. He was a patient fighter that was working to find his rhythm. At the bell, Caffery charged out with full confidence, eagerly stepping to his prey, except this time he tasted three hard left-jabs. When he tried to counter with a jab of his own, Numwar quickly threw a short right-hand over his jab, followed by a left hook to his liver. For a split second, the Englishmen seemed to pause until Numwar followed with another left hook to the chin.

Numwar was now working like a well-oiled machine as he began to put his deadly combinations together. A double jab left-hook and straight right-hand combinations bounced off the redhead's face. Caffery tried to shoot another jab, but before he could fully extend his left arm, Numwar pressed forward and landed a debilitating right-uppercut to his heart. It landed with such force that Caffery lurched forward unable to breathe.

Caffery finally caught his breath, as Numwar cut loose with an explosive left-hook to his chin, dislodging Caffrey's mouthpiece. The crowd was silent for a split second before erupting into a thunderous noise.

There was still five seconds left in the round when the referee stopped the count at five. The cornermen of Caffery rushed into the ring to help him to his feet. Numwar ran to his corner as Xavier jumped into the ring to congratulate him.

"Son, you were terrific," he said, proudly hugging Numwar. "You finished him off just like I wanted."

"I just couldn't get loose in the first round," Numwar explained. "But I finally found my rhythm. I was looking for an opening, anything that would give me the edge. Who would have thought that right-hand under the heart would turn out to be a beautiful finishing touch?"

"The time is two minutes and fifty-five seconds of the second round," shouted the ring announcer. "The winner by kayo and still undefeated...the number one middleweight contender in the world...Numwar Nasser!"

The ring doctor was still examining Caffery. The wicked body punching by Numwar had raised an egg-sized cyst on Caffery's rib cage, just under the heart.

"I've been around boxing, maybe thirty years and I've never seen anything like this," stated the doctor in shock.

The pay-per-view announcers replayed the knockout several times. They were impressed. "I think Nasser is going to be a tough nut to crack," said commentator, Wells Witherspoon. "With him in the picture, the middleweight division is going to get pretty nasty over the next year."

———— ⊙ ————

It was now twenty minutes before the main event. The house was packed with movie stars, rappers, rock stars, politicians, and nearly every well-known athlete in the world. Hordes of beautiful women swiveled by as celebrities marched up and down the aisles looking for their seats.

In Hiwatha's dressing room, there was complete calm. St. Claire had just finished wrapping the champion's hands. Hiwatha examined the gloves he would wear into battle and was pleased. St. Claire proceeded to grease Hiwatha's face and loosened him up. In the last moments before battle, Hiwatha was as supple as a seal. He was surrounded by his entourage and Floyd Nash.

Though their relationship was not one of closeness, his younger brother Kyle had asked to attend the fight. Hiwatha finally decided to take Caroline's advice and start getting to know his brothers. After all, they were his only family. Mitch stepped in to take care of the arrangements.

It was a suffocating hot night. Unusual for Las Vegas this time of year. Thinking ahead, St. Claire had given Hiwatha a couple of salt tablets with his earlier snack. He was covering all bases.

———⟫⟪(⦿)⟫⟪———

A short walk down the corridor, Magnificent was in his dressing room, dancing lightly on his toes, moving effortlessly, shooting his punches in short bursts. He was not as fluid as Hiwatha, but he was graceful and elongated, with an awe-inspiring reach.

Magnificent stopped and held out his arms. Silently, Charleston and his other trainers placed on his robe. It was white satin, trimmed in gold with his name displayed on the back. He looked twice the size he was at the weigh-in. Magnificent slowly slipped into his matching gold-trimmed trunks and shoes. He had to be the most imposing physical specimen ever to walk into the ring for a world middleweight title bout.

A uniformed police officer ducked his head into the door to inform the camp how close they were to fight time. "Ten minutes, champ. Then we go to the ring."

With that, his entourage and handlers began to clap and shout, "Work, work, ah work, work!" When the music started to play, they continued their chant on their walk to ringside. As they came closer to the ring, Magnificent felt a familiar chill run up his spine. It was that strange feeling a fighter gets the night of the fight. It's that unique connection between the boxer and his public. It's what makes one love the roar of the crowd. Magnificent quickly put on his game face while entering the ring. It was a grim, almost determined look.

Charleston, following directly behind, looked as though he were going to the electric chair. As he instructed Magnificent to begin moving to stay loose, gone was his usual swagger and bravado. Not knowing how long it would take prince charming to come out of his dressing room, he wanted Magnificent to stay focused.

"It's time. It's time," said the guard as he opened Hiwatha's door.

St. Claire immediately stood in front of Hiwatha with

Floyd Nash alongside him. Kyle squeezed in next to his brother and grabbed his right arm. The other members of his team closed in around them as several police officers guided them to ringside. They looked like an onrushing football squad.

"Hiwatha, I know you're going to bring the championship home," Kyle whispered in Hiwatha's ear. "I know you can do it. I've always been proud of you. Take it to this guy."

Hiwatha looked over at Kyle and smiled. He further acknowledged his brother's presence by putting his arm around him for the first time.

The spotlights in the arena hit Hiwatha's team as they left the tunnel to begin their fifty-yard walk to the ring. The television cameras picked up his team's images and showed them worldwide. When they zoomed in on the face of Hiwatha "Absolute" Jordan, the crowd went wild as they began to stomp their feet to the music, nearly shaking the roof off the arena in anticipation. As the champion came closer to ringside, the crowd got even louder.

When Hiwatha stepped through the ropes, the crowd rose to their feet to give a round of applause. Hiwatha bowed to all four sides of the ring, then began lightly shadowboxing. St. Claire grabbed him by the shoulders and looked directly in his eyes.

"You are ready. I've never seen you so sharp. You are the best fighter in the world. I truly believe it. Now all you need to do is execute our plan."

Hiwatha smiled at St. Claire as he began to bend at the

waist, stretching his legs to stay loose. He was prepared to fight to the last drop of blood, just like "Mr. Pitiful" opposite him in the ring.

Wonderful Magnificent took a deep breath. It was the moment he'd been waiting for when your dream meets reality.

"Remember, long left-jab. Keep this clown turning. Don't be out there, dropping your hands. Be cool and work on him," said Charleston. "You're much better than this guy. Box him like there's no tomorrow. Let's go to work, baby! Let's go to work!"

The announcer stepped to the microphone, loosening his tie to begin delivering an important message.

"Ladies and gentlemen, welcome to the "showdown," brought to you by International Sports Incorporated. This pay-per-view bout is scheduled to be televised in hundreds of cities in the United States and numerous countries around the world. This fight is sanctioned by World Boxing Incorporated. And the World Boxing Federation in association with Nevada State Athletic Commission. This world middleweight title fight will be under the combined rules of WBI and WBF boxing organizations and the Nevada State Athletic Commission.

"I would like to introduce to you two great champions. Fighting out of the red corner, wearing white trunks with gold trim, and still undefeated. This is his sixth defense of the title."

The crowd began to roar as the announcer continued.

"This young man has done everything asked of him. To get to this point tonight, he has destroyed everything in his path. He really needs no introduction to the world over. Please welcome the WBI world middleweight champion, *Wonderful Magnificent!*"

Magnificent stepped forward and bent at the waist then rose fully extended with his gloves reaching skyward. His upper body looked impressive under the lights. The crowd stood in applause and continued to stomp their feet as the announcer continued.

"Ladies and gentlemen, fighting out of the blue corner, he is wearing red trunks with black trim. He tipped the scales yesterday at one-hundred sixty pounds. He too is, undefeated. This is his eighth defense of the title, and he is a former Olympic gold medal winner. May I introduce the WBF world middleweight champion, the classy and very popular, *Hiwatha "Absolute" Jordan!*

The thunderous applause remained unabated. Hiwatha stepped forward and bowed to all sides of the ring. He then blew a kiss into the close-up camera. There would be several million women in the morning who would swear it was meant for them.

The bell rang several times to silence the crowd as referee James Harris summoned both champions to the center of the ring to hear his instructions. Magnificent tried to stare a hole into his adversary, but Hiwatha kept his eyes on his opponent's rib cage.

"I want a good clean fight. Obey my commands at all

times. Remember, Magnificent and Jordan, protect your-selves at all times.

They touched gloves and returned to their corners. They looked like racehorses ready to charge from the gate. Both of their trainers quickly spoke their last words.

"Left jab...work the left-jab," Charleston whispered into the ear of Magnificent. "Let's show the world who's boss. Tonight, I need you to kick this chump's ass."

In Hiwatha's corner, St. Claire was calm as he gave his final instructions. That's the kind of man he was when everything was on the line. St. Claire knew how thin the line was between pain and glory. As he moved through the ropes, he looked back at his champion.

"Be patient, Hiwatha. Size him up and be sharp. I don't need you to be the tiger tonight. I need you to have the instincts of the prey. If you're really the best in the world, show me tonight."

The tension was palpable. Sitting ringside, Mitch Danton was sweating profusely. Though they appeared calm, St. Claire and Charleston were on edge. They both felt as if it were them in the ring, fighting for their professional careers. Antonio Rosanni, on the other hand, was pleased and genuinely calm. He knew much of the world was watching this boxing epic unfold.

Mr. Wright and some of Charleston's other trainers crammed into their cheap seats. One of the fans in attendance asked Mr. Wright what he thought would be the outcome of the fight.

"Gonna be a good one. Both guys can do it all. It's tight. It's tight," he spoke with the assurance of a boxing professor.

The bell for the first round rang. Wonderful slithered out of his corner. Though his movements appeared graceful, he was on the prowl circling his foe and staying on the perimeter. Hiwatha was feinting with his head and shoulders, looking for an opening or a way to set a trap.

They both shot several jabs. Much to the surprise of Hiwatha, his opponent's left-jab was finding him, touching him up a bit. They each threw wild right hands that were missing the target. The speed and skill of both champions were breathtaking. As the first-round bell rang, Wonderful landed a sharp jab. Hiwatha instantly smelt his own blood faintly in his nostrils.

"Relax, relax you're fighting too hard," explained St. Claire. "You need to slow down and pace yourself. This guy is a good boxer, so you're gonna have to out-think him."

"He's a good boxer, but I intend to stretch him," Hiwatha said, smiling at his trainer.

On the other side of the ring, Charleston was laying down the law. It was apparent to the crowd he was excited and wanted the victory.

"Keep pushing him back. Control his little ass with the jab. He's running already. Take it to this punk. Show him how the boys do it in Chicago."

Magnificent did not respond because he was in a real fistfight. It was best to stay focused on his game plan. Continue putting it all on the line while punishing Hiwatha.

Before the night was over, he was going to make sure that Hiwatha "Absolute" Jordan respected him.

The next four rounds were boxing as high art and drama. Their tactics were sound coupled with their execution of boxing basics had the crowd on edge. The skill level of the combatants would have made the great boxing legends proud.

The goal of Magnificent was to pound Hiwatha's flesh into the canvas. Though he was slightly leading and scoring with the jab, he was not dominating. His right-hand was not accurate; Hiwatha was slipping it entirely and countering with his left-hook.

During the fifth round, Hiwatha pressed his advantage by finally wiping the smirk off Wonderful's face with a blistering left-hook, right-hand, left-hook combination. Hiwatha began working swiftly, maneuvering Wonderful into the ropes, landing a jab off the chest of his taller opponent, then grazing him with a screaming over-hand-right. He then missed with a follow-up left hook.

"Get off the ropes!" shouted Charleston from the corner. "We're not relatives at some damn family picnic. Back this chump up!

Wonderful shoved his tormentor back and spun around to shoot a left-hook to the liver. Hiwatha worked to block the punch, except the move, was followed by a whistling straight right-hand that landed high on Hiwatha's forehead.

For a second Hiwatha was dazed. He reflectively raised his gloves to his face, only to be caught again with a straight left and another right-hand at the bell.

The crowd was at a fever pitch watching the two war-rior's heat up to the task. With each passing round, Hiwatha found himself reaching back for answers in his boxing book of knowledge. Wonderful was hunting him like a hungry timber wolf. His pinpoint precise combinations were being answered by the bionic left-jab and the "bazooka" right-hand of Wonderful Magnificent.

At one point in the eighth round, punches were flying so fast, and furious the boxing experts had to gasp in amaze-ment. It was evident to the crowd that the two champions were facing their worst nightmare in the ring.

Wonderful felt pain he'd never felt before on the right side of his face. He was equally as fast as Hiwatha, but only for the proverbial one-two-three. Each time he shot a vaunted "bazooka" right-hand, it was now answered with a sizzling left-hook.

After this fight, not even the young Cassius Clay or Ray Robinson could match Hiwatha. He was blessed with God-given speed, but it was not helping him right now. Tonight, he could not escape his offensive scores without paying a heavy toll.

Each time Hiwatha scored; his taller opponent punished him. This was the first time in his career Hiwatha was having trouble getting pass the jab and straight right-hand of an opponent. Wonderful Magnificent had perfected that part of his deadly arsenal. There was an ugly mouse now devel-oping under the right eye of Hiwatha. It was the result of a laser left-hand. "Don't worry about the eye," St. Claire told Hiwatha as he worked on the swelling of the cheekbone and lower eyelid with his end-swell. "I need you to hang in there. We're past the midway point. It's time to land this damn plane. Make him hit the runway."

Wonderful's lungs were burning from fatigue and the adrenalin running through his body. He was almost oblivious to the frenzied instructions from Charleston as he spit water from his mouth into a small plastic bucket noticing his own blood mixed in. This was war, and no directions from General Charleston was going to save him from what he was facing in the ring. Magnificent stood as the bell for the tenth-round rung.

"What do you think, man," a fan asked Mr. Wright?

"This is a scientific war. These guys are pulling out all the stops. I got Wonderful ahead by a hair, but Hiwatha is as slick as thirty-five-cent fish," Mr. Wright answered with little interest.

Mr. Wright and the other trainers from Charleston's gym were nervously focusing on the fight, knowing at this point, it could go either way.

Wonderful started the round by swiftly landing two snapping left-jabs, then stepped back to let Hiwatha's jab fall short. Deftly, Magnificent stepped to his right and landed a cracking right-hand to his kidneys. It sounded like a gunshot.

"Wonderful's starting to work on him now," said a hopeful Mr. Wright. "All he has to do is stick to the game plan.

Then we can all go home very happy."

Furiously, Hiwatha fought back, landing a sharp jab to the nose of Wonderful. As he tried to answer with a jab, Wonderful slightly moved his left hand allowing Hiwatha to explode with and overhand-right off his chin, followed by a wicked left hook to the temple.

Wonderful's legs turned to spaghetti beneath him. A tuning fork was going off inside his head. Hiwatha instinctively leaped on him, swift, but calm. He feinted his hurt foe. Then with deadly precision, shot a right-uppercut and left-hook to his chin. The crowd stood and began cheering.

"He's hurt, he's hurt!" screamed the pay-per-view announcer. "Wonderful looks like he is in very deep trouble. Hiwatha "Absolute" Jordan has suddenly come alive here in the last two minutes of the tenth round."

For the last eight seconds of the round, Wonderful wrapped himself around Hiwatha and held him until the bell rang. Everyone who had not already been standing stood as the bell rang to end the tenth round. They cheered and stomped their feet. They shouted loudly for the world to hear.

"Jordan, Jordan, Jordan."

As Wonderful wobbled to his corner, Charleston leaped into the ring and quickly sat his battered warrior down on the stool.

"Goddammit! You're dropping your right hand! Keep your fucking hands up!" he screamed. "Man, I'm gonna stop this shit."

"No, don't stop it, man, don't stop the fight," Wonderful pleaded.

"Then you'd better box this man! Tie his little ass up and walk him around until you clear your head. Just box and clear your head. And remember to keep your right hand up."

"Deep breath, deep breath," St. Claire told Hiwatha.

He knew his man had expended a lot of energy taking the play out of Magnificent. Now he wanted him to slow down and think.

"Take your time. Set this guy up and skillfully place your shots," St. Claire said calmly as the eleventh-round bell rang.

Wonderful started the round trying to be safe, keeping the fight on the outside so he could maintain a distance between him and his tormentor. He tried to jab and move, but Hiwatha was not giving up. He continued to throw punches even though his biceps hurt from the numerous punches he'd already thrown.

Mid-round, Wonderful feinted a jab and landed a beautiful left-hook, right-hand combination that stopped Hiwatha in his tracks. He was dazed and trying to ignore the pain. He immediately charged forward but missed as Wonderful skillfully circled away from him. Hiwatha found his target again, landing several deadly combinations.

"That's it, that's it," shouted Charleston as he leaped into the ring at the sound of the bell. "It's close as hell, but I think we got the lead. We got one more round. Box this man! Box him!" he pleaded urgently.

Across the ring, St. Claire, also was speaking to his

champion. He too wanted Hiwatha to skillfully place his shots.

"Stop walking straight at this man. Side to side and put your shots together," he said while handing him a bottle of water. "Drink this. This is your time to rise and shine. Pick up the pace."

St. Claire knew this fight had been a war. Both men used all their skills, going for a knockout. The exchanges between them were simply breathtaking, even for a seasoned boxing fan. When Wonderful would land a straight-left-right, Hiwatha would counter with a left-hook, right-hand, left-hook combination. When Hiwatha put together a dazzling combination, Wonderful would answer with long powerful right hand to the head and kidneys.

Hiwatha's right eye was almost shut. In the last round, both men would be straining for victory. The body punching had been so unrelenting that each man would pass blood by morning.

The boxing fans going into the final round sounded like one constant loud, piercing noise while both corners were working feverishly during the rest period.

St. Claire was working diligently over his man, giving calm and expert advice. On the opposite end of the ring, Charleston roared and cussed up a storm. Each of them was looking for the final ingredient that might ensure their advantage in pursuit of victory.

In the twelfth and final round, Wonderful and Hiwatha touched gloves and proceeded to fire punches from every angle. The last thirty seconds had to be among the most vicious ever fought in the history of boxing.

Hiwatha landed an over-hand-right that shook Wonderful to his toes. He visibly sagged but did not go down. As Hiwatha moved in, Magnificent countered with a vicious right-uppercut and left-hook to the body, followed by a straight right hand to the head. Wonderful had put such leverage on the final right-hand that it caused Hiwatha's neck to jerk violently.

In the final ten seconds, they stood face-to-face and pounded each other. Hiwatha's right eye was discolored, swollen and appeared to be closed.

Wonderful too had taken a beating but didn't have the extensive marks. His wounds were mostly internal. Still, blood flowed from his left nostril with both eyes swollen and bloodshot.

At the final bell, the referee had to forcefully pull them apart. The crowd's roar went unabated for at least three minutes as each man raised his arms in victory. They each had solidified their respective places in boxing history. The crowd settled down as the ring announcer stepped to the microphone.

"Ladies and gentlemen, I will read the scorecards as follows."

Wonderful Magnificent stood in his corner, totally relieved the fight was over. He was confident while waiting for the judge's results. Charleston, on the other hand, was nervous. The match was too close to call.

As the announcer continued, Hiwatha was being toweled off by St. Claire. You could hear half boos and half cheers from the crowd as the announcer read the first judges scores.

"Judge Mark Anderson scored the bout 120-118 for Magnificent. Judge Dolph De Witt scored the bout 120-118 for Jordan. And Judge Manuel Sousa scored the bout 120-119 for the winner and new undisputed middleweight champion of the world *HIWATHA "ABSOLUTE" JORDAN!* The crowd was split, and many of the fans were in an uproar refusing to be silenced.

Charleston was devastated. Wonderful stood frozen in a daze as one of the pay-per-view announcers shoved a microphone in his face. In disappointment, he pushed the microphone away and quickly left the ring, headed for his dressing room. His entourage was not far behind.

Hiwatha, who was still short of breath, attempted to do an interview with the pay-per-view commentator, but could barely speak. He asked to keep the interview brief but eventually cut it short to exit the ring, holding an ice bag on his right eye. His handlers and entourage were leaping up and down in victory.

Kyle had never been behind the scenes in boxing and was devastated to see his brother in this condition. He made his way through Hiwatha's entourage to quickly put his arm around Hiwatha's waist.

"I'm very proud of you," he spoke into Hiwatha's ear. "I was scared to deaf watching you. That was a hard fight, but I'm glad you won. Just put your arm around my shoulder and let me help you to your dressing room. Keep your head up. You're the champion tonight. Take a deep breath. Everything will be all right. I'm right here to help take care of you."

Kyle was deeply touched to share this special moment with Hiwatha who could only look at him in appreciation through swollen eyes. St. Claire walked behind them, neither happy nor sad. He knew Hiwatha had taken severe punishment. To make matters worse, St. Claire was sure Magnificent would demand a rematch. No, he was not overly joyous.

Hiwatha was coming through the tunnel, heading toward his dressing room. His entourage was still cheering and shouting in unison.

"We're number one! We're number one!"

Caroline and several reporters were heading towards the elevators to attend the press conference. As they approached, Hiwatha noticed her through swollen eyes. He could not speak but asked one of his minions to hold up his belts. Caroline gave him a half-smile, then turned and continued down the corridor towards the elevator.

Hiwatha stood amid his entourage and several reporters trying to get his attention. He watched Caroline as she disappeared around the corner. He no longer heard the screams of his entourage or acknowledged the reporter's questions. He was silent.

Chapter 14

THE PRICE OF LOYALTY

The hotel room was dark. Hiwatha was lying down on the rubbing table, naked, still holding an ice bag to his severely swollen right eye. St. Claire's expert fingers tenderly kneaded the champion's flesh.

"You were great tonight, my son. This fight will go down in history right alongside Frazier-Ali and some of the others," he said at a whisper.

"Man, I'm hurting all over," moaned Hiwatha. "I felt like my lungs were about to burst. I put it all on the line tonight."

Suddenly there was a knock at the door. St. Claire stopped to answer. After looking out the peephole, he opened the door, and Mitch Danton stepped inside.

"How you feeling, champ?" he asked.

"I'm sore all over and tired," Hiwatha stated earnestly.

"Well, it looks good for you to surpass your projections on the fight," Mitch explained. "I should know more when we finalize the numbers on the pay-per-view. Then maybe we sit down and see what's next. Antonio already wants to do a rematch," Mitch said, trying to get a feel for what was next on the menu.

"Wait one minute," St. Claire responded as he continued to massage Hiwatha. "The champ needs a rest. That was a war out there tonight. Or didn't you see it? He's got to take at least six months off to let his body heal."

"St. Claire's right man, I need at least six months to rest up. Besides, it's going to take me that long to count my money," Hiwatha said half-joking.

"How is your eye?" asked Mitch.

"I guess it'll be all right," responded Hiwatha. "Right now, all I want is for this swelling to go down and for the soreness to go away. I've been blessed. Tonight, I won a fight that could have easily gone against me. Maybe it's time to quit. I've done more than most. I've made my mark. I'm going to go home and evaluate things."

Mitch was almost in a state of shock and relieved at the same time. Retirement had crossed his mind too. St. Claire was definitely happy to hear those words. He could care less if Hiwatha ever fought again. He wanted no more traffic with Magnificent, plus another rough bout with Numwar Nasser. It would suit him just fine if his prize pupil went out on top.

All three men were eminently richer. Tonight, they reaped a financial windfall setting St. Claire and Mitch up for life.

Hiwatha laid his head back on the table, realizing the price he paid for his share. Hiwatha had been hit as never before. His handsome face was now swollen; he tasted blood and felt bile in the pit of his stomach. His lungs had burned with a fire that he still felt nearly two hours later. Though Hiwatha had won, he realized that to fight Magnificent again would be more of the same. Maybe next time it would be him on the short end of the decision.

———— ◉ ————

Magnificent was still in a daze. The fight was close, but he thought he had won the biggest fight of his career. He had hurt Hiwatha several times and was ahead on the scorecards more than once. Still, Magnificent was honest with himself. He heard the turnings fork go off, reverberating in his head. Again, he pulled himself together, closing the eye of his opponent and left raised welts under the other. How could he have lost his championship belt? To make matters worse, while enduring insurmountable pain, he was listening to Charleston embarrass him in front of his entourage.

"Damn, man, you had him beat! You had the chump beat! You might never get this chance again. What's wrong, you can't win a big fight?" asked Charleston in a most acerbic tone.

Oblivious to the other people around them, Charleston continued in his cutting manner, stalking up and down the suite in front of Magnificent, who sat there both hurt and tired.

"You're a damn choke artist, a fucking front-runner. I made your ass. Put you in position to take over boxing, and you punk out," he practically spat at Magnificent as he spoke.

Suddenly Magnificent erupted in anger. In the past, Charleston had been almost like a father who Magnificent trusted emphatically, but lately, he had begun to doubt his motives. Now in his darkest hour, Charleston had the nerve to belittle him.

Magnificent knew he had fought a great fight. He had come within points of victory and established himself as a true champion, even in defeat. Charleston words pricked his pride and heart.

His mind raced back to his conversations with Wendy. He thought of Tony Speaks and how Charleston had treated him after his title loss. He also thought of Tony Francis, whom he knew to be a boxing genius. Francis had built Charleston's pipeline of talent by working diligently every day in the gym. He too was dealt an unsavory hand. With that running through his mind, Magnificent in pain managed to leap to his feet.

"Fuck you, man!" he bellowed at Charleston.

Charleston's head jerked around in disbelief to look at Magnificent's face. Charleston was a fool to actually think he was bigger than life, more significant than Magnificent. He still thought he had the upper hand. Sometimes the devil can truly trick you into thinking that way.

"What the hell did you say?" Charleston asked as if he

was talking to his disobedient child.

"Man, I know you don't care about me or anybody else," Magnificent responded. "You're a fucking clown, dancing for money. You want all the glory and recognition without taking a punch. So, nothing I do will be good enough for you. You made plenty of money off my black ass and everybody else you've touched. So what? I lost a fight, but I've also won many."

Magnificent was right in Charleston's face, looking down at him. None of his handlers bothered to get between them. They wanted to see him kick Charleston's ass. Though they prayed the situation would escalate, they said nothing rather than expose their true feelings in front of Charleston. Magnificent continued shouting.

"If I'm not good enough, we can end this shit right here. Why did you fuck over Speaks and Francis?" he asked the now-silent Charleston.

"Yeah, just what I thought, you punk. You think you're going to do me the same way. I see how you are. You think I'm some kind of Frankenstein monster. Roll me in and out to fight," Magnificent shouted as he stumbled towards Charleston.

"Tell you what. You can hold your breath before I ever work with you again. I know you have beaten me out of money, taking under the table deals with Shapiro behind my back. You son-of-a-bitch. You're a fraud and the worst kind of human. If you died tomorrow, I would spit on your grave. I don't need your ass anymore. Get the fuck out of my life."

Charleston was shouting back, but still being careful. He knew Magnificent had several inches on him, so keeping his distance was necessary. It didn't matter how many rounds Magnificent had fought that night. Charleston suspected he had at least one more left in him. Magnificent grabbed Charleston by the collar and pushed him towards the door.

"You little, motherfucker, get out my room and go get my money. If I weren't in pain right now, I would simply kill you with my bare hands. No one has produced for you like I have, and no one else ever will if I have anything to say about it."

He feinted and faked a punch. Charleston quickly stepped back as if he were going to counter. Magnificent looked at him in disgust as he turned and walked into the bedroom, slamming the door behind him. He did not want his handlers to see the tears that had begun to form in his eyes.

It was now time to swallow his pride and call Wendy. He needed her in his life more than ever. He was finally ready to make a commitment to their relationship, even if it meant marriage. Wendy understood him in ways he could no longer deny. She had been right in her assessment of Charleston and the other people around him.

As Magnificent sat there holding his hand to his bandaged rib cage enduring the pain, it was clear he needed to put his ego aside. He remembered the last words Wendy said to him before slamming the front door to his house.

"I need a man sensitive enough to hold me in his arms

when I've had a bad day. Not just because he wants to have sex. If that's not you, then stay the hell out of my life until you're ready to give me what I deserve. Money and trinkets have little value if traded for true happiness. One day you'll learn these people don't care about you."

Magnificent grabbed his cell phone from the nightstand hoping Wendy would answer. He had so much he finally wanted to say. Most of all, he owed her a sincere apology for the way he had treated her.

Unfortunately, when Wendy heard his voice on the other end, without saying a word, she quickly hung up the phone. When he tried calling back, her phone went directly to voicemail.

Magnificent laid back on the bed in physical and emotional pain. He could still hear his entourage in the other room talking about Charleston, but he remained in deep thought about Wendy. Magnificent was not upset that she wanted nothing to do with him. It was apparent he had disappointed her. For that he was sorry. When his flight arrives in Chicago tomorrow, he needed to resolve this with Wendy face-to-face. He was ready to do whatever it takes to fix the situation.

Immediately, Charleston knew he'd gone too far. He thought about going back into the suite and making peace with Magnificent, except in the back of his mind, he felt covered with the signing of Numwar Nasser. Besides, he had grown to resent Magnificent's sudden independence. The boxer had begun to overshadow the manager. The final straw was when he was made to take less than his customary fifty percent.

"Fuck that ungrateful ignorant buffoon!" Charleston shouted loud enough for Magnificent to hear as he slammed the door of the suite, quickly pulling his cell phone from his pocket.

Charleston started making all the necessary calls to the hometown media to cast aspersion on Magnificent. In this area, he felt he could win because Magnificent was basically a good guy and would not respond. On the other hand, Charleston was a vindictive man, therefore, would continue to go out of his way to discredit Magnificent.

"I'll show this motherfucker," Charleston began to tell his cronies.

He was consumed with himself, not understanding that it was indeed a performer's market. Magnificent was now a household name that no longer needed the services of Charleston.

This was something Charleston would never admit as long as Numwar Nasser was waiting in the wings. He had already left several messages for Antonio and Mitch, hoping to get Nasser a title shot. He would not be leaving the limelight without playing his Ace card.

———————

"This was a very successful promotion," Antonio said as he spoke to Mitch by phone. "We exceeded all my expectations. To tell the truth, I'm going to do another promotion.

At first, I was undecided. You know boxing is a slimy business. These people add a new meaning to the art of the deal."

Antonio laughed as he thought of the experience. Money really meant nothing to him. Not like it did to most people. He liked the thrill of winning at all cost. He loved a challenge.

"You know, Mitch, I'm going to be patient and see what the market can bear. I was wondering what you may have heard about the breakup of Charleston and Magnificent?"

"Well, I hear it was pretty bad. Charleston really said some very derogatory things after the fight and Magnificent walked. I didn't know Charleston was taking fifty percent from him at one point. The good news is I hear he is going to fight again and get himself a new trainer."

Mitch knew deep down that Antonio despised Charleston but was too classy to let that get in the way of making money.

"You know, Charleston is a fool," Antonio stated frankly. "I'll bet he's playing the hunch that Nasser is going to beat your guy, and possibly Magnificent."

"Well, that's a tall order, even for Numwar Nasser," Mitch laughed. "But if the price is right, we will accommodate him. I'm getting used to Charleston's ego trips."

"I guess you're right," responded Antonio. "I've had enough for the day. I'm going to dinner and ponder the thought. Talk to you soon, Mitch."

Mitch hung up the phone, satisfied that he was able to

get his fighter such a hefty purse. He was more pleased that he was now connected to one of the most powerful men in America. Antonio Rosanni was a man who liked to know all the facts. He had the best accountants, lawyers, public relations team, and talent scouts. He also paid them to be the best because he was not cheap or miserly like most millionaires.

The movie king had caught the boxing bug. Antonio didn't want to appear eager to Mitch, but he wanted to put together a match between Jordan and Nasser, with the winner fighting Magnificent. Antonio felt his money could get him around the rematch clause. He had learned a lot from his up-close encounter with the boxing world, but he needed to find a real boxing expert.

Antonio had many contacts within the press, and it was time he called in a few favors. He had thoroughly researched Charleston and found out how he built his empire. He knew he discarded those who could not deal with his style of doing business. His staff had uncovered a "sleeper" in Tony Francis.

Antonio knew Francis was a student of boxing. He became more interested when he found out it was Francis who had built the pipeline of talent and advised Charleston on opponents. Francis could do it all. More importantly, he was clean-living. Untouchable was the way Antonio liked them.

Unfortunately, Antonio wasn't the only person thinking of Francis. At that moment, the object of his thoughts was also being considered by Wonderful Magnificent.

"Man, I really don't want to be involved in boxing any-more," expressed Tony Francis. "I'm really tired of it. I bust-ed my ass for Charleston and what did that get me? What has it gotten you?"

"Now, I have made money," replied Magnificent.

"Yeah, you made money, but look at what you got screwed out of."

"Look, man, I need you to train me. Really, I need you to be more than a trainer. I'm looking for someone I trust to also advise me. Frankly, I trust you," Magnificent said from his heart.

This was the third time Magnificent had called Francis. It was strange because they had known each other for al-most eight years and had never worked together. This didn't mean Francis was not aware of Magnificent's strengths and weaknesses. He had studied Magnificent like an art student would study an Ernie Barnes painting. He had taped all of Magnificent's bouts, including acquiring copies of any ama-teur ones.

In turn, Magnificent had studied him. One day in the gym, he asked Francis to spend some time helping him pol-ish his left-hook. At the time, that was his weakest punch.

Magnificent had watched how Francis magically molded youngsters into national and Olympic champions. He had often talked to Francis about the history of boxing and knew he owned a tape library second to none.

Magnificent knew that some boxers who hadn't worked

with Francis, found his ways strange, but Magnificent understood they were a mixture of discipline and compassion. It was just what he needed. Working with another big-name trainer who wanted to be out front was out of the question. His days of sitting on the sideline were over. For now, he was going to be in the driver's seat.

The biggest hurdle to overcome with Francis was that he had passed the LSAT exam and was trying to get into law school. Francis was annoyed that Magnificent was trying to distract him, and it was working.

Magnificent knew boxing was Francis gift. Fortunately, they both shared one thing in common; getting revenge and retribution from Charleston. Becoming a team would assure that.

"Look, man, I know you can bring out the best in me," continued Magnificent now on his fifth call. "I've already gotten a lawyer, but he doesn't know boxing. You and I will make a good team. If you do this, I will pay for law school. You won't regret it."

That got Francis attention. This time he was listening more carefully. Magnificent's persistence was wearing on him.

"Okay, Wonderful, call me when you're ready to go to work. There's just one thing; I must have the last say on all opponents and dates. I won't work with you under any other conditions. So, tell all your cronies hanging around I'm not there to play games with them. When we go to work, I don't want anything but the best from you and everyone on your team. Is that a deal?"

"Sounds good to me, man," Magnificent replied.

"No, I'm asking you, do we have a deal, because I have no intentions on wasting my time. Before I do that, I'd rather keep doing what I'm doing."

"Yes, man, we have a deal. Is there anything else you want?"

"Yeah, to be paid what I'm worth. I no longer do this shit for glory."

"Man, I'm going to pay you. How do ten percent for training me and five percent for everything else sound to you? I already got someone who will handle the negotiations, and I've agreed to pay for law school. You can't ask for anymore."

This was more than Francis had anticipated. Charleston would have never been as fair. He knew that Magnificent was making him a huge offer.

"Sounds good, I'm on board," agreed Francis.

Magnificent hung up the phone before Francis could say another word. He was glad to finally have worked out a future for himself. The initial feeling of uneasiness was gone.

It had been more than three months since he fought Hiwatha. Now Magnificent was about to start his new journey. He was happy knowing that his and Francis success would now profoundly be dependent on one another.

Chapter 15

WHEN HEAVEN CRIES

Hiwatha was enjoying his layoff from boxing. His only regret was his inability to spend quality time with Caroline. They were at least on speaking terms, even though Caroline still refused to let him back into her heart, and definitely not her bed. It didn't help his cause that Victoria was close to her delivery date, and the issue of paternity still loomed heavily over their relationship.

Victoria had stuck to her story, still insisting that Hiwatha was the father of her child. At this point in his life, Hiwatha no longer cared. He was ready for fatherhood, but just wished it were Caroline who was pregnant. She still held his heart; therefore, he was not open to being emotionally involved with someone else.

Yes, Hiwatha had started to entertain the idea of dating other women, but nothing serious. He had experienced true love, which made him look at life differently. Hiwatha was an old fashion guy that still liked to put pen to paper when it came to intimately exposing his feelings. It allowed him to say on a blank canvas what he may not be brave enough to say in person.

Hiwatha had written Caroline several letters over the past few months but was reluctant to send them. He didn't want to appear desperate. More importantly, Hiwatha respected the position she'd taken regarding his situation with Victoria. He didn't have the right to force her to deal with something she wasn't ready for. Even he at times struggled to deal with Victoria. Still, that did little to comfort him, so reading the letters he'd written to Caroline worked as some sort of self-therapy. A way of keeping her presence in his life. He wasn't ready to give up on the possibility of them eventually being together. At least, for now, they were maintaining a friendship. Hiwatha pulled the latest letter from his drawer and began reading it.

My Darling Caroline,

How I miss your friendship and laughter. I wish I could change what has happened between us. Losing your love is such a high price to pay for my stupid mistake. Please know that I do love you and ask for your forgiveness with all my heart. I know that you feel I will never change, but for your love, I will.

Please understand that I'm offering you happiness. I know that you cannot accept this without a real change of heart. I respect you as a woman and have grown to understand and appreciate the position you have taken. I'm a patient man. I'm not just asking, but willing to wait for you and your forgiveness.

With all my love, your friend,
Hiwatha Jordan

When Hiwatha finished reading the letter, he sat daydreaming about their last night together and remembered her playful spirit. It saddens him to think the situation may not work out between them. Hiwatha started to place the letter in the drawer of his nightstand but was startled by a loud knock on his bedroom door. Hiwatha laid Caroline's letter on the bed. It had to be Franklin or his brother Kyle.

Since the fight, Kyle was spending more time at the house. Hiwatha had grown quite fond of him and even became a regular at Kyle's college football games. This made Kyle somewhat of an instant celebrity, especially since he was already ranked as one of the top college players in the country. When Hiwatha opened his room door, he could tell by the look on Kyle's face, something was seriously wrong.

"Hiwatha, it's Mitch on the phone," Kyle said with a sense of terror in his voice. "Something has happened to Victoria and the baby."

Hiwatha stood frozen in the doorway, attempting to process what Kyle was saying as he shoved the phone in his hand and took a seat on the bed. Hiwatha slowly put the phone to his ear and remained silent as Mitch informed him that Victoria had been in a severe car accident in Miami and was rushed to the hospital. Unfortunately, the doctors were unable to save her. Hiwatha was immediately overwhelmed with emotion and some sense of guilt before his thoughts turned quickly to concern for the baby. He knew Victoria was due any day. He couldn't understand why she was driving alone. Someone else must have been with her.

He started drilling Mitch until he learned the doctors were able to save the baby by cesarean. It was then and there that Hiwatha's world changed.

By the end of their conversation, Hiwatha learned that the hospital was holding the baby under observation. They also needed him to take a paternity test. In case of death, Victoria had told the doctor Hiwatha was the father of her child and wanted him to have custody if anything happened to her. Now the hospital needed proof he was the biological father. Otherwise, they would have no choice but to release the baby to Victoria's family, who was already visibly upset and fighting the release of the child to Hiwatha.

Victoria's mother Maria was aware of Hiwatha's public denial that he was the father, and secondly; she knew the child stood to inherit Victoria's estate. The press had already gotten wind of the story, and soon it would become national news. Mitch finally asked Hiwatha what he wanted to do.

"I don't know, man, give me a minute," he replied. "This is not something that happens every day. I need to think."

Hiwatha was visibly shaken but still tried to hold his composure while attempting to digest the information. He was facing a life-altering decision that was not at the forefront of his mind ten minutes ago. If he refused to go, Victoria's family would get the child, and he could go on with his life, unquestioned. The problem would be if he later had a change of heart and wanted to know the truth. Then there would be a court battle to face. Could he live with not knowing? Hiwatha finally asked Mitch what he should do.

"Be a damn man and go get your child," was Mitch's harsh response. "For God's sake, the woman would have never told the doctors on her deathbed the baby was yours if she didn't believe you were really the father."

"Okay, go ahead and arrange a private flight," Hiwatha responded. "Kyle and I can be at the airport in a couple of hours. Let the doctor know I'm coming."

Mitch knew that even with Hiwatha's money, the whole ordeal could take a few days to resolve. He advised Hiwatha that he could be in Miami for a while.

Hiwatha was ready to do whatever was in the best interest of the child. The magnitude of the situation was beginning to sink in. Before hanging up, Mitch informed Hiwatha that a crowd of reporters were in front of the hospital and the doctor was going to call him back once he was able to arrange a way to get Hiwatha in. "Thanks," Hiwatha said, as he hung up the phone and headed for the shower.

Kyle was still sitting on Hiwatha's bed and heard Hiwatha's commitment to Mitch that they both were going to Miami. Now he was trying to decide what to do. He knew his brother needed him, but he would first have to cancel several of his plans.

As Kyle reached for the phone, he noticed Hiwatha's open letter to Caroline lying on the bed. Out of curiosity, he read the letter. Based on his previous conversations with Hiwatha, Kyle knew the letter would never be sent to Caroline, especially after today.

———— ((●)) ————

Caroline sat in her living room, watching the story of Victoria Santiago unfold on television. It was on every station. Her death was now confirmed, and a large crowd of fans and reporters were gathered outside of the hospital and at the gates of her estate. They were now running a clip of Victoria's family talking to the press as they left the hospital.

"It is a sad occasion for us," her mother Maria said through a river of tears. "This is like living a nightmare, but God has blessed me with a grandson. We're praying for his health, and the moment we can bring him home."

Caroline thought of Hiwatha. How would he handle the situation? Was this really his child? She began to feel guilty about the way she'd been acting. She didn't know Victoria but felt part of the story unfolding before her eyes.

Caroline began questioning whether the position she'd taken with Hiwatha was the right approach. She still loved him. Was it right to keep her distance knowing he probably needed her? For a moment, she thought of being by his side. If nothing, she hoped he would at least try to be there for Victoria's child and family.

———❖———

Hiwatha's stretch pulled up behind the hospital around eight o'clock that evening. It felt like days had passed, not just a few hours. Hiwatha had a lump in his throat and a headache from the stress of dealing with the news of Victoria's death. He was trying to do the right thing, so he continued to push himself.

Inside, Hiwatha was afraid of the truth and how it might affect his life. What changes would he have to make? Would he be happy if the child was his, or disappointed if it was not? All these thoughts were scrambled in his head. He was hoping Victoria's family was not inside the hospital. He couldn't face them right now.

As he and Kyle entered the hospital, they were ushered into a waiting area. A nurse appeared about five minutes later. Not knowing which one was Hiwatha, she spoke to both of them.

"Mr. Jordan, the doctor, will see you now."

Hiwatha stood and followed her down the corridor. He began to have flashbacks of visiting his dad in the hospital. Nathan had been ill off and on for the last two years of his life. Hiwatha was crushed when he finally passed away. Now it felt uncomfortable being in hospitals.

When Hiwatha entered the small examining room, Dr.

Barry Stiles was waiting.

"Good evening, Mr. Jordan," he said with a pleasant voice. "I'm sorry to have to meet you under these difficult circumstances. I'm Dr. Stiles."

He extended his hand to Hiwatha and asked him to take a seat. Hiwatha was nervous and continued to stand.

"I appreciate your support and understanding of the situation, Dr. Stiles. Just let me know what I need to do."

"Right now, we need to establish paternity. That can take a few days depending upon the Lab's backlog. How long will you be in Miami?"

"As long as it takes," Hiwatha quickly replied. "In the best interest of the child, I would like to resolve this as quickly as possible."

"Then we're on the same page," Dr. Stiles replied while putting on latex gloves.

The doctor looked intently at Hiwatha. He was honored to meet him, but as a professional, he would not show it. Instead, Dr. Stiles continued to inform Hiwatha of the current situation.

"If the child is yours, you will have to sign the birth certificate before we can release him to you. Just in case, I would try and come up with a name. It's a boy."

Hiwatha's heart stopped at the thought of possibly having a son. He was not ready to grasp the concept of coming up with a name. The doctor was moving a little too fast. Hiwatha first wanted to know whether the baby was his.

Apparently, Dr. Stiles wasn't having this problem. He was

approaching the situation as if it was a matter of formality.

"You know, Hiwatha, Victoria referred to the child as Sacory."

"Were you her doctor?" Hiwatha asked.

"Yes, I was in the operating room. Victoria pleaded with me and the other doctor on duty to call you in the event something happened to her. She also told me to tell you she loved you."

With that, Hiwatha's eyes filled with tears. Dr. Stiles could see he was visibly shaken. He helped Hiwatha to a seat and asked him if he needed a moment alone.

"Yes, please. I just need a few minutes. I'll be all right in a moment."

Dr. Stiles handed him a box of tissues, removed his latex gloves, and left the room. Hiwatha put his head in his hands and cried. He was ashamed of himself. As many times Victoria had told him she loved him, he never believed her. Due to his feelings for Caroline, Hiwatha had questioned whether the child was his, even though the truth was staring him in the face. It was at these times Hiwatha wished his life wasn't so public.

———— ((●)) ————

Hiwatha spent the next few days in his hotel room with Kyle, unable to eat. He had declined to see the child until after the results of the paternity test.

Victoria's family was now making their case for custody in the media by severely attacking Hiwatha's character and pointing to his initial denial of paternity. Hiwatha had not responded, even though Mitch and Antonio had asked him to. He was overwhelmed with guilt and basically felt her family had a right to their position.

"Mitch, until I know the truth, there is nothing to say," Hiwatha spoke quietly into the phone.

Mitch didn't like that Hiwatha was allowing Victoria's family to take front and center. He was thinking of the loss of his own two children.

"Mitch, listen, if this is my son, I will fight like hell for custody if it comes to that, but I spoke with Dr. Stiles. According to him, if the results are in my favor, the family doesn't stand a chance in court. I should know something by morning. If the child is mine, we'll be on the next flight out of here. I've already arranged for Ms. Reed to fly down with everything I need to take the baby back to Virginia Beach. I can handle things from here."

Mitch was still concerned but decided to back off. Hiwatha was right. They should wait for the results. It was no use going to battle with Victoria's parents if they didn't have to.

———((●))———

The next morning, the hospital called and Hiwatha could barely contain himself. The results were positive, and Dr. Stiles wanted him to come to the hospital immediately to get his child. Victoria's family was in the lobby with the media, causing a big scene with the hospital staff.

Hiwatha quickly hung up the phone and had Kyle call downstairs to get the car brought around front. Ms. Reed was thrilled to have a baby in the house and began gathering items in a duffel bag to take to the hospital.

When they exited the elevators, they had to push through the reporters in the lobby and outside the hotel. Flashbulbs were going off in their faces, and the television cameras were rolling. Several cars containing additional press followed their route to the hospital.

When they arrived, the entrance to the hospital was packed with more media. Victoria's fans and supporters were also waiting out front. They shouted at Hiwatha through the limo's tinted windows and threw several eggs and trash at the car. Hiwatha couldn't wait for this ordeal to be over.

Inside the hospital, Victoria's family was still waiting in the lobby. Several security guards met Hiwatha around back and escorted him to a room near the nursery. He sat there for a moment until Dr. Stiles entered the room with a nurse holding the baby.

Hiwatha's world stopped as the nurse pulled back the blanket and handed the baby to him. His eyes again, filled with tears as he pressed the baby to his chest. He was overcome with emotion.

"Mr. Jordan, we have some paperwork for you to sign. Have you thought of a name?"

Dr. Stiles asked as if he were the proud father.

"Yes, Sacory Nathaniel Jordan," Hiwatha said with tears

still in his eyes.

"Yes, that's nice. That's really nice," Dr. Stiles replied as he laid the paperwork on the table.

Hiwatha knew what needed to be done before leaving the hospital. After thinking about it for several days, it was time to speak personally with Victoria's parents. They needed to know that he was genuinely sorry about Victoria's death. Meeting them face to face at a time like this would be difficult. He felt guilty for the way he had treated Victoria. She really didn't deserve that.

Now with her death, he had to turn the focus to the future of his son. He needed to know what part her parents wanted to play in their grandson's life.

Hiwatha asked Kyle and Ms. Reed to take Sacory back to the hotel and prepare for their flight. Hiwatha waited until they left before completing the paperwork. He then asked Dr. Stiles to arrange a meeting for him with Victoria's parents, who were still in the Lobby, making their custody case with the media.

Dr. Stiles asked Hiwatha was he sure about meeting them in light of the current situation. Hiwatha felt in his heart; it was the right thing to do.

"It has to be done before I leave the city," Hiwatha explained. "It would not be right to leave without giving my condolences. No matter what I'm going through, I'm leaving with a son, a blessing I don't believe I deserve. They've lost a daughter, and I can't deny that this is their grandson. I'm sure Vicky would want me to do this."

Dr. Stiles shook his head in approval and left the room. He soon returned with Mr. and Mrs. Santiago and then excused himself. He knew the situation could potentially be ugly. It was apparent Victoria's mother Maria was quite upset.

"How dare you come down here and take my grandson," Maria said with disgust. "That is all we have left of our daughter."

"Mrs. Santiago, I am deeply sorry about the loss of Victoria. I know how much she meant to you and your husband."

Hiwatha barely got the words out of his mouth before Maria slapped him open-handed across the face. Hiwatha instinctively stepped back. It was now obvious where Victoria got her temper. He stared at Maria for a moment. Through her anger, Hiwatha saw the hurt in her eyes and felt he probably deserved that one.

"How dare you say you're sorry," Maria said, practically spitting on Hiwatha. "You, no-good bastard. My daughter loved you, and you treated her like trash. So, don't stand here and act like you have any remorse. You can go to hell."

Hiwatha took another two steps back to keep his distance. Mr. Santiago had just grabbed his wife to stop Maria from lunging in Hiwatha's direction. Though Victoria's father agreed with his wife's position, he continued to restrain her so he could hear what Hiwatha had to say.

"I don't give a damn what he has to say," Maria shouted, pointing directly at Hiwatha's face. "We intend to fight tooth and nail, you hear me!" she screamed.

Hiwatha slowly raised his eyebrow. He had no intention of going through a court battle with them. Sacory was his son, and nothing was going to change that. Hiwatha was a man with not only position but money. Mrs. Santiago would soon find out that he too was prepared to fight for his son.

Hiwatha proceeded to give Victoria's parents two options; money or an opportunity to be proper grandparents to his son. If they chose money, he was prepared to write them a check then and there and disappear. If they wanted to be a part of their grandson's life, he would welcome their help in raising Sacory.

In Hiwatha's mind, Victoria had already made her decision when she asked the doctors to contact him. He would not press her parents for an immediate decision.

"You son-of-a-bitch!" Maria shouted. "I can't believe you! Who in the hell do you think you are? You think we're some kind of trash? You think we don't have money? We don't need your money. We want our grandson, so just take your uppity black ass back to whatever hole you crawled out of. I don't care how much money you have, you're still black, and in this country that makes you a nigger."

"Is that what you think of your grandson?" Hiwatha asked with the look of shock on his face.

He paused briefly to collect his thoughts. They had just lost their daughter. It was not his intention to insult them, but it was clear that the conversation was going in the wrong direction. Hiwatha took a deep breath before continuing.

"Look, I know both of you are upset over the loss of Vicky. Believe it or not, so am I. If there is anything I can do, please let me know."

With that statement, Maria reached around her husband again in an attempt to slap him. Hiwatha quickly turned his head and stepped back. Like a warrior getting ready for battle, Maria took off her shoe and hurled it at Hiwatha as he turned to leave. Hiwatha ducked and hurried for the door. This meeting was over.

"I have to go," he said softly. "This is not going well. Call and let me know what you decide. Again, I am very, very sorry."

He held out his hand to leave them his business card. Maria was now uncontrollable, and her husband was exasperated trying to hold her back. He asked Hiwatha to leave his business card on the counter. Gladly was Hiwatha's thought.

When Hiwatha stepped outside the door, he was happy to see two security guards waiting. He asked for their help in avoiding the media. They informed him that Dr. Stiles had a car waiting for him in the back of the hospital. Hiwatha loosened his tie, then unbuttoned his shirt. He was relieved this ordeal was finally over.

Chapter 16

THAT'S THE WAY LOVE GOES

"I'm not taking your shit anymore! You must think you're dealing with one of your groupies! If that's the case, then you are sadly mistaken!"

Once again, Theresa was relentless and determined to have her way with Charleston.

"Get out of my house right now!" she shouted. "I don't want to hear one more damn lie from you Charleston!"

"Please, baby, please listen to me," he begged. "You know I love you more than anything."

Charleston knew Theresa would not wait forever no matter how much she loved him. Unfortunately, now was not a good time for him. The IRS was at his door, and his wife Danielle had also taken a more profound interest in his business affairs.

"Baby, I've got all types of problems," Charleston continued. "So, bear with me. Please, just give me a little more time to straighten this out. I'll make it up to you once I get Nasser his title shot. I'm going to divorce Danielle so we can be together."

Charleston obviously thought this information would bring Theresa to her knees, but his words now seemed to have no effect. Instead, Theresa picked up a blue lamp from her table and hurled it at Charleston just missing his head.

"You lying bastard!" she shouted. "You are a no-good motherfucker! Get the hell out of here!"

Charleston tried to embrace her, but she slapped him so hard across the face it sounded like a small-caliber pistol. He slowly backed away and walked out of his lover's home. As he drove down the street, he dialed her from his cell phone.

"Don't be this way with me. Please don't be this way. I love you," Charleston said, pretending to sob into the phone.

Theresa slammed the phone down without even responding to his plea.

———— ◈ ————

The papers were now full of stories about the split between Charleston and Magnificent. Charleston's attacks on Magnificent had been vicious. At every turn, he belittled him. Magnificent chose not to take part in it. Instead, he was talking to the press about his future in boxing. The more he spoke about his new partnership with Tony Francis, the more furious Charleston became. He felt both of them had betrayed him. The situation was making him more desperate by the minute. He was worried about the IRS audit and called Shapiro Einstein to borrow money. Shapiro didn't mind giving up thirty thousand here or there. In his mind, he was buying future leverage against Charleston. When it came time to promote a bout between Magnificent and Nasser, Shapiro planned to be front and center.

Charleston was trying to borrow so much money that even the underworld figures that had obliged him in the past were now laughing. In the end, they would still come through for him as long as he continued to give them ringside seats, access to his fighters, and other connections.

One of his moneylenders was a man by the name of Ruben Savala. He was a complete sucker. Savala loved boxing because he was able to launder money. He and Charleston traveled all over the country with their women in tow. Charleston had convinced Savala to buy a gym in Arizona and throw money behind Red Ink Boxing Promotions.

Charleston still owed Savala close to four-hundred thousand dollars, but he got lucky. Savala suddenly died of a blood clot taking Charleston's debt with him.

This pattern would occur again. A local drug kingpin by the name of Lancey Howard also was a benefactor of the now financially strapped Charleston. He was a flashy type of guy that drove expensive cars, wore beautiful suits and lots of jewelry. To legitimize himself, he wanted to manage boxers.

Charleston was looking to unload one of his bad investments. He had a fading junior welterweight by the name of Hector Machado who Tony Francis had advised him against signing.

Machado had excellent skills but didn't like to fight. He purposely stayed injured. Still, smooth-talking Charleston was able to maneuver him into a top contender spot for the junior lightweight title. Machado, who had floored champion Billy Marks in the third round, was suddenly pulverized for the next seven rounds. Then in the eleventh round, Machado was knocked out, but tells everyone he quit.

Charleston wanted to unload Machado in the worst way. He sold his contract to Lancey Howard for twenty thousand dollars. Never mind that Charleston already owed Lancey one-hundred thousand dollars.

Lancey became very close to Charleston. He even had dinner at Charleston home on numerous occasions. Unfortunately, this friendship didn't last the test of time, either. Lancey was assassinated gang-style in public. When Hector Machado learned of the murder, he called Charleston who made sure the conversation was brief.

"Look, man, I'm not your manager anymore. I wish you the best, but I'm busy right now," Charleston said abruptly ending the call. Once again, Charleston changed his number.

———— ((●)) ————

Mitch was trying desperately to reach Charlotte. She had not answered his messages in two weeks. Mitch was worried and suspected that something was wrong. The situation with Hiwatha and Victoria had brought him back to reality. Back to the day, he heard the news of his children's death.

Mitch stood trembling as he phoned Charlotte's sister Avery in Los Angeles to check if she had heard from

Charlotte. When Avery also confirmed she hadn't spoken with Charlotte, Mitch swallowed his pride and asked for her help.

Avery listened with compassion as Mitch told her the details of their separation. Towards the end of their conversation, Avery told Mitch to make arrangements for her to fly to Virginia Beach by the end of the week. That would give her time to make sure the kids could stay with their grandparents. She then tried to assure Mitch they would find Charlotte.

"Mitch, it's no use in telling you not to worry. My sister has been a little crazy lately. Even I know that. Still, it's not like her not to call. Something else could be wrong. Let's pray; she's all right."

Avery knew more than she was willing to tell Mitch. Though she was genuinely concerned, Avery didn't want to betray her sister's confidence. She was hoping Charlotte hadn't gone too far with Roscoe.

Avery sensed upon meeting Roscoe that he was using Charlotte and warned her to stay away from him. Since her previous attempts had failed, this time she would insist Charlotte go back to Mitch and leave Roscoe alone. Avery needed to find a way to reach Charlotte before Mitch.

<hr>

Mitch hung up the phone and tried to compose himself. He had a meeting scheduled with Hiwatha in the morning, but his gut feeling told him Charlotte desperately needed him. To avoid dealing with the loss of their children, Mitch had buried himself in boxing, telling Charlotte it was for their future. Now he realized how selfish he'd been. Outside of arranging therapy, Mitch hadn't been there to help Charlotte deal with her grief. In the morning he planned to tell Hiwatha he was taking time off to spend with Charlotte. It was time to seriously work on their marriage.

———————⊸«❰❱»⊷———————

With all these thoughts swirling around in his head, Mitch had a restless sleep. While in the shower, he began to rehearsed what he would say to Hiwatha. He hadn't told Hiwatha about his separation from Charlotte. Now with Hiwatha having just arrived home with the baby and the upcoming fight with Pete Sherry, Mitch began to have second thoughts. He hit the bathroom mirror with his fist in frustration. The glass shattered and fell to the floor and sink. There I go again, thinking about everybody else but Charlotte, he thought to himself. When does my life become important?

After a few cups of coffee, Mitch pulled himself together and made the drive to Hiwatha's house. As he entered the door, you could feel the excitement from the staff. There was a new baby in the house.

Kyle greeted Mitch as he ran through the Foyer with a baby bottle in his hand.

"Hey Mitch, hold on!" he said, sprinting up the stairs. "I've got to give Hiwatha this bottle. I'll tell him you're here."

Mitch walked into the Study to wait. That was the one room in Hiwatha's house he loved. They'd strategized and made many deals there. Some of which had made them both very rich.

Mitch took a seat behind Hiwatha's desk. There was a full picture window that gave him a view of the lake. His thoughts were of Charlotte and their children. Six months ago, he made more money than he'd ever had in life, but to Mitch, it was not worth losing his marriage. He couldn't remember a time since the loss of his children that he'd felt so depressed. Reality lay upon him like a wet blanket. Still, he felt his soul embracing it.

Mitch didn't bother to acknowledge Hiwatha as he strode into the Study, wearing white linen pants and match-ing shirt. Hiwatha had a glow on his face. The excitement of having his son was in the sound of his voice.

"Hey Mitch, I thought you were coming upstairs to see the baby. He's beautiful, man, which means he doesn't look like me."

As Hiwatha came closer to the desk, he noticed Mitch did not move. He paused for a moment, suddenly realizing that something was wrong. Mitch back was to him, and his head was in his hands facing the window.

Hiwatha noticed the bloodstained bandages and be-came more concerned as he stepped around the desk to get a better view. Mitch didn't look like himself. Whatever was going on, Hiwatha sensed it was serious. Though Mitch worked for him, Hiwatha still respected Mitch as a friend and father figure. He put his hand on Mitch's shoulder to comfort him.

"Mitch, what's wrong?" Hiwatha asked with concern in his voice. "What happened to your hand? Talk to me, man. You don't look so good."

Mitch did not respond. Instead, he continued to stare out the window, not knowing what to say, or where to begin.

"Mitch, can I get you something to drink? Maybe you need to lay down. You're worrying me. What do you need me to do?" Hiwatha pleaded.

"I need some time off," Mitch finally said with sadness in his voice. "I'm exhausted and need to take care of some personal things."

Hiwatha remembered moments like these with his father. His dad had raised him alone. During his childhood, they had faced many difficulties together. Hiwatha still missed him every day. He thought of these things as he answered Mitch.

"Sure man, take all the time you need. My tune-up fight with Pete Sherry isn't for another eight weeks. I still got another week before I start training. St. Claire and I can handle it."

Mitch lifted his head as tears slowly filled his eyes. Hiwatha rested his hand on Mitch's knee. He wanted him to know it would be all right, but first Hiwatha wanted to know what was wrong. How could he help him? Hiwatha brought up the fight with Pete Sherry again.

"I'll postpone the fight if necessary. I don't have to fight this guy. I'm only doing it because you and Antonio put it together."

Due to the agreement Mitch had already made with Antonio, he didn't want to interrupt business.

"No, don't do that," Mitch responded. You and St. Claire continue to move forward. I've got to find Charlotte. I haven't been able to reach her in weeks. I don't know what I will do if something has happened to her."

Mitch began pouring his heart out, even telling Hiwatha how he truly felt the day he lost his children. Hiwatha thought of his son as he listened to the pain in Mitch's voice. Though it had only been a few days, he couldn't imagine his life without Sacory.

Hiwatha helped Mitch move to the sofa facing the expansive fireplace. He could see how worried Mitch was about Charlotte. Still, Hiwatha was uncertain how involved he should get; therefore, he just continued to sit and listen.

Hiwatha didn't understand how Mitch could be so smart in business, but blind in other aspects of his life. There should have been some clues, even he knew what Charlotte had been up to? How could Mitch not know? Her sexual encounters were no secret. Many people had seen her in the company of Roscoe Evertoni. The guy had a reputation for being a playboy and using rich women.

After an hour of conversation, Hiwatha finally went over to his desk and retrieved the large envelope containing photos of Charlotte and Roscoe given to him a year earlier by Floyd Nash. Hiwatha hadn't even bothered to look at the pictures. They were in his possession in the event Charlotte ever tried to blackmail him again. Though Hiwatha was reluctant to get involved, he knew Mitch desperately needed answers.

"Mitch, I probably should have given you this a long time ago, but I thought you knew what was going on with Charlotte," Hiwatha said with the sound of hesitation in his voice. "Since you never discussed intimate details of your marriage, I assumed you wanted to keep your relationship private."

Though he had just told Mitch a lie, Hiwatha nervously handed him the envelope hoping to not raise any suspicion regarding the extent of his own relationship with Charlotte. Mitch looked strangely at Hiwatha as he took the envelope to open it. As the graphic pictures of Charlotte's life unfolded, Mitch put his hand over his mouth in disbelief.

"Who is this guy?" he asked Hiwatha. "He's got Charlotte using drugs. What the hell is going on here?"

Mitch thought for a moment. It was now coming to him. That's why so much money was missing from their accounts. Could that be why Hiwatha was having Charlotte followed? How could Hiwatha have known that? Mitch wanted answers and began to question Hiwatha.

"Why didn't you give this to me before?" Mitch asked in anger. "This is my wife, for God's sake."

Hiwatha began apologizing to Mitch. He didn't want to jeopardize their friendship any further than he already had, so he kept telling Mitch to not involve him. It was their marriage, not his.

"Well, you were involved enough to have my wife followed," Mitch responded. "What was that about?"

"I don't know, man. I was afraid of your reaction to me checking up on Charlotte. It really was not my business, but I heard things. People talk, so I did it out of concern for you."

"Afraid of my reaction, or afraid to tell me what the fuck is really going on here? I'm not stupid. I know you, Hiwatha. You would never have Charlotte followed unless you were protecting your best interest."

"Look, man, you are my best interest," Hiwatha snapped. "You wanted to know about Charlotte, now you do. Isn't that enough?"

"No, that's not enough," Mitch said as he got up from the sofa. "You see, I've busted my ass for you."

"Yeah, and you've gotten paid very well for busting your ass. So, don't give me that shit," Hiwatha responded in defense.

"Is that all you think about...money? I don't give a damn about money right now. I'm standing here talking to you about my wife, and I deserve the fucking truth from you. Don't play games with me. You see, I'm not one of your sorry ass flunkies."

Mitch held his hand to his head for a moment, trying to think of what to say next. He was angry and sensed Hiwatha was not being completely honest with him. Mitch had witnessed how Hiwatha treated women. He slowly walked towards Hiwatha with a stern look on his face.

"I guess in your world you just love 'em and leave 'em. Isn't that what Caroline thinks about you? Isn't that what Vicky thought?"

Mitch, you don't know what you're saying," Hiwatha said as he backed away from Mitch. "You're just upset. Let's concentrate on finding Charlotte."

"You son-of-a-bitch! Did you sleep with my wife?"

"Mitch, please, I don't believe you're asking me that."

Mitch looked in Hiwatha's eyes because he wanted to know the truth. He couldn't believe he was asking Hiwatha that question either. Still, he knew there was more to the story. Mitch grabbed the envelope from the sofa before leaving.

"I'm done!" he shouted. "You and me, Mr. Playboy, we're through! I don't need a client or friend like you!"

"Mitch, wait, man, it's not what you think. I am your friend. You're like a father to me."

Mitch rushed to open the front door. He turned to take one last look at Hiwatha.

"Well, I guess you just have to get another daddy. I'm gone."

Hiwatha grabbed Mitch by the arm in an attempt to stop him from leaving. He couldn't afford to lose him right now. Mitch was his rock. No one would protect him with such devotion.

"Wait, Mitch, don't leave like this. We can work this out. Let me help you. We're a team. I would never do anything to hurt you."

At that moment, Hiwatha felt like a stranger to Mitch.

"I want you to remember something. There is no loyalty in boxing. You know it, and now I know for certain. So, go ahead and find yourself another ass kisser. You fighters usually, do."

As the door slammed, silence fell in the Foyer. Hiwatha stood there, unable to move. He wasn't prepared to lose Mitch. Hopefully, this would eventually blow over.

——⫸«(◉)»⫷——

Over the next few weeks, Hiwatha remained heartbroken and distraught over the situation with Mitch. St. Claire sensed something was wrong. Hiwatha was merely going through the motions in training.

St. Claire was aware of the problem between Hiwatha and Mitch. Though Hiwatha was trying to take care of it, Mitch would not answer his calls or the door when Hiwatha dropped by. During his last visit, Hiwatha decided to leave Mitch a letter explaining everything. He owed his friend no less than the truth.

Now, on fight night, Hiwatha seemed listless and fatigued. St. Claire didn't want his champion to get hurt, but Hiwatha had just been briefly stunned by journeyman Pete Sherry's left-hook.

It was Hiwatha's first bout since his epic battle with Magnificent, and he wasn't concentrating on the fight. His rhythm was off, and he was a step slower. As the bell rang to end the second round, St. Claire went to work.

"Look, man, you're falling short with the jab. Feint this clown's socks off and get your left-hand working. What's the matter with you? Are you listening to me? We got to win this, man. I need you to shoot the right-hand and then cut loose with the left-hook. Take your time. Let's go to work. You're the champ, aren't you?"

St. Claire was looking straight in Hiwatha's eyes. He could tell something was wrong but was hesitant to stop the fight since it looked like Hiwatha could still pull it off. St. Claire continued to speak as Hiwatha assure him he would be ok.

"Well, show me you're still the boss with the hot sauce. Don't let this man take another round from you. This guy is a bum, so treat him like one."

Hiwatha shook his head in agreement. He thought of Sacory and Kyle sitting ringside and swiftly as a carpenter fitting a door for its hinge, he went to work quickly pumping two hard left-jabs into Sherry's face. He feinted a right-hand and doubled up on the jab again. He then crossed a hard right-hand and followed it with a crisp left hook to the ear of his slightly stunned opponent.

Hiwatha then slid to his right side and cut loose a left-hook, right-hand, left-hook, right-uppercut, left-hook, over-hand-right combination that nearly decapitated Sherry. His body appeared to fall in sections. Blood trickled from his right ear.

The referee reached the count of six before Sherry started to get up. As he rose, Sherry told the referee he was all right. Like a surgeon putting in the final stitches on his patient, Hiwatha placed his own fistic touches. He slammed a wicked left hook to the side of a weakened Sherry.

As Hiwatha retrieved his left hand from his bent-over opponent's side, he sent a digging left-uppercut to his chin then followed with a right uppercut to the jaw and a whistling left-hook to the body. Sherry was out before he hit the canvas. The crowd was still cheering in the background as Hiwatha spoke into the commentator's microphone.

"I'll be glad to fight Magnificent, Nasser or both! I'm ready, so bring them on! They don't want to mess with me!"

Hiwatha spoke with an arrogance that was unbecoming of him. St. Claire was now sure there was something wrong with Hiwatha. They would have to settle the situation with Mitch. It was definitely affecting Hiwatha, whether or not he wanted to admit it.

Tony Francis was at his home just outside of Washington, D.C. watching the fight on television. He was taking notes and noticed that Hiwatha was now vulnerable to right-hands. He saw him several times drop it while throwing left-hooks. The discoloration from the fight with Magnificent was no longer in Hiwatha's right eye, and the slight swelling in his right cheekbone was gone.

Francis knew Hiwatha was still number one but felt that Magnificent could take him. He also wanted an opportunity to prove to Charleston that he was the best.

As Theresa sat on the beach in Antigua, she was livid with Charleston and thinking of several ways to get even. A month earlier, she had attended a fight between Numwar Nasser and David Fontaine. Charleston didn't allow her to attend major fights involving his fighters. He said it was too risky. Theresa sensed he was still stalling. For a long time, she had gone along with Charleston, but her ego could no longer stand by and warm his bench. In her mind, life would be complete if she could have him.

Theresa was thinking about how she had acquired two ringside tickets from Dr. Andrew McIntosh, head of the state athletic commission and another of her suitors. For weeks she had put Charleston on hold. He was incensed and had called several times to say so.

"Why are you treating me like this," he would ask harshly. "I've been good to you, and still, you treat me like a dog. I ought to kick your ass," Charleston threatened.

Theresa laughed. She knew Charleston would never harm her. She held the phone away from her ear as he continued.

"You'd better not be seeing anyone. I'm the one paying your damn bills. Don't forget, I gave you that house, and I'll take it back if I have to."

"I'm going to do whatever I please, whenever I please and with whom I please," Theresa responded.

"What in the hell does that mean?" Charleston asked.

"You know damn well what that means. If you mess with me, Mr. Orlando, you will regret it. Now you don't forget that. I can take my shit back too."

With that fatal comment, Theresa hung up in his face. Charleston had no idea Theresa was planning to attend the Nasser / Fontaine bout with a girlfriend from New York. The night of the fight Theresa spotted Charleston's wife Danielle in the front row opposite them and was determined to make her presence known.

Theresa was dressed in a blue velvet dress, exposing her shoulders so she could show off her most exquisite jewelry. She was beautiful, and it was confirmed by the compliments she'd received.

Theresa never let her eyes waver from Danielle. To the point, she missed Numwar Nasser's sixth-round destruction of David Fontaine. Theresa was there to make a statement, thereby forcing Charleston to make one too.

Dr. McIntosh had also given Theresa a post-fight press credential, and she was now waiting in the press conference area. She saw Danielle standing at the bottom of the short flight of stairs leading to the stage. Charleston was leaving the podium and about to take her arm when Theresa decided to approach.

"Good evening, Charleston," Theresa said in a friendly tone. "Is this your wife?"

Theresa extended her hand to Danielle, who did not respond. Charleston stood there, stunned, thinking of his next move. Before he could speak, Theresa continued.

"I'm finally glad to meet you, Danielle. It is Danielle, right?"

"Do I know you," Danielle asked?

"No, you don't know me, but you should. I'm the one who has been sharing my bed with your husband for over two years. The one he claims to be leaving you for. Why don't you tell her the truth Charleston, while we're all standing here?

Theresa spoke like a presidential candidate while Danielle tried desperately to remain calm. She finally threw her head back and looked directly at her husband.

"Yes, Charleston, why don't you tell me?"

Though Charleston had a lump in his throat the size of Texas, he was not going to tolerate being one-upped by Theresa. Today he intended to shut her performance down without a scene.

"Look, baby, I don't know this woman. She's obviously crazy."

Charleston looked directly at Theresa. His eyes were pleading with her to back off.

"Look here, lady, I'm a happily married man," Charleston said as if he didn't know Theresa. "I have no idea who you are or what you're talking about. You may have slept with one of my fighters, but not me."

Charleston grabbed Danielle's arm to make a hasty retreat to his hotel suite. Danielle's eyes remained fixed on Theresa as Charleston pulled her from the room. Theresa continued delivering her menacing smile. They both knew the truth had come to light.

Once inside their hotel suite, Danielle cursed Charleston severely as she packed her bags to leave. She knew without a shred of doubt; their marriage was not only broken but finally over.

Theresa, on the other hand, was not finished. Her lover had rejected her in public, and now he would pay.

As she sat on the beach in Antiqua taking in the sun, she went over the names, dates, dollar amounts and recordings of her conversations with Charleston. Theresa had also eavesdropped on conversations Charleston had with several money-lenders.

Charleston had been foolish to let his guard down around Theresa knowing her connections extended to law enforcement at the state and federal levels, some of whom would love to do her a favor. Theresa was sure the Internal Revenue Service would want to know why all those cash loans were never reported. Where was the money trail leading to their payback? She knew Charleston had funneled money through his company Elite Boxing, Inc.

Theresa contacted her long-time friend Donald Bogle who had once worked for the federal government. He now was an investigator with the Justice Department. At Theresa's, insistence, Detective Bogle had Charleston under surveillance. Every inch of his business dealings and phone conversations were being recorded. Theresa was a woman without remorse.

Over the following months, Charleston would feel as if he were walking under a proverbial cloud. As Theresa took in the view of the beach, she continued to smooth on suntan lotion, knowing even the slick Mr. Orlando could not escape her spider web. Now all she needed to do was allow the pieces to fall into place.

———⸺«(●)»⸺———

Danielle sat on the bed, crying. Charleston had gone too far this time, and even he knew it. As he reached for Danielle, she pulled away and continued sobbing. "Look, baby, it won't happen again. I promise." It was a half-hearted apology, and Danielle knew it was a lie. Their relationship was over. "Don't cry, baby. It'll be okay. You'll see. We can get pass this. That woman is nothing to me."

Danielle jumped from the bed in anger. Her sudden movement startled Charleston. Although she was still crying, Danielle broke out into one long stretch of laughter. It seemed to come from the depths of her soul.

"You fool, Charleston," she began. "These tears are not for you. These tears cover the road I've traveled in my life. They represent the mountains I've climbed and the freedom I'm going to have without you. I've endured some shit being married to you, so these tears are for the life I've put on hold, the two children I lost in childbirth and the two I bore for you and raised. I have had to endure degrading looks from my friends and family because they know my husband's a whore."

"Now you wait one damn minute," Charleston shouted as he rose from the bed.

"No, you son-of-a-bitch, you wait a damn minute. You're leaving this house just as sure as my name is Danielle Orlando."

"I'm not going anywhere," Charleston shouted back. "I built this shit. I made it possible for you and our children to have a good life. If it weren't for me, you'd be in the projects with your relatives."

Danielle began shaking her head. She had lost all respect for Charleston. So deep were her wounds, she was willing to kill him if she had to.

"You don't want to be here, Charleston. This place is no longer your home. If you eat one more meal here, I'll poison you. I am no longer in love with you. We cannot live under the same roof anymore. I want you out of this house, right now. If your car is still parked in my driveway come morning, I will burn it. Do not call me, and do not ever come back to this house again. When these tears are gone, I'll be finished with you."

"I'm not going, anywhere," Charleston shouted. "If anybody's leaving you can bet it's you. This is my shit. You haven't brought a damn thing. If it weren't for me, you'd be on welfare still living in the projects with your momma. Not wearing furs and diamond rings. Getting your hair and nails done at upscale salons. Who do you think paid for that fancy car you drive?"

Danielle had heard enough. She reached into her nightstand drawer and retrieved the forty-five-caliber pistol she'd recently purchased for the occasion. She stood and pointed it directly at Charleston.

"What the fuck are you doing?" he asked as he moved toward the doorway with his hands up in the air.

"What does it look like I'm doing?" Danielle asked. "If you don't leave this house right now, I'm going to blow your damn head off. Now back up! Get what you can carry and get the hell out. If you so much as say one more word, I'll shoot you dead in the eye. Then I'm gonna step over your dead body like the piece of trash you are."

She cocked the gun and aimed at him with both hands. Charleston stood frozen in the doorway for a moment. He could not believe his life was about to change at this very moment.

Danielle continued to point the gun at Charleston. The look in her eyes confirmed she was willing to shoot. Danielle tilted her head to the side, then hunched her shoulders like she was playing a starring role in a movie.

"Don't worry, baby, God will forgive me," she said in a purposeful tone. "He never said anything was wrong with killing the devil."

With that, Danielle fired one shot, hitting the top of the doorway. Charleston ran through the hallway, down the flight of stairs and out the front door. He didn't stop until his car was at least a block away.

Chapter 17

WITH TEARS IN MY EYES

The curtains were drawn. The hospital room was dark. The patient was totally alone and in excruciating pain. Their head was wrapped tightly with white bandages. Even though the medication was starting to wear off, the patient didn't make a sound. Instead, they were listening to the jumbled mix of thoughts swirling around in their head.

The promoter had canceled the scheduled title defense against Justin Cooper. The fight was just a stepping stone to the proposed rematch against Wonderful Magnificent. Unfortunately, it was derailed by unforeseen circumstances. A week before the bout Hiwatha came back to the corner after a sparring round and told St. Claire he was experiencing fuzziness and blurred vision.

"I'm through for the day, man," he told St. Claire. "I don't feel well. I don't understand what's wrong with me."

St. Claire was concerned. Hiwatha had never cut their training short. He always left that decision to St. Claire.

On the drive back to the hotel, Hiwatha was quiet. His

body was telling him something was seriously wrong. He began to worry about Sacory. What would happen if he were not there to care for him?

When they arrived at the hotel, Hiwatha instructed St. Claire to immediately arrange a private plane back to Virginia. Then call Antonio and cancel the fight.

"What's wrong, Hiwatha?" asked St. Claire. "I've never seen you act like this."

"It's my head. I'm in pain. I feel dizzy, and my vision is blurred. That's not normal. Maybe I'm just tired, but I don't think I should fight."

St. Claire did as he was instructed. Antonio was not happy but also became concerned about Hiwatha. He told St. Claire to make flight arrangements for Washington, D.C. Antonio had a friend, Dr. Marvin Webster, who was a brain specialist at the John Hopkins Hospital. He wanted Hiwatha to be checked out by him immediately. St. Claire got off the phone and began making reservations for a private flight.

Hiwatha was in his hotel room, struggling to complete the task of packing his luggage. When St. Claire finished making their flight arrangements, he came in to inform Hiwatha there had been a change in plans.

"Hiwatha, we are not going to Virginia," St. Claire said with concern. "Antonio is making arrangements for you to see a specialist in Washington, D.C. I think this is the best decision for you. Right now, we both need answers. You can't go home, not knowing. We don't know if this is something serious that needs to be taken care of immediately."

Hiwatha sat on the bed in surrender, then nodded his head in agreement. He would contact Kyle an have him go by the house to check on Sacory and Ms. Reed.

Later that night, Hiwatha and St. Claire landed at National Airport, where a car was waiting to take them directly to John Hopkins Hospital. Dr. Webster was there ready to examine Hiwatha, take x-rays, and perform a brain scan. He called in three other specialists to look at the results, and they all confirmed his diagnosis. There was a small mass at the front of his brain. It may have started initially from the swelling caused by a previous injury. They were not entirely sure but did know it had to be removed as soon as possible.

When Dr. Webster explained the diagnosis to Hiwatha, he was nervous and scared. All he could think of was his son. Who would be there for him? Hiwatha had gone through life, not fearing death. How could he? His profession demanded you put your life on the line each time you entered the ring. Every great fighter knew there was no defensive line in front of him. No Running Back coming up the middle, and no one to pass the ball to. When a fighter entered the ring, he was alone. Hiwatha was a warrior that never considered the consequences of death. Now, with Sacory in his life, he had the best reason of all to live.

As Hiwatha lifted his head, Dr. Webster could see the fear in his eyes. Hiwatha needed answers...answers he did not have.

"How serious is this?" Hiwatha asked in a slow, deliberate voice.

"If it's not cancer, we can remove it, and you can go on with your life, except I would suggest you find a profession outside of boxing," answered Dr. Webster.

"It's too soon to talk about recovery time until we know exactly what we're dealing with. Thank God you didn't go through with the fight. Be patient, and we should know more after the surgery."

Dr. Webster admitted Hiwatha to the hospital then began preparations for his surgery. Hiwatha had St. Claire phone Kyle to tell him the doctor recommended surgery and he wanted Kyle, Ms. Reed, and Sacory to board the next flight to Washington, D.C.

"Were you able to reach Kyle?" Hiwatha asked St. Claire. "I will not go through with the surgery until I see my son."

"They will be here," answered St. Claire. "Don't worry. Kyle would never let you down."

Hiwatha looked over at St. Claire. He wanted to tell his friend how afraid he was. Instead, they both sat in silence, waiting for uncertainty to reveal itself.

—————⊙—————

Hiwatha lay in his hospital bed, waiting for a medical answer. Maybe even a miracle. The surgery was finally over. Kyle had been by his side through it all. Even Vincent had driven over from Baltimore to check on him. His newfound relationship with his brothers had turned out to be a blessing. When his father was alive, he never encouraged any communication or told him of Kyle and Vincent's existence.

Even in death, his father hadn't mentioned them.

Over the past year, Hiwatha had gotten to really know Kyle. They had shared stories, laughed, and became comfortable enough to show their vulnerabilities. Hiwatha had grown to not only love Kyle but trusted him. He couldn't imagine life without their friendship.

On the other hand, Hiwatha still felt a distance between him and his brother Vincent. What he knew about his life he'd learned from Kyle. It was sad they now had to build a relationship under these circumstances.

Hiwatha began looking back on his life and career in boxing. There was no denying he was "The Gold" to media and fans alike. Hiwatha was nervous about the test results. He was praying for an opportunity to move on. Try something different. Most of all, experience fatherhood.

The doctors hadn't told him anything. They had to know something. Hiwatha's mind continued to race as he tried to block out the pain. He thought of the Olympics, the adulation from fans, the fame, championships, and money. What would he do when the cheering stopped?

Hiwatha thought of Caroline. He still loved her and wanted them to spend their lives together. Would he be able to do that? Would she ever forgive him? Hiwatha, out of shame, continued to pray. He had let money and fame distance him from God. It didn't seem right to ask for help now. Hiwatha thought of his father Nathan and prayed anyway.

At that moment, an awful pain shot through his head,

and he screamed a deafening, piercing shriek. Immediately the nurses came running into the room, followed by Dr. Webster, who was in the waiting area talking to St. Claire and Kyle.

"What's wrong, Mr. Jordan?" Dr. Webster asked. "Are you in pain?"

"Yes, yes, I am in pain," Hiwatha responded. "I can't take this much longer. Where is my son? I thought he was here. Didn't I see him earlier? Where is Kyle? My brother, Kyle, is he still here?"

"Yes, Mr. Jordan, your brother, is in the waiting area. I'll get him as soon as the nurse gives you something for the pain. In a few minutes, you won't feel anything. It's only been a matter of hours since the surgery. You need some rest. We have a lot to talk about in the morning."

Hiwatha grabbed Dr. Webster's gown so tightly it tore at the shoulder. The pain was unbearable. Hiwatha had survived unsurmountable abuse during his career and could not conceive of the pain he was feeling right now in his head. Dr. Webster knew Hiwatha was also a bit delirious.

St. Claire and Kyle stood in the doorway, hoping to see Hiwatha. They had been worried since the surgery. Dr. Webster motioned for them to stay back.

———————

The news ran through the gym like a hot tip on a racehorse. Sportswriters and every news outlet were running stories about Hiwatha Jordan's potential brain surgery and retirement from boxing.

Tony Francis was ahead of the game. His sister Debra coincidently was one of the nurses on staff at John Hopkins Hospital assigned to care for Hiwatha. She informed Frances of Hiwatha's brain surgery. The mass they'd found at the front of his brain was benign. Still, Debra didn't think Hiwatha would fight again since that would go against the recommendations of his doctor.

Francis immediately called Magnificent, who was crestfallen by the news of his rival's illness. He cared less that his next multi-million-dollar payday had just gone up in smoke. Magnificent asked Francis to check with Debra to see if it would be alright if he came to visit. At the very least, send flowers so Hiwatha would know that I'm thinking of him.

Francis next call was to Antonio Rosanni. Through their conversations regarding Magnificent's career, they had built a professional relationship over the past few months. Antonio was aware the illness of Hiwatha would require a change in strategy. The two briefly discussed Hiwatha's medical condition before moving on to the topic of a proposed bout between Magnificent and Nasser for the vacant title. It made perfect sense with Hiwatha now on the sidelines.

Antonio asked Francis to get information on the managerial status of Numwar Nasser. With Magnificent's break from Charleston complete, coupled with all the other problems Charleston was having, Numwar just might have to look for other managerial options.

Antonio was positioning Mitch to be the man who filled

the space. He knew Mitch was having personal problems but hoped they'd be over soon.

Antonio also had Francis on his list of future contacts. He knew he needed to somehow get Francis out of the clutches of Magnificent and onto his payroll.

———————⟨⟨●⟩⟩———————

Danielle hung up on Charleston for the tenth time. She was starting to make peace with their situation and now wanted to be free. Her plan for divorce was in motion.

Earlier that day, Danielle received a call from a detective Boyle, asking to meet with her. She knew it would be related to Charleston, but any information that would help her with the divorce was welcomed.

Detective Bogle sat in the back booth of Wrights Coffee House, waiting for Danielle to arrive. He had done the background investigative work and only needed a few more pieces of information before it was time to move in on Charleston. Detective Bogle wasted no time getting to the point once Danielle took a seat in front of him. He reached in an envelope and slowly laid pictures of Charleston and Theresa Tarver one at a time on the table in front of her.

"Mrs. Orlando, these photographs show your husband with a woman named Theresa Tarver. I have taped telephone conversations recorded from his cell phone and other locations. Some of the tapes are a bit graphic."

"How graphic?" Danielle asked, not surprised.

"Well, on some recordings, you will hear obvious sexual

cohabitation taking place."

Danielle looked at the photographs and immediately recognized Theresa. Detective Bogle began playing one of the recordings. Danielle quivered slightly. A small tear formed at the edge of her eye. The sounds and voices obviously belonged to her husband. Danielle looked across the table at detective Boyle.

"Okay, what is it that you want to know?" she asked in surrender.

There was no doubt her marriage was over. To assist with her divorce, Danielle asked Detective Bogle for a copy of the tape. She wanted to get even with Charleston and Theresa.

Danielle left the meeting thinking of her marriage to Charleston. She drove around for hours before parking her car outside Theresa's home. Danielle sat for a while, debating whether to knock on the door. Although she had come to terms with her decision to divorce Charleston, Danielle still felt a need to confront the woman who had turned her world upside down. She wanted to kill Theresa.

Danielle studied the well-manicured lawn while thinking of the years, she'd spent loving Charleston. Now it was apparent she'd been living a lie. Theresa was proof of that.

Danielle tossed her cigarette out the window and placed the gun back in the glove compartment. She rested her head in absolute surrender on the steering wheel of the car. For the sake of her two children, it was time to let go. Not do anything stupid.

Danielle picked up the phone lying in the seat next to her and dialed Francis number. When Francis answered, Danielle, started the engine of her Mercedes and drove off. She decided to let the magic of time heal her wounds.

———— «()» ————

Hiwatha's recovery was slow. He took to wearing hats to cover the scar that was still healing. When he was not resting, his time was spent taking care of Sacory.

Kyle was still in college but occasionally visited on the weekends to check on Hiwatha and spend time with Sacory.

Over the past year, Kyle had created a charity to benefit children from his old neighborhood. After attending one of Kyle's events, Hiwatha made a substantial donation to help Kyle turn his vision into reality. Tonight, they were preparing to attend a star-studded dinner at an upscale hotel in Baltimore. It was a gala benefit set up by Kyle's charity to raise money for his inner-city scholarship program.

Hiwatha was scheduled to be the guest of honor. To assure he kept his promise, Kyle and Vincent were on their way to pick up Hiwatha, Sacory, and Ms. Reed. Pressed for time, Hiwatha was rushing around his bedroom, still trying to find the right suit to wear. Franklin was helping Hiwatha by browsing through racks of clothes in the opposite room. They both knew Kyle would be arriving shortly. Sacory sat on the floor, watching his father as he played with one of his superhero toys.

When Kyle arrived, Hiwatha was pleasantly surprised to see his brother Vincent with him. He hugged them both before helping Franklin load his bags into the limo. They would have time to catch up on their drive to Baltimore.

Vincent had recently started his own architectural design firm and wanted Hiwatha to know how things were going. Hiwatha was happy his brothers turned out to be men of profound character. He had to at least give his mother credit for that.

Hiwatha smiled as he watched Vincent and Kyle play with Sacory. It was a blessing that his son would grow up knowing his uncles.

Vincent leaned forward in his seat as he began to talk about his new business venture with Hiwatha and Kyle. He couldn't wait to finish decorating the office so they could see it. Hiwatha laid back in his seat and patiently listened to Vincent while the smooth grooves of Frankie Beverly and Maze played softly in the background.

When the limo began to approach the venue, Hiwatha quickly changed the subject to the night's program lineup. He wanted to know the time Kyle had scheduled him to speak. Hiwatha had worked on his retirement speech all week but now was hesitant to use it. Sometimes it's better to just let your heart flow.

"I don't want to give a prepared speech," he told Kyle. "I can't remember half of it, and the ending doesn't work. I'm just going to speak from the heart and live with whatever comes out my mouth." "I'm sure whatever you do will be just fine," responded Kyle. "We're here now, so brother its show time."

As they entered the hotel parking lot, Hiwatha was surprised to see such a large crowd of fans and media at the entrance.

"Kyle, it looks like you did an excellent job," Hiwatha commented. "I wasn't expecting to see this many people."

"Well, all I said was the undisputed king of boxing had an important announcement to make."

"I think you said a lot more than that," replied Hiwatha.

As the limo door swung open, the camera lights began to flash in their faces. Two security guards stepped forward to guide them through the crowd towards the entrance.

Once inside, Hiwatha immediately started shaking hands with many of the guests in attendance. He was being pulled in different directions to take pictures and make light conversation. It was a relief to finally make his way through the crowd of people and to his table.

Antonio Rosanni, St. Claire and Floyd Nash were already seated to the left of him at the table. As usual, Antonio had two beautiful women with him. St. Claire and Floyd had come alone. Ms. Reed took Sacory from Hiwatha's arms and sat down next to St. Claire.

Hiwatha, Kyle and Vincent began shaking hands with several of the guests in their vicinity before taking their seats. Numwar Nasser and his two brothers were at the table to the left of Hiwatha along with several people from the Nevada State Boxing Commission. To the right of them was Tony Francis and his sister Debra along with Wonderful Magnificent and his beautiful wife, Wendy. Magnificent got up from his table to greet Hiwatha personally.

"Man, I'm glad to see you out and about. I was a little worried about you," Magnificent said with sincerity. "What happened to you made me think more seriously about my career in boxing. Seeing you today does make me feel better."

"It's good to see you too," responded Hiwatha with a smile. "When I saw you coming over, I thought about ducking under the table to block your bazooka right-hand."

They both laughed before Magnificent responded. "Well let's just hope neither of us has to worry about that again. I'm willing to put that in the rear-view mirror for now."

"Thanks for coming," Hiwatha replied, still laughing. "And thanks for the flowers. It meant a lot to know you were thinking of me. Maybe later we can have a chance to talk privately. Play some golf or have dinner sometime."

"I would like that," Magnificent said, shaking his hand. "Dinner sounds good. That would give you a chance to meet my wife, Wendy."

"Yeah, I heard you got married," responded Hiwatha. "Good for you. We all have to settle down sometime. I will make sure to get your information from Antonio. When you have time, I would like for you to think about coming to Virginia Beach and having dinner at my house. If it's ok, I'll call you to work on a date that's good for you. Since you say we're putting boxing in the rear-view mirror, maybe I can get you to play a little golf while you're there."

"Well, as long as you don't play golf like you land left-hooks,"

Magnificent replied as he walked back to his table.

This exchange was the most words ever spoken between the two competitors. Their lives and careers, though different, had been so closely entwined. Now that Hiwatha is retired and the stage lights have gone down, they can finally approach friendship.

Loud chatter could be heard throughout the ballroom as dinner was being served. From the stage, the master of ceremonies announced that the program would start right after dinner. Hiwatha sat watching Sacory being passed from one dinner guest to another before finally reaching him again. He knew Sacory eventually would tire out, and Ms. Reed would take him upstairs to their suite.

As the guests slowly calmed down, the master of ceremonies began going through the long list of introductions. Several celebrities were there to specifically speak in support of the charity. They also took the opportunity to talk about Hiwatha's career and say some special words to him. Several guests sang touching songs as a huge screen was lowered to show clips from his career, and several of his memorable knockouts.

Hiwatha laughed when they showed pictures of him and Sacory at an amusement park. A tear came to his eyes when the clip ended with an old photo of him and his father. How befitting he thought as the noise of the crowd rose to a tumultuous crescendo.

"Ladies and gentlemen, may I introduce to you the man we are honoring tonight. He's the undisputed, undefeated middleweight champion of the world, *Hiwatha "Absolute" Jordan!*"

Hiwatha rose from his seat and proceeded to the stage. As he stood next to the podium, he bowed to the audience. When he leaned in to speak into the microphone, the applause did not abate. Looking out at the crowd, he felt chills flow up his spine. He pointed to Kyle, Vincent, and Sacory and mouthed thank you, before addressing the audience. It was as if he were preparing to give a presidential acceptance speech.

"I would first like to thank the Northington Scholarship Foundation. My brother Kyle is doing an excellent job inspiring our youth to embrace higher education. The money raised will help many young students fulfill their dreams. One day they too will be proud contributors to our community."

"I am a blessed man. I've realized my dreams ten-fold. Tonight, I would like to thank all of you for supporting my career in boxing. I'm still in the prime of my career so I would be lying if I told you I didn't want to box again. I love being the undisputed middleweight champion of the world. I have ducked no man. I'd like to fight this man over here (pointing to Numwar Nasser). Or fight Magnificent again. He, too, is a great champion. One of the best I've ever seen or had the honor of sharing the ring with. The money I would earn fighting either one of them would be astronomical.

Hiwatha paused for almost ten seconds. Tears had begun

to fill the corner of his eyes. His throat was knotted up as emotion overcame him. St. Claire also had tears in his eyes as he thought of the years, they'd spent working together. When he regained his composure, Hiwatha continued.

"But due to my injury and successful brain surgery, I have decided to retire from boxing. Tonight, I relinquish my undisputed middleweight title." Hiwatha loosened his tie before continuing to speak.

"Lying in my hospital bed, I had time to think and evaluate my life. Thinking, though necessary, can be painful when you're faced with the truth. I had to ask myself, what is enough? How much farther do I want to go in boxing? Most of all, I had to answer one question. What is most important to me? I guess we all ask that at one time or another."

"When you're on top, you tend to forget there is a bottom. Well...I now know, there is a bottom from which I came a short time ago. When the doctor looked me in the eye and told me I needed to give up boxing, that was my bottom. Unfortunately, that is where I needed to go to get my answer."

"So, today, I can tell you from the heart that I seek a new trophy in life...being a good father to my son. That is worth more to me than any belt, or title I've earned. I'm grateful to have him in my life."

Hiwatha paused again as he looked down at Ms. Reed, holding Sacory. He blew a kiss to both of them before ending his speech.

"I have a friend who is not here tonight. He was very

instrumental in my career. I love him like a father. He and my trainer, St. Claire Robinson, kept me in line and always told me the truth. Any awards or accolades I receive; I share gladly with them."

"St. Claire has been the foundation on which my career was built. Without him, you probably would have never heard of Hiwatha "Absolute" Jordan. He was my first and only trainer. With the blessing of my late father, Nathaniel Jordan, St. Claire has taken the boy within me and made a champion. I never attempted to enter the ring without him, but it was my friend and adviser, Mitch Danton, who was never afraid to tell me like it is.

Mitch completed the package that you know today as, Hiwatha "Absolute" Jordan. I respect him for that. I am sorry that he could not be here to share this moment, but he is forever in my heart and in my prayers, thank you, Mitch."

"I would also like to thank my brothers Kyle and Vincent for showing me it's never too late to change your life. It's never too late to forgive. It's never too late to love."

"Honestly, I could be here all night thanking all the special people who took part in my career, but there is one very important man here tonight that I don't want to forget. His family name is well known to the world of entertainment. He is planning to do some great things in the sport of boxing. Please welcome, Mr. Antonio Rosanni."

Antonio stood as the crowd applauded, then raised his glass to Hiwatha in approval. Hiwatha was now ready to make his exit. He looked sincerely at Antonio as he spoke.

"A very special thanks to you, Antonio. Only you could have pulled off the Fight of the Century, goodnight."

Hiwatha bowed to the standing-room-only crowd one last time. Many of them had tears in their eyes as they watched the sunset on the career of a great champion. They applauded for nearly three minutes.

Hiwatha posed briefly for several photographers and film crews before leaving the stage area. As he made his way back to his seat, Magnificent and Tony Francis rose to pay their respects to a great champion. In his own way, Magnificent did admire Hiwatha. He reached again to shake his hand in honor.

"I guess it's all up to me now," Magnificent said with a smile. "I'm proud of you. Class all the way, baby."

Hiwatha shared a laugh with his former rival, although his heart was breaking at the thought of his career in boxing ending. He wanted to be anywhere but, in a room, full of people.

Hiwatha was shaking Tony Francis hand when he felt the vibration of his cell phone. He pulled it from his pocket and notice it was Franklin, calling from the house for the third time. Hiwatha quickly excused himself. He held his hand to his free ear to better hear what Franklin was saying.

"Hiwatha Charlotte's sister Avery called to tell you they found Charlotte. I told her you were at an event in Baltimore so she understands if you cannot make it, but felt you should know they have taken Charlotte to Sentara Hospital in Virginia Beach."

Hiwatha thanked Franklin for calling then quickly clicked off his phone. Hiwatha hadn't spoken with Mitch since the day he left his house in anger. He missed his friend tremendously but had kept his distance out of respect. This was different. Whether Mitch liked it or not, Hiwatha was going to make an attempt to be there for him.

Hiwatha stayed at the event a little longer to speak with several guests who were considering large donations to Kyle's charity and to make sure Ms. Reed knew of his plans to check on Charlotte and Mitch. He assured Ms. Reed he'd be back to the hotel to pick them up by morning.

———————

Mitch stood over Charlotte's hospital bed looking at her swollen face and lips, the bandages on her hands and the awful bruises on her legs. He knew she was in pain.

"Charlotte, where did I fail you," asked Mitch.

"You didn't fail me," replied Charlotte. "I failed you. After the death of Davin and Lorie, I did not want to live anymore. I was such a coward. I couldn't bring myself to take my own life, though I thought of every way possible to do it. Oh, I hated that you had something meaningful in your life. You seemed so strong. You went on with life, but I couldn't."

"Charlotte," Mitch said softly. "If you only knew, there isn't a day that I don't die a million times over when I think of our children. I pray a lot. I ask God to soften the pain. I bury myself in my work. I smile, but I'm not happy. How can I be? I, also lost a part of me, a part of us that can never be again. I need you to be my wife and love me the way you used to. We can be strong for each other."

"Mitch, you don't know what I've done," replied Charlotte. "I have made a mockery of our marriage. There is no way you can be with me now."

"Oh, yes, I can," Mitch quickly responded. "I promised you for better or worst. I will not leave you like this. There's a clinic on the west coast where you can stay for a few months. You'll be close to Avery and the kids, and I'll buy us a nice home in Los Angles so we can start over. We can finally sell our house here. Get rid of all those sad memories. Start fresh. I just need to know who did this to you."

Charlotte turned away from Mitch to rest her face on the pillow. She did not want to involve Mitch or cause any more trouble.

"Mitch, let's put this behind us," Charlotte replied. "I don't want to get you involved. No one else needs to get hurt."

Mitch pulled a photo of Roscoe from his pocket and insisted that Charlotte look at it.

"Is this the guy?" he asked several times. "Look at the picture, Charlotte."

Charlotte looked over at Mitch, and then at the photo of Roscoe, he was holding in his hand but did not speak. Instead, Charlotte turned over and put her bandaged hands alongside her face and lay back on the pillow. Mitch had his answer. He pulled the covers over Charlotte's back to make sure she was comfortable before leaving.

"Charlotte, I want you to get some rest. Take comfort that no one will ever lay a hand on you again. I give you my word."

Mitch couldn't wait to get out of Charlotte's hospital room to leave a message on Antonio's voicemail. He knew Antonio was attending the dinner for Hiwatha; therefore, Mitch was surprised when he answered. Mitch could hear the crowd in the background. Still, he wasted no time making his point.

"Antonio, this is Mitch. I am at the hospital in Virginia Beach with my wife. She is not doing well."

"I am sorry to hear that," Antonio said in a sympathetic voice. "But at least you have found her. Is there anything I can do?"

"Yes, there is," Mitch stated with conviction.

Mitch desperately needed help, and now was the time to ask. Mitch proceeded to tell Antonio about Charlotte's condition and the person he knew to be responsible. Antonio listened with great compassion and then spoke coldly and directly.

"Mitch, I will have my assistant contact the clinic and arrange for your wife's stay. You will not have to do anything. You are welcome to stay in my condo in LA until you find other accommodations. It's pretty close to the clinic. The choice is yours. Now, regarding the asshole who did this to your wife, send me all the pictures and information you have on him. In a short time, this guy will regret the day he was born. I will talk to you in a day or two. Now go, take care of your wife."

With that, Mitch pushed the end button on his cell phone and slid down the wall in the hospital corridor. As time passed, Mitch didn't even notice the people parading back and forth in front of him. All he could think of was Charlotte, his children, and the years of emotional pain he'd endured.

Mitch suddenly felt the presence of someone standing over him. He could tell by the expensive shoes and finely woven fabric of the suit; they were well dressed. Even the scent of their cologne smelled of success. Mitch looked up just as Hiwatha began to speak.

"Mitch, I know I'm the last person you want to see," conveyed Hiwatha as he took a seat on the floor next to Mitch. "I had to come when I heard you found Charlotte. How is she?" he asked with concern.

Mitch looked like he hadn't showered or shaved in ten days. Hiwatha rested his hand on Mitch's knee to comfort him. Hiwatha never wanted anything to come between him and Mitch. That is why he paid Charlotte the money. He was still hoping their friendship was strong enough to get pass his betrayal.

"I had to come," he stated again to Mitch. "Whether you believe me or not, I am a friend and have been since the day we met. I want to thank you for everything you've done for me. When I later realized Charlotte was your wife, I should have been honest with you. I am hoping one day you'll forgive me."

"There is no one to forgive, Hiwatha, except myself," Mitch replied as he placed his hand over Hiwatha's.

"I read your letter, and I thought about it a lot. You did not know she was my wife, Hiwatha. And I do not want Charlotte to know that we've discussed this. If you had told me about Charlotte the night we met, I would have never gotten involved in boxing. I would still be getting my law practice off the ground, basically drowning in my own self-pity. In a sense, you saved me. You became the inspiration I needed. A pleasant distraction. You were young, talented, and amid a rising star. Yes, my friend, you were indeed a blessing to me. Unfortunately, we both know things will never be the same. You're retired now. My services are no longer needed."

"Yes, I know that. I officially retired from boxing tonight. So, you're right, our relationship will change. That doesn't mean you can't still be part of my life. It's important to me that we remain friends. That's worth tomorrow."

"Hiwatha, we will always be friends," Mitch assured him. "After all, that's worth tomorrow to me as well. Besides, you can't play baseball. Who else is going to teach Sacory how to throw a curve-ball?"

Mitch and Hiwatha both laughed. Knowing how much they'd shared, they stood to embrace one another like father and son.

"Charlotte is in a bad way," Mitch informed Hiwatha. "It may not be a good time to see her. Maybe some other time."

"I understand," replied Hiwatha. "You take care of

Charlotte and I will talk with you soon. Everything is going to be fine. You'll see. If you need anything at all, please call me. I will always be there for you."

Mitch nodded his head in approval as he watched Hiwatha flow down the corridor and through the white double doors. His black trench-coat flowed in the wind. Mitch felt as though he were watching life change right before his eyes as the doors closed behind Hiwatha. Now all Mitch needed was to make sure the man who had caused Charlotte so much pain lived long enough to regret it.

A week later, Mitch was relaxing in a chair on the balcony of Antonio's condo, enjoying the California sunshine. As he read the article about Roscoe, it was clear things were looking up.

The newspaper headlines read, "Former tennis star Roscoe Evertoni found dead in his Virginia Beach home from a drug overdose. His family is requesting an autopsy, but no foul play is suspected."

Mitch sat back and smiled. He would continue to take a break from boxing until Charlotte was better, then begin working with Antonio on a Magnificent / Nasser bout.

With the retirement of Hiwatha "Absolute" Jordan, Wonderful Magnificent would surely become the new king of boxing. Tony Francis would definitely see to that. Together they now have an opportunity to set boxing on its heels.

Mitch picked up a newly released boxing magazine

from the table and flipped to the article where Francis and Magnificent were telling the story of how it all began. Mitch laughed as they talked about one of the old trainers at the gym, Mr. Wright. Everybody knows a guy like that.

Mr. Wright still worked for the City of Chicago Recreation Department grooming young champions. At two o'clock each day without fail, he opened the gym. Young kids that didn't weigh even sixty-five pounds soaking wet sought his expertise.

"Mr. Wright! Mr. Wright! I want you to make me a champion? I want to be champion of the world, like Wonderful Magnificent," they would shout as they entered the gym. "Will you help me? Please, Mr. Wright."

Gone was the presence of Charleston Orlando. Though Numwar was training every day, Charleston hadn't been to the gym in months. Numwar knew it was time to consider making some changes. He wasn't about to let anything get in the way of his potential opportunity to fight Magnificent, especially not Charleston's surmounting problems. Numwar consulted with his attorney, then put the word out that he was looking for new management.

Chapter 18

A CHANGE OF HEART

Maria Santiago was standing in the expansive living-room of her daughter's estate. It was nearly two years since Victoria's death, and she was still grieving. Although Maria had two other children, the loss of Victoria was still unbearable.

Victoria had touched Maria's heart in a way no one else could. They shared a friendship that stretched beyond the boundaries of their mother and daughter relationship. Maria not only missed her daughter but her closes friend.

She felt tears forming in her eyes as she patiently watched the moving company lift the last piece of furniture. Most of Victoria's valuables had been auctioned away to help fund her favorite charities. The lion share of the estate was put into a trust fund for her son, Sacory Nathaniel Jordan. His name lingered in Maria's mind.

The last time Maria had seen her grandson was at the hospital shortly after Victoria's death. Maria remembered holding him tightly to her chest as she wept. What kind of life was Sacory having without Victoria?

Maria felt guilty for not being there for Sacory. That clearly was not Victoria's intentions. Maria had slowly come to realize that Victoria must have really loved Hiwatha. Otherwise, her decision to let him raise Sacory made no sense.

Victoria's father, Edward, had made his decision shortly after their meeting with Hiwatha at the hospital. Edward desperately wanted to be part of his grandson's life but knew Maria was still bitter about the situation. He patiently waited for Maria to have a change of heart.

That was Edward's hope the night he convinced Maria to watch the recording of Hiwatha's retirement speech. Their son, Ramiro, had given it to him a few weeks earlier.

Edward looked over at Maria who was intently watching the event unfold, he was hoping to see some sign of surrender on her face. Though Maria was deeply touched by Hiwatha's words and unyielding devotion to Sacory, she tried not to show it.

Maria had to admit to herself it was an eloquent speech. She realized why Victoria fell in love with Hiwatha. Right before her eyes, he'd captivated the entire audience with his charm and intellect. That package would be hard for any woman to resist.

Hiwatha was more than a world champion. He was a man of strong character that was blessed with something money just can't buy. By the end of Hiwatha's speech, Maria herself had tears in her eyes.

As Maria stood looking out the window of Victoria's estate, she was thinking of Hiwatha and Sacory. In her hand was a letter she'd written to Hiwatha a week earlier. Maria held it to her chest and prayed. No matter how difficult, it was time to move forward with life. The task of settling Victoria's estate was complete. Now Maria was ready to make a decision regarding her grandson. She watched the moving van pull away from the house. As the gates leading to the estate opened, Maria felt her own heart expanding. It was time to love again.

———⊙———

Charleston entered his office in a state of disarray. He quickly rushed pass his secretary without speaking and closed the door to his shrine. Charleston sat at his desk, looking at all the awards and testimonials to a great career in boxing. What a ride, he thought to himself. For many years, he'd lived a champagne lifestyle.

As he leaned further back in his chair, his travel down memory lane was interrupted by his secretary, Marsha Lewis who had just opened his office door without warning.

"Charleston, there is someone from the Justice Department here to see you."

Charleston turned around in his chair with a look of surprise on his face.

"What is this all about?" Charleston asked.

"Mr. Orlando, I'm Donald Bogle from the Justice Department. I'm serving you with a warrant to search the premises and remove any records or files we deem necessary to our investigation. We hope that you comply without incident. I would advise you to contact an attorney."

For the first time, Charleston was at a loss for words. With a look of disbelief on his face, he walked around to the front of his desk to accept the warrant from detective Bogle before stepping into the hallway to contact his attorney.

Over the next few weeks, the Justice Department questioned Charleston's association with drug dealers and worked to indict him on money laundering charges. Behind the scenes was his former lover, Theresa Tarver, working feverishly to assure his demise.

Theresa had contacted the Internal Revenue Service about Charleston shady business deals. They were now auditing Charleston and pursuing him for over a million dollars in back taxes.

Charleston was also going through a divorce. Danielle stood to receive a large settlement, plus half of all property.

The boxing magazines and tabloids were having a field day with Charleston Orlando stories. Even one of the cable sports stations did a feature story on his fall from grace.

Theresa laughed as she watched the segment aired on television. She had finally gotten Charleston where she wanted him. So deep were the roots of her revenge, when Charleston phoned, Theresa, laid the phone down next to her so Charleston could hear her making love to another man. It turned her stomach to think she once loved him. Now, like all his former fighters, Theresa took pleasure in destroying him. Satisfaction for her would be looking directly into Charleston's eyes when he finally had his day in court.

———— ◦《◉》◦ ————

Hiwatha sat comfortably on the sofa in his bedroom, wondering how different Sacory's life would be if Victoria were still alive. Though challenging at times, fatherhood was agreeing with him. Sacory had stolen his heart. He was a terrific kid with an even temperament and warm spirit. Something he surely must have gotten from the Jordan side of the family.

Victoria was full of passion. You weren't getting anything over on her, especially if she saw it coming. In some ways, Hiwatha missed her. Not romantically, but it would have been nice for Sacory to have such a dynamic woman for a mother.

The overwhelming guilt Hiwatha felt at times hadn't gone away. He still imagined what Victoria must have endured because of the embarrassment he'd cast over her life and career.

These thoughts ran through Hiwatha's mind as he nervously opened the letter from Maria Santiago. He had waited almost two years for Victoria's parents to make a decision. Their first meeting at the hospital wasn't under the best of circumstances. Hiwatha knew what it was like to grow up without a mother. He wanted Sacory to have some connection with Victoria's family, so he prayed the letter would be a new beginning.

Over the past two months, he'd been devastated by the news of Caroline's engagement to Lance. Without boxing to occupy his mind, Hiwatha became restless and appeared to be somewhat depressed. Ms. Reed and Franklin often checked on him, while Vincent kept blowing up his phone.

Though Kyle was away finishing his last year of college, he often came up with excuses to drive up on weekends to keep Hiwatha company. A bit of good news could change everything.

Though Hiwatha had made several attempts to open his life to Victoria's family, until now, Maria and Edward had not responded. Hiwatha took a deep breath and said a silent prayer before reading Maria's letter.

Dear Hiwatha,

I was deeply touched by your retirement speech. I am happy to know that you and Sacory are doing well. Edward and I finally settled Victoria's estate. Our lawyer will be contacting you shortly concerning the trust fund that was set up for Sacory. I want to thank you for the pictures you sent of him last Christmas. He has Victoria's eyes, but I must admit Sacory is a split image of you.

I want to apologize for not contacting you sooner. I realized it took a lot for you to face Edward and I under such extenuating circumstances. It speaks to your character and sense of responsibility.

If you are agreeable, during the Thanksgiving holiday, we would like to visit with you and Sacory. It would be a long-awaited blessing.

In closing, I want you to know that we truly loved Victoria with all our heart. She was our only daughter, and we will always miss her. There is no price anyone can ever put on that. We hope to hear from you soon.

Sincerely,
Maria Santiago

Hiwatha placed the letter on the table then looked over at Sacory, who was sleeping soundly on the bed. "Yes…God is good," he said out loud to himself. "In the morning, I'll tell Franklin and Ms. Reed to help me plan a special family dinner for Victoria's parents."

All sorts of thoughts raced through Hiwatha's mind as he looked at the picture of him and St. Claire holding his championship belts. He was thinking of all they had shared over a lifetime. Hiwatha had missed having St. Claire close to him. It was time to reach out and allow a new beginning to unfold. He would invite St. Claire and his wife, Ella, for Thanksgiving. His boxing career may be over, but his friends were forever.

Hiwatha reached for the phone to first call Kyle and Vincent. He knew it wouldn't be a family dinner without his brothers there to celebrate. He laid back on the sofa, waiting for Kyle to answer.

"Hey, man, what you up to?" Hiwatha asked excitingly. "I hope you're sitting down. I have some good news."

Kyle could hear the joy in Hiwatha's voice as he told him about the letter, he'd received from Victoria's parents.

"This is good news," responded Kyle. "I thought they would never come around. It just goes to show you that life has a way of working things out."

"Yeah, but I can't do this without you. So please don't make any plans for the holiday. I want you and Vincent to be here. It would mean a lot to me."

"I will not let you down," responded Kyle. "I'll let Vincent know before he makes other plans. I'm happy to hear things are finally moving in the right direction."

Kyle was aware of the emotional changes Hiwatha had gone through over the past two years. He had been there to listen and help his brother with Sacory after Victoria's death. Although things appeared to be coming together, Kyle knew in his heart, something was missing. It was a void not even Edward, and Maria Santiago could fill.

———— ◉ ————

Xavier and Numwar looked around the plush offices of Antonio Rosanni's executive suites. They were honored to receive such an invitation. It had been a long road, but today they were signing a deal that would decide the next undisputed middleweight champion of the world. A mega-fight between Nasser and Magnificent. It was difficult for

Numwar to contain himself. This would be the most money he'd ever made in his career.

"This is it," he told Xavier. "This is what I've been waiting for my whole life. The moment when your dreams finally align with reality. It's a beautiful thing."

Xavier did not respond. He was caught up in the moment. Not even Numwar's rumblings could intrude on his thoughts. As he and Numwar walked down the corridor leading to the conference room, Xavier was in awe of the expensive artwork and numerous pictures hanging on the wall of famous movie stars.

"Pretty impressive, I would say?" Came a voice from behind them. "Can I get you, gentlemen, something to drink?"

Numwar and Xavier both turned around to look at the beautiful woman coming toward them. She extended her hand to greet them.

Xavier introduced himself, but Nasser could not speak. He was instantly captivated by her presence. After a moment of silence, Numwar finally managed to respond.

"Good afternoon. I'm Numwar Nasser. We're here to meet with Mitch Danton."

"Yes, I know," she quickly replied. "I'm Destiny Ross. Mr. Rosanni hired my firm to do the public relations for the upcoming fight. So, we'll be working together over the next few months. Please have a seat while I get you something to drink. I'm sure it was a long flight. You're probably tired."

"Oh, we're all right. Don't trouble yourself," said Xavier.

"It's no trouble. It's my job to make sure you're

comfortable. I hope you're hungry. I took the liberty of ordering lunch. I found an excellent deli nearby."

Destiny looked over at Numwar. She made a mental note of how refined he looked in his tailored suit. To her, Numwar was not drop-dead gorgeous, but definitely handsome in a very masculine sort of way. That's a plus for any promotional campaign.

Destiny sensed Numwar was nervous and contributed it to him signing the biggest deal of his life. She was just happy to be on-board. Over the last year, Antonio's business generated a lot of revenue for her firm. Now with an opportunity to work with Numwar, her five-year plan just became three.

Antonio had already given Destiny background information on Numwar. She knew this fight was Numwar's chance to step into the limelight, and Destiny had just the right publicity campaign to support his rising star.

Numwar got up from the table to take in the view of Los Angeles from the large conference room window as Destiny left to get them something to drink. What a big city Numwar thought to himself. This was a long way from the poverty of his hometown in Antigua. His life was about to change. It was hard to keep it all in perspective.

Numwar thought about his friend Wiley. It would have been great if he were still alive to share this moment. The road to the title had been tough. The only thing standing between him and the title now was Magnificent.

Numwar was confident about winning the title. He had

done so a thousand times in his mind. He held his breath for a moment and slowly began to exhale. He was desperately trying to calm his nerves before Mitch arrived. When he heard Destiny's voice coming from the hallway, he quickly turned to face the door.

Destiny returned to the conference room holding a tray full of drinks. She was anchored by a group of people who began setting up an array of sandwich platters. Numwar was pleased to see Mitch enter the conference room behind them. It was time to sign his contract and catch a flight back to Antigua to celebrate with his family.

Mitch pulled the contract from his briefcase and began explaining to Xavier and Numwar the terms of the deal. Though he had already gone over the contract with his lawyer and advisor, Numwar still listened carefully. He wasn't the type of guy who liked surprises. Not after waiting years for a shot at the title.

As Numwar signed the contract, several reporters waited with Destiny outside the conference room. This would be an enormous story by the time Antonio's promotional team finished.

Working on the new pay-per-view deal put Mitch back in all his glory. Charlotte's recovery had gone well. They were once again happy in their marriage.

Charlotte persuaded Mitch to purchase a piece of property outside of Los Angeles near her sister Avery. This would allow Charlotte and Avery to begin their plans of opening a modeling school. Eventually, Charlotte's goal was to turn it into a full-blown agency. Mitch was happy that Charlotte finally found something to fill her days.

Before placing the signed contract in his briefcase, Mitch stood to allow the cameras to get a picture of him and Numwar shaking hands. By nightfall, Mitch would be in Chicago preparing for his morning meeting with Wonderful Magnificent and Tony Francis. Yes...this would be another mega-promotion. Mitch could feel it.

Caroline was standing in her living room, looking at an envelope addressed to her from Kyle. It had been sitting amongst a stack of mail on her desk for a few days.

Caroline was surprised to receive a letter from Kyle. She hadn't spoken to Hiwatha since the announcement of her engagement to Lance. She nervously opened the letter hoping everything was ok.

Caroline,

I hope all is well on your end. Hiwatha is doing much better since his surgery. Enclosed you'll find a letter he wrote to you some time ago but never mailed. You know pride can be a hell of a thing for a man to overcome. This letter is one of many unsent. The rest are in the drawer beside his bed. I am sending this letter without his knowledge because I know you need to hear what he has to say from him and not me.

When he heard about your engagement to Lance, he did not sleep for weeks. Hiwatha truly loves you, and right now, I think he needs you in his life. Please come to see him before you go through with this. We're having a special dinner on Thanksgiving. Hiwatha would be surprised and thrilled to see you.

Call me if you decide to come. I will take care of the flight arrangements.

Sincerely,
Kyle Northington

Caroline took a deep breath before reading Hiwatha's letter. Her heart and soul stopped in time. It wasn't that Hiwatha hadn't said these words before. Caroline was just finally ready to hear them. She rushed to the phone to call her brother Stevie whom she knew would help her make the right decision.

When Stevie informed her of all the things, Hiwatha had done, especially to help their mother, tears filled her eyes.

"Why didn't you tell me this before?" she asked.

"Hiwatha asked me not to," replied Stevie. "I gave him my word. Hiwatha didn't want you to feel obligated to be with him. You know how close Mom was to his father. He did those things because of his feelings towards Mom, not you. I've told you a thousand times you were making a mistake. I've always known the guy really loved you. I believe deep down inside you love him, too. So, swallow your pride and go see him. What do you have to lose? If you have any doubt. Or just the fact you're considering this at all means you can't marry Lance without knowing the truth."

Caroline sat quietly in her living room for hours, thinking about her conversation with Stevie. Even if it was too late for her and Hiwatha, she still couldn't marry Lance. It was time to listen to her heart, face her fears, and take a chance.

Caroline needed to figure out how to break off her engagement to Lance. Even though they had broken up and gotten back together so many times, she still didn't want to hurt him. Lance had been her college sweetheart. Still, it was wrong to marry him, knowing how she truly felt about Hiwatha.

Caroline hoped Kyle was right and it wasn't too late. She knelt down and prayed for some divine intervention.

⸺•《《◊》》•⸺

Hiwatha and Sacory were playing out back by the lake. It was Thanksgiving, and there was a chill in the air. Hiwatha was spending quality time with his son before his numerous guess arrived that evening. He was excited that St. Claire and Ella would be there.

Mitch and Charlotte were in town to finalize the sale of their house. When Mitch called, Hiwatha invited them to dinner. Though Mitch had kept him abreast of Charlotte's recovery, Hiwatha hadn't seen either of them in a long time.

Hiwatha and Magnificent had kept their promise to play golf and keep in touch. Lately, they spoke often by phone about Magnificent's upcoming fight with Numwar. After Magnificent signed the contract to fight Numwar, he flew to Virginia Beach with Tony Francis to discuss various strategies that would work in Magnificent's favor.

Hiwatha took the opportunity to invite both of them to his home for Thanksgiving. Magnificent and Francis knew that the counsel of Hiwatha and St. Claire was invaluable, so they both agreed to be there.

Magnificent also knew Wendy would be excited to get away for the holidays. He was satisfied with his decision to marry her. They both had finally found happiness within their relationship.

Tonight would be a special night for all of them. Even Sacory would finally have a chance to spend time with his grandparents, Maria and Edward.

Hiwatha picked up Sacory. It was time to head back to the house and begin preparations for the evening. When Hiwatha opened the patio door, he saw Kyle, leaning on the refrigerator, drinking a beer. He gave him a look of disapproval. It was way too early for that, especially with all the work they still had to do.

Kyle started smiling as Hiwatha stepped into the kitchen. He pointed toward the stove, where Caroline was busy cooking breakfast. Caroline turned around to face Hiwatha, who was still holding Sacory in his arms.

"Why don't you two take a seat and have some breakfast," she said in a matter-of-fact tone.

"I should be finished in a few minutes. How do you like

your eggs, Mr. Jordan? Did you and Sacory have a nice walk this morning?"

Hiwatha stood frozen in the doorway, wondering what to make of the situation. What was Caroline doing here? Who had invited her? Caroline looked back at Hiwatha and pointed to the table.

"Why are you standing in the doorway? You need to close the door. It's cold outside. Sit down and make yourself comfortable. You look like you've never seen a woman cook breakfast before?"

Caroline adjusted the strap on her apron and continued flipping pancakes. She made sure to turn her back to Hiwatha. She didn't want to acknowledge the bewilderment showing on his face. Not knowing what to say, Hiwatha followed Caroline orders and slowly sat down at the table. He placed Sacory in the seat next to him.

Hiwatha looked at Kyle and raised his eyebrows, silently asking what was going on. Kyle hunched his shoulders, signaling he didn't know. No reason to let on that he had invited Caroline. Instead, a smirk appeared on his face.

Kyle knew that his plan was working. He could see that Caroline's presence was like receiving the perfect gift on Christmas. Except it was Thanksgiving.

Caroline began humming a song as she moved about the kitchen. Hiwatha sat there, observing every move she made. He had never seen Caroline cook before, so this was definitely a surprise. He knew Ms. Reed would be upset. She hadn't allowed anyone to cook in her kitchen, except

St. Claire. Using her cookware was a serious matter. Up to now, she had never dealt with another woman in the house.

As the shock slowly faded, Hiwatha began to smile. He didn't totally know what to make of Caroline's performance but decided to play along. His butler Franklin walked into the kitchen with a perplexed look on his face.

"Mr. Jordan, what do you want me to do with Ms. Davis bags?" Franklin asked in an annoyed tone.

Before Hiwatha could speak, Caroline turned and looked at Franklin as if he were a complete idiot who obviously didn't know she was the new lady of the house.

Caroline moved quickly to the doorway leading to the front of the house and peeked out. She then placed her hands on the sides of her hips.

"Franklin, whether you know it or not I intend to be here at least until Sacory is grown."

Caroline then pointed her cooking spoon at Hiwatha who was sitting at the table holding Sacory for confirmation. Franklin looked at Hiwatha for direction. He would never consider taking orders from one of Hiwatha's women, especially after the way Caroline had looked at him. Franklin only answered to the man who signed his paycheck.

Hiwatha stumbled over his words. He didn't know what Caroline was up to but didn't want to ruin the moment by saying the wrong thing, so he decided to entertain her intrusion.

"Uh, I guess you can put her bags in one of the guest rooms, Franklin."

"Mr. Jordan, I hate to be a bother, but can I speak with you for a moment in private?"

Hiwatha handed Sacory to Kyle and followed Franklin out to the front Foyer to see what the problem was.

Hiwatha was shocked to see the amount of luggage Caroline had left in the Foyer in no apparent order.

"Mr. Jordan this is absolutely ridiculous," Franklin stated in frustration. "You know several guests are coming for dinner this evening."

"Franklin, it will be okay," replied Hiwatha. "Let me find out what's going on."

"Oh, you don't know? Now, that's a damn shame," Franklin responded as he opened the front door and pointed to two men standing next to a moving van in the driveway. They both recognized Hiwatha and waved at the champion.

Hiwatha put his hand over his mouth to contain his laughter. He finally realized what was happening. If this was the way Caroline wanted to play it, he was going to sit back and allow her to entertain him. Hiwatha closed the door then bent over in laughter. This was a gesture only reserved for Sacory lately.

Since his retirement from boxing, he'd been depressed spending most of his days in the bedroom in silence, especially after the news of Caroline's engagement. The laughter felt good to his soul.

"Franklin, you have to admit, the lady, certainly knows how to make a statement. Just tell the movers to unload the truck out back near the guest house. They can store

Caroline things in the adjacent garage for now. You can put all these bags in one of the upstairs guest rooms. I'm going back to breakfast."

Franklin leaned back, rolled his eyes, and gave Hiwatha one of those, you must be crazy looks.

"Mr. Jordan, it's early in the morning. That's too many bags for me to concern myself with, and you want me to help the movers. I don't know about you, but I'm not interested in being the wide receiver, punt returner, and kicker around here."

Hiwatha raised his hands in the air while backing out of the Foyer. Franklin stood there with a look on his face that said, I'm quitting. He spoke under his breath as his boss returned to the kitchen.

"Lord, I hope this boy knows what he's doing," Franklin said as he kicked one of the bags of luggage towards the stairs. "This woman got the nerve to try an move into a man's house on Thanksgiving with no notice. I don't know why women feel they can do this type of shit. I got other things to do today."

When Hiwatha returned to the kitchen, he quickly took a seat at the table. It was important not to miss one minute of Caroline's act. I guess this was her way of finally saying yes, to him. It was bold, but a beautiful thing. How, what or why she was there didn't matter.

Hiwatha walked over to the counter, stood close behind Caroline then slipped his arms around her waist. His emotions had gotten the best of him.

Hiwatha knew for Caroline to show up at his house without warning took a lot of courage. She needed to know he was happy to see her. Hiwatha leaned down to whisper in her ear.

"You need any help?" he asked. "You know I am at your service."

"Really, then set the table like you've got some manners," Caroline replied as if to ignore Hiwatha's advances. "Now move out my way. I've got work to do this morning. You people are moving around here like there's nothing to do. We've got a dinner to prepare for tonight. I'll bet you invited the whole youth community center and every friend you know."

Caroline kissed Hiwatha on the cheek as she slipped from his embrace and moved quickly to the refrigerator. She paused to get a good look at Sacory before kissing him on the forehead.

"Boy, I can see you gonna be just like your father. You already got that dangerous smile. I guess I'll have to start running women away from the house when you turn twelve."

She winked at Kyle and mouthed a thank you to him. She felt this was where she belonged. Although Caroline couldn't see Hiwatha behind her, she knew he was still staring at her. When you're in love, there are rare moments when you can have private conversations without saying a word.

As they ate breakfast, Hiwatha continued to stare at Caroline. He was thinking about the time he'd spent with her on the press tour. That was when they fell in love. With her here, it felt like yesterday. Hiwatha was glad to have Caroline back in his life. He could move on. Really step away from boxing. Finally, have a real family to love.

After breakfast, Caroline began cleaning the dishes. Hiwatha watched her for a moment before going over to the sink and politely turning off the water. "You don't ever have to do that," he told her. "That is not what I need from you. How about we take a walk before it gets too busy around here?"

It was still brisk outside, so Hiwatha went to get her a jacket from the front closest. He wanted to be alone with Caroline so they could talk privately. It had been a long time since he'd held her in his arms. Hiwatha thought of how much he wished for her visit when he was in the hospital. He wanted Caroline there the night he retired. To share all of those significant moments was important. Hiwatha needed Caroline in his life. Today, he was not going to let his pride get in the way. As they made their way pass the lake, Hiwatha grabbed Caroline's hand. He wanted to ask what happened with Lance but decided to leave well enough alone. She was there with him. They could move forward from here.

"Thanks for coming," Hiwatha said, looking directly at Caroline. "I've missed you."

Hiwatha pulled the collar up on her jacket while thinking of what to say next. Even though there were many things he wanted to tell Caroline, he tried to keep the conversation light. This was a special moment for both of them.

As Hiwatha looked over at the moving van parked in the driveway near his guest house, he broke out in laughter. Caroline looked over at him, wondering what was so funny.

"Ms. Davis, that was a pretty good move showing up with the moving van. Franklin almost lost his mind. You had to think pretty hard about that one. Not even I have the balls to pull that off."

Hiwatha was trying to make Caroline feel comfortable, so he continued to tease her. That was a bold move for Caroline and definitely out of her character.

"Yeah, I knew that would get you," Caroline responded while thinking of how much work it took to get there.

Once she decided to leave Los Angeles, Caroline wasted no time packing and quitting her job at the agency. Plan "B" was to keep moving toward home if things did not work out with Hiwatha. There was no turning back; she had broken it off with Lance. It was Hiwatha who held her heart, and Caroline wanted to know if they still had a real chance at love. So, she boldly posed the question to Hiwatha.

"Now that all my things are here, you can either put me out or let me stay. Which is it going to be?"

"Well, hell, you must have packed everything you owned. That's a lot of stuff to unpack don't you think? Like I said, that's a big moving van. I guess my only option is to let you stay. I'm not getting into a fight with your brother over leaving you stranded."

Caroline turned to seriously look at Hiwatha. For her,

that was the wrong answer.

"No, there are other options," she replied. "You don't have to let me stay. I'm fully aware I was taking a chance showing up at your house today. I'll stay only if you want me to."

Caroline wanted a direct answer from Hiwatha. She had read the letter he'd written more times than you can count. Now it was time for a face-to-face commitment from him.

Caroline knew she hadn't been there to support Hiwatha. She was prepared to hear no, but in her heart, she was praying Hiwatha would say yes.

In truth, Hiwatha had been honest with Caroline. It was her lack of faith in him. It was hard for her to believe that a man in Hiwatha's position would consider being faithful to her. When she saw how beautiful Victoria was, that brought out insecurities Caroline didn't know existed. In reading Hiwatha's letter, she finally found the courage to face him. Caroline not only owed Hiwatha an apology, but she needed to thank him for all that he'd done for her mother.

"Stevie told me what you've been doing for our mother," she said softly. "I want to thank you. After all, you've been through, you're truly amazing."

"Caroline, I didn't do that for you," Hiwatha responded with humility. "When we were growing up, your mother always treated me like I was her own son. Sort of the mother I've never had. That meant a lot to me."

"Yeah, I know she's always been sweet on you, even when we were kids. Still, you didn't have to take care of her.

So for that I am genuinely grateful. I also want to apologize for not believing in you. I was wrong for not being there when you and Sacory needed me. I really have no right to just walk back into your life, expecting to pick up where we left off. I do understand if this is terrible timing. I just couldn't live with myself if I hadn't at least tried to see you. I want you to know that I still love you. You're right. This is by far the craziest thing I've ever done. So please say something before I melt."

Hiwatha put his hand to Caroline's lips to silence her. He wanted this to be a memorable moment for them.

"Caroline, I very much want you to stay," Hiwatha said to comfort her. "I still love you too. With all my heart, and yes, I still, want us to get married. For a moment there, I had given up hope. I didn't...."

Before Hiwatha could finish, Caroline leaped into his arms. She didn't need to hear anymore.

"Mr. Jordan, I accept without any doubt. I love you. I knew it the day you kissed me in the elevator. I've just been foolish, insecure, and afraid I'd wake up, and it would all be a dream."

"This whole thing has been a terrible misunderstanding," she continued to confess. "It's all my fault, but I want to make it up to you. I even quit my job."

"Yeah, sure, you did," Hiwatha responded. "I need proof, Ms. Professional. I don't believe that for one minute. You without a job. Where's your resignation letter?"

"That big truck over there is proof enough," she said,

pointing to the guest house. "You said yourself, I didn't leave anything behind. I walked into the office last week and handed the vice president my resignation. All it said was six words. I'm going to get my man. Can you believe that?"

Hiwatha held Caroline in his arms and kissed her. He made sure it was one of those slow passionate kisses. The kind babies are made of.

They embraced for a long time before deciding to head back to the house. What these two were thinking surely couldn't be done in broad daylight.

Caroline looked at Hiwatha and began singing one of her favorite songs by Marvin Gaye and Tami Terrell, "Ain't No Mountain High Enough." Hiwatha thought of when they were kids, playing music in front of his house. It was then that his dreams of becoming a world champion were born. He laughed and prepared to start singing with her.

When his solo part came, Hiwatha kissed Caroline on the cheek while pulling her close to him. They started slow dancing as he sang the words to the song in her ear. They were finally two lovers entwined forever.

Kyle and Sacory were watching from the kitchen window. Kyle was smiling as he held Sacory's hand up to wave. He knew it was rare to find someone in life that could touch your soul. It is one of the greatest feelings. Has anyone ever touched your soul?

THE END

EPILOGUE
LEGENDARY TRAINER BILL "POPS" MILLER
1925 – 2012

When I was told Diana was writing a book about boxing; I knew her husband Alex Sherer would have been proud of her. He too was a student of boxing and made his mark as a trainer. As my wife Beverly and I read through the chapters, we were saddened by the thought of losing Alex but blessed to have so many wonderful memories. He was like a son to me.

There were many days the trainers at the Kronk Boxing gym sat around talking stuff. We had great debates about the sport of boxing, and Alex loved to get everybody fired up. The other trainers were fueled by pure emotion, but Alex was the kind of guy who had already been to the library and looked it up.

At that time Alex worked for Emanuel Steward as a scout and trainer. He had an excellent eye for talent and developed many young fighters; such as Michael Moorer, Jemal Hinton, Donald Stokes, Frank Liles, Gerald McClellan, and Tony Robinson. He also scouted and trained two Olympic Gold Medal winners for the 1984 Olympics. Most people would remember him as the trainer who guided Thomas Hearns to winning his sixth world championship title against Virgil Hill.

He was a good guy, but Emanuel never would be fair and pay the man what he was worth. Bill Gates is a billionaire not just because he's a creative genius. The guy was smart enough to pay those who were loyal to him. He knew loyalty has a price. In the chapter of the book The Price of Loyalty, this was captured so well.

Everyone has a right to the American Dream. When your purpose becomes, I can have it, but you can't, that's no longer a dream, that's an agenda.

This fact, along with other broken promises caused great resentment, not only between Alex and Emmanuel but Thomas Hearns, the other trainers and fighters as well. Everybody put in hard work at the gym developing fighters, scouting talent, building champions. We didn't take too kindly to Emanuel showing up the night of the fight working the corner.

I never, in particular, grew to dislike Emanuel the way others may have. I had been around him a long time. So, I knew what motivated the guy. Back in the early sixties, I was his trainer when he won the National Golden Gloves Bantamweight title.

I always knew Emanuel's greatest asset was his ability to be a good talker. So, I didn't have any problem with him using that to his advantage. Others thought of him as self-serving. It was clear to his fighters that he was no longer a trainer. He became better at selling promissory notes. When those notes became due, he was left to survive on his reputation. And these days I guess that's enough to get you to the Boxing Hall of Fame.

Alex and I understood that some fighters are ruined in the gym by bad trainers. A good trainer must understand the art of patience. There is a big difference between a teacher and a trainer. A real trainer will spend time with a fighter outside the gym. From day one, if you care about your fighter, the most important thing is to protect him. Not that they can't take on great challenges, but you have to know when they are ready. If not, you will ruin their career and possibly their quality of life.

I respected Angelo Dundee as a trainer, but he was not good at developing fighters from scratch. The one thing he did have in boxing was great connections. No one can doubt a need for that, especially after working with the greatest heavyweight of all-time, Muhammad Ali.

Ali was trouble for any heavyweight. He had speed and could take a good shot. His lay-off from boxing in the late sixties and early seventies solidified him as a hero to many people but robbed him of his best years as a fighter.

I will always have great admiration and respect for Ali. Not many people are willing to sacrifice glory and money for the good of all people. When a fighter entered the ring with him, he was not only coming up against some of the best talent in boxing, he was fighting a man of great conviction. The peoples champion. And for that Ali would make you pay.

In World Champions Only the one thing trainer's St. Claire and Charleston have in common, is their eye for raw talent. They instinctively knew when they saw it. To make a lot of money in boxing, you should have something unique to offer, and both of their fighters were blessed with talent.

People often say that styles make fights; such as a strong puncher against a skilled boxer. Well, you should also know that styles identify trainers. In World Champions Only, Charleston worked to protect his own interest, while St. Claire worked to protect his fighter.

In the chapter Showdown, their fighters Wonderful Magnificent and Hiwatha "Absolute" Jordan collide for the Fight of the Century. It was a contest of wills, and the battle was not only between the fighters but the trainers.

When you know your fighter is getting ready for the fight of his career' your honor is also on the line. This was captured so well in the book; it reminded me of some of the greatest fights I've seen in boxing.

From the day I opened my eyes, I believe I was destined to spend my life in boxing. During the early 1930s, I was a young boy growing up in the West-In of Cincinnati, Ohio. Back then, you knew where you could go and where not be when the Sun went down. Boxing became my refuge from the harsh racism and poverty I faced. My Uncles boxed professionally, and I spent most of my childhood watching them train in the gym.

One of my friends at the time was Ezzard Charles. He won all of his forty-two amateur fights. It was unspoken, but in the gym, we could be men. We were both dreamers who wanted a better life, not just for us, but our families. We were so below the poverty line that you woke up some days knowing you probably wouldn't eat. To save your parents the embarrassment, you just didn't ask.

When Ezzard and I left Cincinnati, we both had something to prove. Ultimately, Ezzard's challenge would be in the ring and mine in the corner as a trainer. No one was surprised the "Cincinnati Cobra" became heavyweight champion of the world in 1950 when he won a 15-round decision against Joe Louis. Unfortunately, he lost it to Jersey Joe Wolcott the next year.

I remember when Ezzard fought Archie Moore three times. This was somewhere around 1946 and Ezzard had won the first two fights. Archie was a tough fighter. If you got in the ring with him, you had to take a good shot. The last time Ezzard fought him in Cleveland I said Ezzard you got to knock him out and he did. Competition in those days was at a fever pitch.

The first champion I met was former heavyweight champion Jack Johnson in New York. Though time had passed, everybody still recognized Jack as the first black man to win a heavyweight title. I was just seventeen. To me, he was bigger than life.

Over time I would meet many great champions such as Joe Louis, Hammering Henry Armstrong, Floyd Patterson, Muhammad Ali and others. I can't recall a time when boxing was not a part of my life.

In the early part of the 20th Century, you didn't have video or instant replay. A trainer couldn't sit home and watch tapes of an opponent. To see a fighter train, you had to go to the gym, listen to his fights on the radio or wait until he came through your town. Even if you were a reporter in those days, you had to be diligent.

At that time, New York was the Mecca of boxing. It was there that my Uncles introduced me to Sugar Ray Robinson. I remember going to fights at Madison Square Garden. It was an exciting time to be young, but not black. Ray and many like us had to find our way in a world that didn't really want us and definitely didn't want to recognize our existence as men. At one brief point, Ray and I actually shared a room. Back then, that was what you had to do.

Ray was dedicated to the sport. He had no problem going the extra mile. We all knew one day he would be champion. Many of us hopefuls would watch him train. If you wanted to figure out what you got, he was the guy you wanted to spar with. Like many fighters who obtain widespread popularity, he stayed in the game too long.

Some fighters as long as they are doing all the punching their fine, but greatness comes when you can deal with an opponent that can not only punch back, he too can take a good shot. This type of fighter is not afraid to meet you center ring or work the ropes. It becomes a fight of mental toughness. No one can help you block a shot. Like my good friend and trainer Alex Sherer would say, "That's when you bite down on your mouthpiece and get with it." You either have heart in this game, or you don't.

One of my most memorable times in boxing was when Ray fought Tommy Bell from Youngstown, Ohio for the vacant 147 lbs. Title. It was an unbelievable fight. By then, Ray had become a hero to all black people trying to rise above poverty. He had a club on 7th Avenue in New York and anybody who wanted to be seen hung-out in his spot. It was what the young people call today the hangout.

We all loved Jazz. Even Ezzard Charles was a double bass player. I would catch him sometimes sitting in with some of the great jazz players. People of all colors seemed to appreciate the talents of real musicians. Music is the one thing that transcends cultural differences, and in my time, Jazz was it. My favorites were Charlie Parker, Dexter Gordon, Miles Davis, and Charles McPherson. All of them spent time at Ray's club.

Back then, Ray had a lot of businesses. Unfortunately, he was not a great businessman, but he tried to give back to his people. Without some level of education, money is a hard thing to hold on to. Those he trusted robbed Ray blind. In the end, he still is one of the greatest fighters to ever live with a legacy that boxing will never forget.

It takes heart and dedication to be a world champion. When I began reading the book World Champions Only, I instantly was captivated. It wasn't just another how-to-help book or an autobiography. It captured the lifestyles of champions, the business of boxing, the training, the women in their lives, and the hurdles every champion must overcome.

I believe the level of television exposure has made a big difference in the way fans view the sport. In my day a fighter could lose a fight and still be perceived as a champion or great fighter. Willie Pep was the #1 featherweight of the 20th Century. He's in the Boxing Hall of Fame. The man had 229 fights with 65 knockouts. Do you think he was worried about his eleven losses? It was three of those losses against Sandy Saddler during their four historic fights that shaped his legacy.

Today you lose, and you're no longer marketable. That's a shame because fighters don't fight as much. They're afraid of not only losing the fight but their marketability. In football just because you didn't win the Super Bowl people don't stop watching their favorite team. That has everything to do with the way the NFL markets the sport. For boxing to keep a foothold on one of America's greatest sports, we have to change that.

Boxing has to continue drawing new talent and generations of fans to the sport. That is why I stayed in the gym well beyond my years teaching young men how to love boxing. I was always looking for the next champion that could excite a new generation. At the end of the day, fans want to see a fighter put it all on the line. Let the corner, analyst and judges worry about how many points are on the scorecard. You're there to do battle, showcase your skills, and take advantage of any opportunity to knock the guy out. Fans want to walk away, saying that was a great fight win, lose, or draw.

In the book World Champions Only Hiwatha "Absolute"

Jordan was a good boxer. His real asset was his ability to make money, excite a crowd, and draw media attention to the sport. He was not afraid of losing, because he convinced people he was there to win. He knew there were others just as talented lurking in the background waiting to take his place.

When I watch Floyd Mayweather, Jr. fight, I know the key to his success is conditioning. This kid is a solid defensive fighter that still loves to train. Acquiring money did not change that. He knows training is fundamental to solidifying a great legacy in the sport. When he gets to the end of his career, his next challenge is to transcend that into a purpose beyond the sport of boxing.

I never liked working with undisciplined fighters. When I decided to put the time in with a fighter, I looked for natural talent and a high level of dedication. Unfortunately, there are times you have to work with what you got. At one time in my life, I trained James Toney. He had an eating disorder. So, I had to handle him differently. I would make him box 7-8 rounds then rest only 30 seconds. He didn't like it at first. Everybody is not willing to go through that. Boxing has to be your number one priority, or you will not make it in this sport.

I cared a lot for James, but over time, I realized the kid was a headache. He also was not good with money. A fighter has to know how to handle having money. A lot of boxers when they get money they're through with training. I use to tell James that the greatest boxer was the Internal Revenue

Service. He would ask, "Pops," do you pay them?" I told him yes, I do. You have to be crazy if you think it's an option.

Mike Tyson learned this the hard way. As long as he stayed up in the Catskills, he was a good fighter. Cus Damato knew Mike was not the kind of fighter you turn loose in New York City with millions of dollars in their pocket. When he lost Cus Damato, he lost his protection. Cus understood the importance of the trainer's personal relationship with his fighter. It is essential to their development. He had proven this in his development of Floyd Patterson. Mike may have been the youngest boxer to win a world heavyweight title, but Floyd was the youngest undisputed heavyweight champion.

I would advise anybody not to fall in love with a prizefighter. They may not be loyal to you because the sport of boxing is not loyal to them. When Ezzard Charles turned professional, the people that were with him, in the beginning, were not there when he got on top.

That's what made Hiwatha "Absolute' Jordan's and his trainer St. Claire characters so uniquely in the book. Hiwatha was loyal to him. If I got anything out of reading this book, I would say it was a well-written lesson in dedication and loyalty. I would recommend reading it to anyone wanting to understand the business of boxing or how to take control of their lives and career.

I'm not necessarily a romantic guy, but Diana did an excellent job of letting you know what motivated her characters. You could feel the emotion between the main characters and understand how their choice of women influenced their lives. I was left to reflect on my own life. Something my wife Beverly might appreciate.

I know many have referred to me as a historian of boxing. The reality is, I spent my life as a passionate student. I've read everything I could find about boxing, whether it was a boxing magazine or the next great autobiography. I saw the rise of fierce competition during the early years of the 20th Century, to the decline of talent in my later years in boxing. I've seen prizefighters go from compromising their economic well-being for championship glory, to becoming economic powerhouses. It's been an amazing journey.

By Bill "Pops" Miller
2009